Silent

Silent

Justice Hawk

iUniverse, Inc.
New York Lincoln Shanghai

Silent

iUniverse, Inc.

For information address:
iUniverse, Inc.
2021 Pine Lake Road, Suite 100
Lincoln, NE 68512
www.iuniverse.com

ISBN: 0-595-32902-0

Printed in the United States of America

For the crewmen of the fleet ballistic missile submarine force…

Acknowledgments

There are many people who helped in the production of this story. First is the production staff: Renee Szeligas and her associates in Chicago. Second is the publisher. Third are those individuals I had the pleasure of knowing during my career in the nuclear submarine Navy.

Preface

From the detonation of the first atomic bombs in 1945, nuclear power has become the main deterrent of another global catastrophe. The United States enjoyed a short era of peace between 1945–1949. In 1949, the Soviet Union detonated their first nuclear weapon. From 1949 onward, the United States and the Soviet Union engaged in an arms build up of nuclear weapons. For some reason, both sides concluded that to have an abundance of nuclear weapons was the key to global supremacy and continued existence.

For the most part, these nuclear weapons were stockpiled in land base arsenals. Delivery vehicles included both bomber aircraft and rockets. Both countries invested enormously into secret, underground, launch facilities.

In the mid-1950s, the United States developed the first nuclear powered submarine, the USS Nautilus. The feats of the USS Nautilus convinced the United States' arms makers that a nuclear weapons platform could be mounted within a nuclear submarine. Hastily, a platform was constructed with existing submarine designs, and the first class of fleet ballistic missile submarines was built.

By the end of the 1950s, the first fleet ballistic submarine was launched, the USS George Washington. By the early 1960s, five nuclear-powered, fleet ballistic missile submarines were in service, roaming the seas undetected. The Soviet Union had no response. The United States surged ahead in the arms race.

From the early 1960s, the United States continued to improve upon fleet ballistic missile submarine designs and payloads. The Soviet Union never caught up.

By the mid-1970s, the Strategic Arms Limitation Talks (SALT) commenced, resulting in a formula for Mutually Assured Destruction (MAD) in the limitation of nuclear weapons. Succinctly, both the United States and the Soviet Union agreed to maintain a stockpile of nuclear weapons sufficient to annihilate one another in the event of an attack by either party.

Though the period between the mid-1970s and late 1980s was tense, the United States continued to leap ahead of the Soviet Union. By 1989, the Soviet Union had redirected so much of their economic resources to the arms race that they imploded. The Berlin Wall was dismantled and their reign over the Eastern European countries came to an end. The Cold War ended, and the Soviet Union ceased to be a Super Power.

This is a story of one Western Pacific deployment aboard a nuclear-powered, fleet ballistic missile submarine in the early 1980s. The story is told from the perspective of an enlisted, nuclear-trained submariner.

I pray this story provides an appreciation for the crews who served aboard fleet ballistic missile submarines. It was their dedication and sacrifice that was instrumental in winning the Cold War.

CHAPTER 1

Pre-deployment Preparations, Apra Harbor, Guam

Andie's

In the early days of the buildup for the Vietnam Conflict, the Seabees constructed a large wooden hut along a backwater portion of the inlet to Apra Harbor. Someone, everyone seems to forget who, named it Andie's. By the time the fleet boats arrived, the more affectionate name for the establishment became Andrew's By The Sea. Andie's really was just a large hut: four windowless, undecorated, inner plank walls covered with tarpaper on the outside and roof. The tables consisted of thick-lacquered, wooden, electrical cable wheels, surrounded by the latest fad in Navy Exchange hard-plastic chairs. A series of portable air conditioning units provided a sanctuary from the tropical humidity of Mariana Islands. A few planks, laid side-by-side and lacquered, served as a bar separating the patrons, mostly sailors and marines, from the staff, also sailors from the commissary group of the naval base. Most patrons relieved themselves along a path leading up to a poorly kept latrine in the back of Andie's that served more as a gathering place for brown snakes. The beverage of choice at Andie's was cold American beer in a can: Budweiser or Olympia. Servicemen, seeking relaxation from the long hours aboard ship, listened to a jukebox as they gobbled down military pizzas, French fries, hamburgers and hot dogs. Coke and Pepsi in cans rounded off the soft drinks. Good lighting deterred the type of reckless, aggressive behavior afflicting similar establishments off base. According to the Navy, life away from homeport was advertised to be arduous. I guess they never let anyone down in that expectation at Apra Harbor.

Outside Andie's, the Navy created a beach and recreational area. Swimming provided instant relief from the tropical humidity. The group activity was volleyball; although, some crews had organized flag football games. At fourteen degrees above the equator with no tradewinds, daytime recreational activities often were limited to air-conditioned spaces.

The walk from a unit, tied up along side the submarine tender to Andie's, was measured by the sweat absorbed in a sailor's clothing. It took a half an hour or so, immersed in air conditioning, to evaporate the sweat absorbed into your clothes. But, you still reeked of sweat. The dried sweat stuck to your clothes. A restraining and uncomfortable firmness, resembling that present in over-starched garments, replaced the comfortable, fresh, fluffy feel of cotton. Long after the patrons had departed Andie's, the stench of their sweat remained. One never forgot that scent. It became a popular greeting in naval outposts during the Vietnam Era.

If you were not thirsty when you departed your boat, by the time you reached Andie's, you could not wait to feel a cold beer or soda in your hands. Your body needed to be fed a constant supply of fluids to survive in these climates until it could acclimatize. Since most moorings at naval outposts were of short duration, crews got quenched in tropical humidity and returned quickly to their atmosphere-controlled, inner-submarine environments. During a typical deployment, a half dozen or so quenchings could be experienced. Cold beer seemed to be the prescription of choice to counteract this quenching. It was no wonder so many fleet sailors develop alcohol-related problems later in their careers. Repeated quenchings in tropical environments over a series of deployments almost condemned the more susceptible sailors to the unfortunate outcomes of alcohol abuse; i.e., disciplinary actions, divorce, child abuse, etc. Like hot metal quenched in cold water, sailors lost their flexibility and hardened. The Navy, for the fleet boat sailor, was a hard life that got harder with repeated exposure.

It is about 9:00 PM right now. A few of the shipmates are sharing a pepperoni pizza over a few Olympia beers, or Olys as they call them. The crew spent an overhaul in the Washington state area and acquired a taste for the fresh mountain stream flavor of Olympia beer. It seems you can feel the cool freshness of the mountain streams whenever you swig on a can of Oly. Oly is lighter than Budweiser. It is a very smooth beer.

In the far corner of Andie's, a marine is taunting about for a fight. From what he is saying, it seems some older marines have teased him about making sergeant so quickly. He blabbers on about how he has never been busted in rank, so he needs to prove his manhood by losing a stripe and being man enough to regain it. It seems like a foolish thing to desire, but in the tropics, with little to do, and a few beers under his breath, he seems willing to undertake the task. We sailors pity the marine. It takes a full year in grade as an E-4 to be considered for advancement to E-5. Sergeant is E-5. If the marine succeeds in his aspirations, he will be reduced to E-4, Corporal, with some suspension. He will need to keep his nose clean through the suspension period and the following year to once again be eligible for the rank of sergeant. A scuffle with sailors on a naval base will bring discredit upon the Marine Corps and further hamper his ability to win his superiors' support to regain his rank. This marine seems unaware of the consequences. It is so unfortunate how his senior enlisted supervisors have persuaded him to follow such a destructive course.

Fortunately, the sailors in the room are paying the marine no mind. His verbal assaults go unanswered. Sailors are smarter than marines. In the Navy, the rank of E-5, Second Class Petty Officer, provides an assurance against mindless, long-hour details that go on for months. No one enjoys swabbing decks at all hours or rising for mess cooking duty before 5:00 AM. Anyone that has experienced those junior-rank assignments has no desire to repeat them. E-5s in the Navy realize how fortunate the benefits of rank are.

Beer and pizza seem to be the highlight of any evening at Apra Harbor. It is no wonder sailors put on a few pounds while mooring in Guam. It is amazing how good a pizza tastes with a beer after working over ten or twelve hours straight. With the soft, lamenting music of the peace movement filling the air from the jukebox, relaxation slowly overcomes us with each round of beer. That is what I remember most about Andie's: the soothing taste of the Pacific Northwest in my mouth and the peaceful lullabies of the gentle people in my ears.

Amazingly, we did not talk about sports or the latest fads. We talked about the boat, our home life, the ports and the wonderful memories of past deployments. We did not even talk about women. There were not any around anyway. At least, there were not any women at Apra Harbor. Some of the local entrepreneurs brought in Asian women to stock the nightclubs. You had to travel off base for them. Going off base meant changing into appropriate civilian attire and hiring a taxi. Since the taxis could not meet you at the gangway from the tender, you had to endure the tropical humidity of the evening and walk past Andie's to connect with a ride. The thought of that sweat-soaked trek discouraged most sailors from going into town.

We ventured into Agana a few times. The evenings we chose to do so were cooler and often involved a ride from the duty military vehicle to the pick up point just past Andie's. The Supply clerks controlled the duty vehicle. Getting to know them was quite beneficial to anyone with off base intentions. For the most part though, non-duty night evenings at Apra Harbor were spent at Andie's.

Duty meant a twenty-four hour shift on the boat. On a typical duty day, you stood two six-hour watches that required your undivided attention monitoring boat parameters. A full workday was expected, unless you were fortunate enough to draw one of your watches during the daytime. After the 5:00 PM chow call, the hour between 7:00 and 8:00 PM was devoted to boat training. New crewmen, on duty days, saw their first free time after 8:00 PM. From about 8:00 PM to midnight, new crewmen either stood watches or studied their qualification requirements. Qualified crewmen could enjoy a movie after 8:00 PM or spend their time as they chose aboard the boat.

Most in-port duty days on deployed fleet boats were Port and Starboard, meaning enlisted crewmen stood duty every other day: one day on and one day off. The day off is misleading. You never got a full day off after duty. You were still required to do a full day's work the next day. Hence, off time was limited to the time after 8:00 PM on your day off. Since Andie's closed at midnight, you had four hours to enjoy a few beers. Typically, this routine repeated itself for the thirty days you were prepping the boat for service in the Pacific Theater. Other than pre-deployment, prepping periods, most other mooring periods were of shorter duration: a few days or so. When you were in port at Apra Harbor, Andie's was your sanctuary from the boat. And, you were glad it was there.

Consumption of beverages was not restricted to the inner walls of Andie's. You could order a cold beer and walk about the environs. After 8:00 PM, Andie's clientele mostly consisted of submarine sailors. Sometimes a few tender marines would stop in for a quick beer, before they continued on into Agana. Otherwise, it was just sailors from the units tied up alongside the submarine tender. For the most part, the tender serviced one fleet boat at a time. That meant that only off-duty crewmen would be present in Andie's after 8:00 PM. You got to know the personnel in your duty section real well. Every night off, they were sipping brews at Andie's. I can still remember the names of the guys in my engineering duty section. Better yet, I can remember where they were from in the United States, whether or not they went to college, what they majored in if they did, what their aspirations were after naval service, etc. I even remember how the naval service turned out for them. I remember it all. Every submarine sailor does. It is the way life was.

The environs of Andie's consisted of the Apra Harbor estuary and the open area between the tender and the outer perimeter gate. There were few trees. In the absence of streetlights, the area was dark. It was very dark. Outside Andie's, the only lighting came from the night lights of the tender and the pier area. The swimming area abutting Andie's was unlit. A few lights were barely visible around the entrance gate, because the Seabees had strung a long extension cord to the guard shack to provide some lighting.

When you stepped outside Andie's, you stepped into a darkness that few of us living in the United States had ever experienced. Unless you were the wilderness camping-type, this darkness was uncomfortable.

In the picnic table area just outside Andie's, on the path to the swimming area, we could talk story over a few beers. After a while, at least for our off-duty section, it became quite popular. That was how we got to know each other so well. The darkness comforted us and encouraged us to speak of ourselves, as if we were cloaked in the sanctuary of our consciousnesses. I suppose it is the same feeling young, summer campers experience when huddled around a campfire: they listen to the sound of the embers extinguishing as we listen to a serenade from the tropical insects. We began to talk.

We learned about disrupted families, strict and disappointed parents, unplanned pregnancies, college failures, law troubles and even some admirable intentions of family support. The stories were endless. Each sailor had one to account for his sitting on the picnic table with us. After hearing a sailor's story, you could not help reflecting on your own situation. Some stories made you appreciate your life. Most were that way for me. But, there were a few that pointed out my weaknesses. Even years after hearing one of those stories, I am still reflecting on what I could have been had I chose differently. Each time the reflection lead back to how important it was for me to have a father figure to advise me. I did not have one. Many of the sailors in my off-duty section had lost their fathers, or their fathers were not there to guide them. The picnic table sessions stressed the importance of having someone available that has been down the tough road of life to guide you. We never forgot that lesson. One never should. It made the job of our supervisors easier, knowing how valuable their insights were. We were good listeners and fast learners. Under the sea, you had to be. The sea was much less forgiving when you were immersed within it.

One of the benefits of the environs of Andie's was the night sky. In the absence of street lighting, the overhead canopy showcased an immensity of stars. None of us ever dreamed that there were so many stars in the sky. In the upper Northern Hemisphere of the continental United States, we could easily identify the main constellations. Here, near the equator, in the absence of ground lighting, we could not identify any of them. It was just all stars overhead. We could have been in a space ship traveling between galaxies. There were so many stars and so close together. The wonder of the universe captivated us. It encouraged us into philosophizing about the nature and the origins of human kind. Until we experienced that awesome sense of infinity, few of us ever considered our insubstantiality in the universe.

The soothing taste of Olympia beer took on new meaning. For once, we appreciated the cool freshness of the water from the Pacific Northwest. Not because it was fresh, but because it was part, a very pleasant part, of the entire cosmos. It was a part of that myriad of stars above us. Olympia beer and we were one with the universe. We were part of the stars. In the silence of the starlight, we opened our consciousnesses to all around us. I never forgot those evenings, even long after I stopped sipping Olympia beer. The beer had nothing to do with it. It was all about recognizing how a part of all this wonder we were. I miss those talks.

On the Boat for a Day Operation

This evening, we need to be strolling back to the boat early. We have a startup and preps before we get underway. For electricians that means we have to remove the shore power cables once the boat is up and running on nuclear power. While in port, the boat relies on electrical power from the naval base or submarine tender to run its equipment. This enables the crew to do maintenance on the power plant, as well as curtail a number of its normal watch standers.

In the old Navy, these in port watches were referred to as "cold iron" watches. "Cold iron" came from the condition of the metal in the steam plant. Without steam flowing through the pipes, the pipes normalized with room temperature. I admit that room temperature in the tropics was not exactly cold, but the temperature was considerably lower than that of steam at saturated or super saturated condition; i.e., some two hundred and twelve degrees Fahrenheit. We still use steam systems in the nuclear Navy, but the "cold iron" watch terminology has faded into the past. Since the reactor piping itself is still at elevated temperatures, it can hardly be classified as cold. We refer to the new watches as shutdown watches to identify with the condition of the nuclear reactor in port.

It has been a practice, one that I still participate in, to raid the galley just after midnight. Most of the crew is asleep, and the cooks leave some quick food: i.e., hamburgers, cheese and eggs, in the chill room near the galley. Three or four of us returned from Andie's and cooked up some eggs on the galley grill. This way, when we are roused for the startup around 4:00 AM in order to be ready to remove the shore power cables at 5:30 AM, we will not be missing breakfast. Knowing what to anticipate is half the survival skills of a submariner. As for toast, sliced bread is always available, as is coffee, milk and juice, twenty-four hours a day in the galley. As long as the midnight chefs clean up after themselves, little is said about their use of the galley equipment. It is a golden rule to clean up after yourself. No submariner ever abuses that privilege.

Everyone knows their job and what is expected of them in the submarine force. There is respect for one another unlike any found in the regular Navy. Most crewmen know one another by their first name or a nickname. Nicknames are popular in the fleet boats, and those nicknames carry over to new fleet boat assignments. I carried the same nickname for my entire career in the fleet boats. That is true for all the old timers. Everyone knew of some submarine sailor called "Asiatic Jack," but few ever knew his real name. That nickname lingered on long after Asiatic Jack retired from the naval service.

This morning, the midnight chefs decided to cook up some sunnies with toast. One of the guys found some ham, and we diced that up into ham omelets. It is amazing how consoling it is to share a ham omelet in the galley at 1:00 AM. Of all the early morning breakfasts I have experienced in twenty-four-hour joints around the world, the most memorable were those shared in a submarine galley. Those breakfasts were like a continuation of the soul sharing experienced on the picnic tables around Andie's. Though on the boat, the conversation gravitated about the performance on board. We talked mostly about experiences related to the boat. Many times we mapped our plan for the upcoming event whether it was a startup or merely removing shore power. This was true, especially, when new electricians or crewmen were dining with us. Upon reflection, the morning breakfasts were like football huddles before a play. Everyone was reminded of his assignments. In some cases, the assignments were explained in detail to the newcomers. Upon further reflection, this huddling was probably similar for the old timers of the "cold iron" era, as well. We just use different, technical language today. It had to be the same. On that thought, it was probably that way in the days of wooden ships and iron men. It probably has been that way since the waves first commenced lapping the sides of ships.

By 5:30 AM, the oncoming electricians are roused to remove shore power. The other duty section personnel have started up the reactor and brought the steam turbines to the point of assuming ship's electrical loads. Once the shore power isolation breakers have been opened, the oncoming electricians remove shore power. Removing shore power involves a thorough tag out of the isolation breakers to insure that the electrical buses connecting to the shore power cables are de-energized. Tag outs refer to two-person, independent checks verifying the accuracy of the isolations and signed paperwork attesting to that verification. Any discrepancy in tag out procedure could result in immediate disqualification from submarine duty. Tag outs are considered a serious matter, and something never to be taken lightly nor violated. With electrical systems, death is a very possible outcome of a tag out violation.

Once the tag out is verified and documented, permission is given to the on-coming electricians to remove the shore power cables. Shore power cables are huge diameter cables. Some may measure as much as ten inches in diameter. The cables connect directly to the ship's internal electrical distribution system. Hence, the sensitivity to ensure the connected bus is de-energized prior to any attempt to disconnect the cables.

From a safety standpoint, death can occur from an exposure to as little as one-tenth of an ampere of electricity. Since shore power cables can carry hundreds of amperes during normal operation, death would be certain if someone tried disconnecting them during normal operation.

The entire removal process takes about thirty minutes to an hour. Most of the time is spent physically disconnecting the cables and then hoisting them onto the pier via a crane or derrick assembly. After a few experiences with the shore power removal, the oncoming electricians have become adept-experts and move about like automatons removing and stowing the cables.

Once shore power has been removed, the tag out of the shore power isolation breakers is cleared and power is reconnected to the de-energized buses via the ship's turbine generators. The ship's electrical distribution system is then aligned for at-sea operation. The senior engineering watch officer makes a report to the commanding officer that the electrical distribution system is carrying full ship's loads and ready to get underway. Once that acknowledgment is concurred by the commanding officer, the ship's crew is ordered to make preparation to get underway.

The electrical crew that just removed the shore power cables makes their way to the engineering spaces and relieves those watch standers that started up the reactor in order that they may change into underway attire and get some breakfast. Within an hour, the entire crew will be at their stations to take the ship to sea. This entire process is accomplished professionally and as routine as going to your mailbox in a small town to get your mail. Most submarine operations are carried out with the same precision and automation.

Once the submarine commanding officer receives permission to get underway from the squadron commander, the order is issued to remove the mooring lines and depart from the pier or side of the tender. Mooring lines are removed in the same manner as one removes a mooring line from small sailing vessel. Submarine mooring lines are just bigger ropes. To depart the pier or tender side, a tugboat is employed to provide the initial, directional-propulsion to acquire the necessary underway angle. Once the underway angle is achieved, the submarine can maneuver its way out into the middle of the channel of the Apra Harbor estuary. For inexperienced commanding officers, a tugboat accompanies the submarine through the channel, edging the ship as necessary to maintain it in the channel, until the submarine exits Apra Harbor and enters the Mariana seascape.

The Apra Harbor estuary is short, so the maneuvering is relatively easy. Only two wide curves bend the straightness of the estuary. The tugboats adjust the fleet boat in these curves, if it steers off course. For the most part, the commanding officers are familiar with these channel curves and compensate nicely, maneuvering their way through them. Within two hours of ordering the crew to make preparations to get underway, the submarine has maneuvered out of Apra Harbor and making its way to its prescribed dive location.

The Maneuvering Watch is the term designated to describe the organization of the crew's activities during the underway period between unmooring and reaching the dive location. This organization requires a full complement of watch standers in order to perform duties in excess of normal underway watch standing. Crew personnel are pre-assigned to these normal and extra watch stations via a posted watch bill.

For the Maneuvering Watch, I always plan to be off-watch. For some reason, my physical make up makes me susceptible to seasickness when the boat is subjected initially to the rolling of the waves. I have little explanation for this. Perhaps, I have a momentary imbalance condition in my ears. Whatever the reason, after the ship is underway a few hours, I am able to ambulate without any regard for seasickness. I just take a little longer to acclimatize to the at-sea environment. Few people, especially sailors, are so afflicted. Those susceptible to this temporary seasickness usually avoid sea duty altogether and join one of the other services.

What is seasickness? Medically, seasickness results from failure of the inner ear to maintain balance during a period in which the walking surface moves in an unpredictable fashion. Seasickness, in its worst state, creates a queasy feeling in the stomach that often results in throwing up. Interestingly, once a sailor has succumbed to seasickness, a tremendous feeling of relief overcomes the victim. That feeling remains for at least twenty minutes until the stomach reaches another state of queasiness. Expectorant follows in about ten minutes. This expectorant-relief cycle continues until the inner ear achieves equilibrium. Often, having the afflicted sailor lie down for an hour or so will hasten the equilibrium condition. Once the inner ear achieves equilibrium, the symptoms of seasickness disappear for the rest of the at-sea period. In the Old Navy, acquiring inner ear equilibrium was referred to as "getting your sea legs."

The one caveat to "getting your sea legs" occurs during high seas state conditions. Tropical storms can agitate the sea surface so intently as to disrupt the equilibrium condition of the inner ear on the most hardened sailors. Although the movies have dramatized the frantic actions of sailors during heavy storms conditions, working in those conditions to rig the ship is in fact quite miserable. Fear, perhaps, is the only anecdote that manages to postpone seasickness under high sea state conditions.

Being assigned to a submarine would seem to elude such arduous experiences; however, there exists patrol areas where the sea state in certain times of the year is difficult to contend. My first experience in such a sea state was my initial assignment to the North Atlantic in February. Our vessel was heaving and reeling at the test depth of World War II U-boats. I never gained more respect for the U-boat crews of the Second World War than I did on that run. Keeping in mind that those U-boats required near surface operation in order to inflict damage on Allied convoys headed to supply Murmansk above Scandinavia and Archangel in the White Sea, the impossibility of the assignment becomes obvious. U-boats would have had to endure thirty-foot swells and remain poised to launch torpedoes at approaching vessels, themselves contending with such a sea state. The arctic conditions of the ocean water made survival from a torpedo attack near impossible. Sudden death awaited the victims of submarine attacks in such an environment.

The Titanic disaster hardly could compare to the plight of the victims on the Murmansk run. Yes, those personnel froze to death in the near-zero-degree water; however, the Titanic ran into an iceberg in a calm sea state. Picture thirty-foot swells and the plight of the Titanic multiplies enormously. Some convoy vessels succumbed to the ice waters without the aid of the U-boats by similarly repeating the Titanic's demise. The convoy vessels broke apart from being slammed by near-freezing, thirty-foot swells that brittle fractured their hulls and engulfed their crews in frigid ocean water.

Fortunately, this day run out of Apra Harbor occurs in tropical conditions. The water is much warmer. Submarine construction has been modified, as a result of the lessons learned from tragic demise of the Titanic and the Murmansk-run, convoy vessels. In this day and age, we only concern ourselves with overcoming seasickness.

Once in the dive area, the Maneuvering Watch is secured. Normal at-sea watch rotation takes effect.

Normal at-sea watch rotation consists of three duty sections alternating six-hour watches. There are four watches each day: Midnight to 6:00 AM, 6:00 AM to Noon, Noon to 6:00 PM and 6:00 PM to midnight. Meals are arranged to straddle the four watches. Major ship evolutions are likewise scheduled to coincide with commencement of a new watch. Ship's routine operations follow the morning: 6:00AM to Noon, watch and the afternoon: Noon to 6:00 PM, watch. Ship's sectional training and entertainment follow the evening watch turnover: 6:00 PM to Midnight. The Midwatch: Midnight to 6:00 AM, is reserved for those activities that would burden or disrupt normal ship's activities. At-sea dumping of trash is one such activity as are power plant realignments.

Since there are three at-sea duty sections and four watches to man per day, the duty sections rotate through the four sections, so that each duty sections stands four watches every three days. Hence, for a routine sixty-day patrol, each duty section will stand some eighty watches while underway. The three-duty-section rotation allows the duty sections to experience all the meal times each three days. There is no monotony of having to wake for breakfast before each watch.

What are the meals like? Actually, they are not that bad. The submarine service gets a larger allowance per sailor than the other branches of the Navy. Accordingly, more can be spent on the rations carried for an underway period. Steak and lobster, affectionately referred to as "surf and turf," for the evening meal are not uncommon. The steak, for that meal, is often filet mignon or choice tenderloin. Chateaubriand has been known to grace the plate for "surf and turf" as well.

For the routine meals, breakfast consists of eggs to order with a selection of bacon, sausage or ham. Upon entering the crew's mess, the oncoming watch stander merely selects the entrée of his choice on a little rectangular, pre-scripted, piece of paper and gives it to the cook. The cook prepares the selection provided him, with priority given to the oncoming watch standers. The egg selection is limited to sunny side up, over easy, over hard and scrambled. Eggs Benedict and Florentine are not available in either the crew's mess or the officer's wardroom. If the demand were sufficient on special days, like Sunday, they could be. The demand just is not there.

A rotating grill toaster continually feeds bread into waiting baskets. The crew can select the type of bread: white, wheat or rye, from a row dispenser located adjacent the rotating toaster. Little butter squares are kept in bowls in the chill room. Adding a few chunks of ice enables the butter squares to be brought to the tables in crew's mess. In another basket-like container, breakfast condiments and jellies are segregated. Strawberry jam is a favorite on toast and is well stocked for the morning meal. Since many sailors enjoy catsup with hash browns, catsup packets comprise the largest selection of condiments, ahead of mustard, mayonnaise and relish. The last bread-spread available is peanut butter that is dispensed from huge tins. The peanut butter of choice is a creamy substance closer to the Jiffy brand than the Skippy brand. It is bulk purchased from a generic distributor. The actual name of the brand, few sailors remember. Affectionately, the sailors refer to it as "generic." Trust me, no one ever looks for that brand for their families at home.

Coffee, tea and hot chocolate are dispended from larger hot water drums mounted against the wall separating the galley and the dining area. Milk: white and chocolate, and ice cream are dispensed likewise a little distance from the hot beverages. Lastly, a kool-aid drink is provided to round off the beverage selection. The kool-aid is affectionately referred to as "bug juice." "Bug juice" is as available as coffee during an at-sea run. Consumption might drain the other beverages; however, "bug juice" lasts forever.

The noon meals offer the major meat entrée for the day. For the most part, it is a form of beef: steak, chicken fried steak, hamburgers, Salisbury steak, tenderloins, grilled beef strips, veal, etc. Other optional entrees include chicken, shrimp, lobster, swordfish, ham and lamb. Pasta selections include potatoes, French fries and noodles. Vegetables range from peas, carrots, corn, string beans, etc. Dessert accompanies the noon and evening meals. Now, this selection can be quite exotic. Baked Alaska has been known to distinguish the tables in the crew's mess. Ice cream is always available from the Dairy Queen like, soft serve dispenser. My favorite dessert was pineapple upside down cake. That treat would appear about four times a patrol. I would put in a special wakeup call to make that meal, if in the event I was not the oncoming or the off-going watch.

When it came to measuring crew morale, one look at the faces of the crew enjoying the noon meal replaced mounds of psychological data. Happy sailors eat well. The Navy runs on its stomach. Keep the stomach happy, and the rest will fall into place. Not surprisingly, the best performing crews had a tremendous affection for their galley and cooks. Consequently, the root cause of a poorly motivated crew could be traced to the galley. A commissary officer appreciative of the relationship between crew performance and the service of the galley will find promotion awaiting him.

The evening meal pretty much mimics the noon meal in selection. Generally, the portions are a little smaller. If beef is prepared for the noon meal, then chicken, ham or some seafood will dignify the plates of the evening meal. It seems the dessert portions of the evening meal were larger. It probably went along with the feeling of relaxation that accompanied the evening meal. Perhaps, having the ship's movie following the evening meal created that sense of relaxation. These were first run movies, too. Some sixty to seventy movies were on loaded prior to patrol. The movie control division, Interior Communications Electricians or IC-men, established a matinee schedule for the entire patrol. One new movie was shown twice a night: one showing after the evening meal and one showing after the Midnight meal or Mid-rats. Naturally, for the movie, popcorn was self-popped in microwaves or hot air generators. Butter was easily melted in the galley on the ovens.

The last meal of the day was Mid-rats, formally called midnight rations. This was a potpourri of leftovers and quick-make items. Leftovers from the noon and evening meal were served along side pork & beans, hot dogs and buns, pizza, cold cuts, cheese and some soup with crackers or French bread. For sailors addicted to fast food outlets, they were right at home with Mid-rats. The selections resembled a combination of foods from delis and brand name fast food outlets. Interestingly, it was Mid-rats that attracted most of the younger sailors whether or not they were the oncoming or off-going watch. I guess it reminded the younger sailors of their hometown hangouts, munching on pizza or junk foods.

Though the crew's mess is a small area: maybe 20 feet by 15 feet, half the crew could be squeezed in there at Mid-rats. Hogs, overcrowding a trough, had nothing on the Mid-rats feeding frenzy. The scene would have made an ideal deodorant commercial! Interestingly, when the hungry horde dispersed, most of the serving trays were empty. Some of the trays even lacked the usual crumbs that accompany bread selections. When leftover desserts, like pineapple upside down cake, were served at Mid-rats, the remaining serving trays were clean. I will not conclude that someone licked them clean, but something like that must have gotten them that way. When you consider how sticky the tray must have been to carry pineapple upside down cake, to see a clean tray afterwards was astonishing to say the least. Well, we witnessed clean trays on more than one occasion after Mid-rats.

The friendly conversations at Mid-rats represented another anomaly. For some reason, sailors were more conducive to talk at that meal. Topics ranged from just about everything back in the world. Unlike other meals where the conversation was more work related and professional, Mid-rats presented an array of topics. Generally, work was not one of the topics, unless a special evolution was planned to take place during the Mid-Watch. Otherwise, sports, theater, women (mostly playmates) and fun things to do back in the world comprised the Mid-rats' conversations. They were upbeat conversations as well. The sailors seemed genuinely excited about what they talked about. It was a pleasure to see their gestures and hear the joy in their voices. When I recall the Mid-rats' conversations, it is hard to keep from smiling. Those were wonderful memories.

Getting Underway

Getting back to the Maneuvering Watch, the typical underway time is 8:00 AM. The Maneuvering Watch is set about 7:30 AM in order to get all watch stations manned and allow time for the topside watches to don their safety vests and muster topside. Safety vests are the flotation devices that buoy a sailor, if he should fall overboard.

The topside watches handle the mooring lines. They have counterparts stationed on the pier to assist them. It is a simple process of removing the eye-shaped loop of the mooring line from around a pier cleat and feeding the line toward the topside watches. It is a practice done so effortless on a sailboat. The trick with mooring lines is that they are 50 to a hundred times larger than the tie-up rope of a sailboat and require a few personnel to handle them. But, it is the same technique. It is just a larger line. There is a science to this removing of the mooring lines. There are generally five lines mooring a fleet ballistic missile submarine to the pier. The sequence of removal may vary depending on the skill of the commanding officer; however, generally the last line removed is the forward line to allow the aft (rear) of the fleet boat to position itself away from the pier and into the channel. The aft end of the fleet boat houses the propeller (screw) used to drive the ship. Once the aft end of the fleet boat clears a safe distance from the pier, the commanding officer will order a light backing bell to reverse propel the ship away from the pier. A light bell is preferred to allow the topside watches time to remove the forward (bow) mooring line and divorce from the pier.

Bell refers to the terms used to indicate ships propulsion. All Stop bell refers to the shutting of the steam throttle or, in automobile terminology, taking your foot off the gas pedal. Ahead One Third refers to stepping on the gas to achieve one third of standard running power. Standard running power refers to a speed roughly equivalent to half the vessels top speed. Ahead Two Thirds is double the speed of Ahead One Third. Ahead Standard is Standard Speed. Ahead is used when the intention is to move the ship forward. Back would refer to an intention to move the ship backward or reverse. Back One Third would refer to moving the ship one third of ship's capable reverse speed. Back One Third is a different speed than Ahead One Third, because the reverse capability of a vessel is not as precise as the Ahead capabilities. Back Two Thirds roughly equates to twice Back One Third. Back Full refers to near top reverse speed. Back Emergency refers to expending all the ship's energy to reverse. Back Emergency is used to avoid collisions.

Returning to the forward speeds, Ahead Full refers to providing one-half of the ship's propulsion energy in the forward direction. Note that one-half of the ship's propulsion energy would propel the ship more than half the ships top speed. Hence, Ahead Full is a more powerful propulsion order (bell) than Ahead Standard. This has to do with the motion-energy law that, simply put, translates: if you double the speed you cube the power required to make that speed. Ahead Flank refers to providing one hundred percent of the ship's propulsion energy to go forward.

Bells are communicated by a system called the Engine Order Telegraph. Mostly, the Engine Order Telegraph has been designed as a magnetic system with a mechanical bell to alert engine room watch standers that a propulsion order has been given; i.e., a sending station located in the control room transmits propulsion orders to a receiving station in the engine room.

The control room refers to the space in a submarine where the commanding officer administers overall control of the vessel. This space is located in the forward end of the boat and contains the periscope stand, the steering and diving station, fire and navigation control and the trim system control board.

For example, the commanding officer orders an Ahead One Third bell. The Engine Order Telegraph operator rings up Ahead One Third by manually positioning a mechanical pointer to Ahead One Third on the Engine Order Telegraph in the control room. Since the receiving Engine Order Telegraph is magnetically connected to the sending Engine Order Telegraph's mechanical pointer, the receiving Engine Order Telegraph in the engine room registers Ahead One Third and rings a bell. The bell continues to ring until the Engine Order Telegraph operator in the engine room acknowledges the order and moves his mechanical pointer to Ahead One Third. Once the receiving mechanical pointer lines up with magnetic pointer on the receiving Engine Order Telegraph, a magnetic signal is relayed to the sending Engine Order Telegraph by moving its magnetic pointer to Ahead One Third to inform the control room that the engine room has acknowledge their propulsion order. The Engine Order Telegraph uses a magnetic/mechanical interface to insure propulsion orders can be relayed during times when electrical power could be limited or lost.

The ship will employ the assistance of a tugboat to navigate the channel out of Apra Harbor. Essentially, the underway out of the harbor is an easy task. Two bends in the channel provide problems for sailors new to the Apra Harbor. Fortunately, every submarine carries a harbor pilot to assist with navigation. The harbor pilot boards the vessel at the pier just prior to unmooring and disembarks after the vessel clears the channel breakwater.

Underway in any channel is a smooth ride. The bow of the vessel merely parts the water like a hot knife pressed against soft butter. That sensation changes dramatically when the vessel reaches the breakwater of the channel. At the breakwater, the vessel begins to heave and yaw to the open ocean currents. Since fleet boats are round bottom with little in the manner of an extended keel, they tend to pitch and roll easily. Seasickness overcomes the crew like the plague until their sea legs kick in to the sudden exposure to the pitching and rolling.

From the breakwater to the dive area, the ride is bumpy. Sailors need to concentrate on each step they make. Often using the bulkheads (walls) for support in order to transit within the ship, the scene truly is inspiring to anyone who enjoys carnival rides. If one of the meals is being served during the transit to the dive area, crewmen busy themselves with keeping the dinnerware on the table, often using their bodies as barriers to the sliding bowls and plates. Interestingly, under these sea state conditions, requesting a particular selection merely requires waiting for the ship to roll in your direction, and all the selections make themselves available at your elbows. At times, the selections manage to elude the containment of your arms and nestle moistly on your at-sea attire. It provides new meaning to the expression: "taking your meal with you."

In an effort to minimize spills from the ship's movement on the surface, Navy-supplied coffee cups provide a fill line, painted around the upper perimeter of the outside of the cup. The fill line alerts the sailor that filling the coffee cup to a point under that line provides some sense of security that the contents of the cup will not spill onto him during a ship's roll. It works! Seldom will any sailor intentionally fill his coffee cup above that fill line while the ship is underway. With the exception of having the coffee cup fall from the dining table, the contents of the cup remain within it during heaving and rolling conditions.

Other dining receptacles likewise have been marked with a fill line. Soup or cereal bowls have a similar line marked on their outer perimeter of the outside portion. Interestingly, entrée plates have the line drawn around the outer perimeter on their inside portion. This even includes the smaller plates: coffee cup holder, dessert plate, etc. The entire vessel's dinnerware containers are marked to ensure safe usage at sea. The detail engineered into safe, at-sea life truly is amazing.

Once the vessel arrives at the dive area, propulsion is reduced to minimum while the crew assesses the depths below for safe submergence. The ship's sonar sensors scan the depths for soundings and the distance from the ocean floor. Underwater, the ship has no eyes. Sound is the only means of maneuvering. To imagine the situation underwater, try maneuvering about a room in your house with your eyes blindfolded. One thing you learn quickly is to measure precisely the distance between each object in the room when your eyes are open. In a way, a submarine does the same thing. Prior to attempting to maneuver blindfolded, the submarine measures, through the use of sonar, the seascape beneath it. Once it feels comfortable with the layout of the seascape, it can proceed slowly to descend into the depths. Dive areas, however, are not new rooms *per se*. Dive areas have well chartered seascapes. The prior-to-submergence sonar scan merely confirms the data already available on the seascape to the ship's diving officer. From our example, this would be like trying to move about a room blindfolded that you previously mapped out a number of times in the past.

Submergence

The dive is a sensitive evolution. When you think about submerging a multi-ton, steel vessel beneath the surface, the integrity of the hull becomes of utmost concern. It would not take much of leak to unimpeded the multi-ton vessel's journey to the bottom of the ocean. Hence, the Golden Rule of Submarines reads: Keep the Ocean Out.

Prior to submergence, a double-independent-check system is performed on all inlets from the sea. By double-independent check, we mean that one qualified submariner checks the proper position of a particular valve that provides access from the sea to the ship's interior. As he checks each valve, he signs verifying that the position is correct for submerged operations. Upon completion of the first sailor's satisfactory check, a second qualified submariner goes back through the first submariner's check of the proper position of the valves to verify that their position is accurate. Once the second qualified submariner is satisfied, he signs certifying the correct position of the valves for submergence operations. A submarine-qualified commissioned officer then reviews the double-independent check and, if satisfied, authenticates the valve check and reports to the control room that the ship is ready to submerge.

Since over one hundred valves may need to be so checked, the process is timely and painstaking. However, for experienced submariners, it can be accomplished quite quickly. Generally, the pre-submergence, double-independent checks are initiated long before the ship arrives at the dive area, so that only strategic valves, called major hull valves, need be checked and/or repositioned. This double-independent check is second nature to submariners. It is almost as routine as putting on your socks. After all, it only takes one missed hull valve to have the date of that submergence etched on your tombstone, or receive the more ominous submarine epitaph: "still on patrol."

Once the ship is ready to dive, the diving officer will announce the dive intention twice and sound the diving alarm. The diving alarm consists of two long blasts from an air horn, or claxon, that sounds like "ouga, ouga." After the diving alarm sounds, the diving officer orders the crew to open the vents to the main ballast tanks and shift water within the ship's water reserve tanks to trim the ship. The main ballast tanks are huge enclosures that straddle the ship's hull like saddlebags on a horse. They are open to seawater at the bottom, but closed at the top to contain the air in order to buoy the ship on the surface. Vents, or hull valves, are located at the top of these tanks to allow for their venting. As the main ballast tanks are vented, air gushes out the vent valves as seawater displaces the air within the tanks. The action of air leaving and seawater rising within the main ballast tanks causes the ship to acquire negative buoyancy and begin to submerge. Since the main ballast tanks are huge, full submergence takes a few minutes.

Once submerged, the ship's angle is adjusted by relocating water within the ship's water tanks to the desired list and trim for underwater operations. On the surface, the laws of physics with respect to water rising to its own level insure the ship is trim. However, once submerged, the water has enveloped the ship, and the trim is now determined by the weight distribution within the ship's hull. Accordingly, to bring the ship to a normal angle, one-hundred-and-eighty degrees, for underwater operation, the diving officer often has to trim the ship by relocating water from one water tank to another. This feat is accomplished by a trim system that consists mainly of a pump that can draw water from one water tank and redirect it to another water tank. The trim system water tanks are strategically located within the ship to be able to adjust list (left or right side tilts) or trim (up or down angles). Since evolutions on the ship may alter the trim, control room watch standers often adjust the trim from time to time. Trim is also adjusted when down or up angles are required for ship's operations.

From time to time, water needs to be taken in or expelled from the ship to adjust buoyancy. For example, the sanitary tanks collect the crew's human refuse. As the sanitary tanks fill, they begin to influence the ship's buoyancy. As they fill, trim water will be expelled from the ship to compensate for the weight increasing in the sanitary tanks. Once the sanitary tanks are full, they will be discharge overboard by the ship's crew with the use of high-pressure air. The discharging of the sanitary tanks overboard will lighten the ship, effecting buoyancy, and require sea water to be pumped inside the trim system from the ocean to compensate and return the ship to its normal underwater operation's buoyancy. This is but one evolution requiring adjustment of the trim system. Many evolutions, like the sanitary tanks, occur each six-hour watch and require adjustment of the trim system.

Underway submergence requires tremendous sensitivity to sound. Sound instrumentation of various capacities performs all sorts of functions. Listening arrays are employed to determine the existence of other submerged vessels. To determine the distance between the keel of the ship and the ocean floor, sounds waves are bounced off the ocean floor with low energy sonar. Active sonar of appreciable strength is seldom used while underway. Though active sonar is quite precise at locating submerged objects and other obstructions, it announces the precise location of its origin to any other submerged vessel, making the sender easily detectable. In the undersea world of submarine operations, silence is golden. Noise is soon silenced!

Like the walking stick of the blind man handled to detect objects, passive sonar feels the ship's way through the ocean. Although the underwater journey seems difficult to imagine, maneuvering benefits from the fact that there are few obstacles in the ship's operating depth of the ocean. Even whales, like all other sea life, stay clear of large submersibles. Submarines never run into whales, sharks or dolphins. The only thing submarines have to worry about is another submarine while submerged and surface vessels when the submarine attempts to surface. Despite the lack of vision underwater, undersea collisions are rare. Far more collisions occur during surfacing operations. This is mainly due to the fact that submarines surface near ports where surface traffic is abundant. It is seldom a lone vessel that a submarine fails to detect. Collisions occur when there are multiple contacts in the area and the sea state is rough.

If the submarine crew is tracking a dozen contacts, often the crew will assign priority to the position and direction of the contacts. Those vessels departing the dive (surfacing) area will be given low priorities for tracking; whereas, those vessels entering the dive (surfacing) area will take up the crew's attention. Collisions tend to occur when a vessel initially reported as departing the dive (surfacing) area will for some unknown reason change course and enter the dive (surfacing) area. Often, due to the attention of the crew on the other vessels, the vessel having changed direction will come upon the submarine unnoticed. This is especially true if the sea state masks periscope visibility of an approaching vessel. If the crew does not routinely monitor the entire dive (surfacing) area, rather than restrict their attention to those previously identified vessels' tracks, the chance of collision will increase dramatically.

Once the crew's attention has been diverted away from a particular vessel, it requires vigilance on the part of the sonar crew to randomly verify all areas around the dive (surfacing) area. This is particular difficult if many vessels have been identified entering the dive (surfacing) area. The hectic conditions of the control room with multiple contacts in the area are akin to a stock floor during heavy trading. It is difficult to put something back in your mind that you have already discounted. You cannot see it. You have to hear it. Since hearing is not our primary sense, it is easy to discount something even if you, in fact, do hear it coming. To be successful in undersea operations, you have to elevate hearing to become your primary sense. Vision must become subservient to hearing. This is especially true during submergence operations when another undersea vessel is detected in the area.

In the days of the twenty-one gunners and sails, entanglements were determined by wind advantage and ship's position relative to the opponent. In undersea encounters, silence, passive sonar and temperature and salinity of water make the difference. If your submarine is quieter running than your opponents, you will best him. Why, because he cannot hear you. If your passive sonar is more sensitive than your opponents, you will best him. Why, because you will detect him long before he detects you. Last, the water conditions can mask an opponent from your sonar.

Sonar depends on constant salinity and temperature conditions of the ocean area of operation. If the ocean area of operation has for some reason layered out from inactivity of circulation, sonar efficiency may be hampered. Sounds emitted by another submerged vessel may be masked by the effect of their bouncing back when they interact with the sudden salinity or temperature layer much different from that of their point of origin. This bouncing back will reduce, often greatly, the sounds perceptible to a submerged vessel on the other side of the salinity or temperature layer. In some cases, the reduce sound will fall below the threshold of sensitivity of a listening vessel or be misinterpreted as a biologic (sea creature) or a vessel at a great distance away.

Bays may acquire odd salinity variations, as may large river delta areas. Different depths in the ocean can stratify into colder or warmer layers. Knowing where these layers are most probable heightens the sonar detection efforts. After all, if an undersea vessel is approaching your area of operation, knowing a temperature layer exists below your current operating depth will enable your vessel to descend under the temperature layer and become undetectable to any vessel operating above the temperature layer. Regrettably, the same technique is available to your opponent. Sudden ascension through a temperature layer is another cause for undersea collisions! Neither underwater vessel is aware of the other's presence.

Today's dive concerns testing some new ship's equipment and getting the crew ready for a long deployment. This is not a deep dive. The ship will operate at normal operating depth and conduct a few training exercises.

The training exercises generally involve a flooding and a fire drill to measure the crew's reaction time. A number of at-sea evolutions will be conducted, as well. One evolution that often attracts attention prior to a long deployment is discharging garbage at sea. Interestingly, the ship does not surface and dump their garbage over the side like was done in the days of sailing vessels. Collecting ship's garbage has become a pastime with foreign monitoring vessels in order to identify submerged vessels operating in their area.

In an effort to avoid detection via refuse analysis, submarines are equipped with an on board trash compactor and ejection assembly. At predetermined times of the day, the crew assembles all trash in a particular room. The trash is compacted tightly into metal cylinders and weighted down with lead. After the trash has been compacted, the metal cylinders are fed into a pressurized ejection assembly. The ejection assembly is sealed then evacuated of water. The loading chamber door is opened and the metal cylinder is inserted. Once the metal cylinder is snuggly inserted into the ejection chamber, the loading chamber door is sealed. The outer ejection chamber door is opened exposing the metal cylinder to sea pressure. Once the outer door is fully opened, high-pressure air is injected into the upper volume of the ejection chamber, forcing the metal cylinder out of the outer door and into the ocean. The lead weights insure the metal cylinder sinks to the bottom of the ocean. Once the metal cylinder clears the outer door, the high-pressure air injection is ceased and the outer door is sealed. The process repeats itself for the next metal cylinder.

For the fire and flooding drills, the ship monitors itself in its ability to perform correctly the damage control procedures for each drill. In essence, the ability of the crew to isolate the effected compartment is of utmost importance in these exercises.

Fleet ballistic missile submarines are composed of four compartments: bow, main, missile and engineering spaces. The bow compartment holds the main sonar sensors, torpedo tubes and torpedoes. Some berthing is available as well. The main compartment consists of three decks (or levels). The upper level contains the control room, sonar monitoring space, radio room, administrative room and the senior officers' staterooms. Crew's mess, the galley, the wardroom, staterooms and some senior enlisted berthing take up the middle level. The lower level accommodates the laundry, refuse collection, and the remaining berthing. The basement of the main compartment holds the ship's battery. The missile compartment houses the missiles, their launch tubes and associated control systems and the missile launch console. The missile tubes extend through the three decks of the compartment. The engineering spaces include the reactor plant and associated systems, the steam turbines, the propulsion turbines and the propulsion train, the major electrical distribution switchboards and the engine room control center.

Compartments are like rooms in a house. Undersea compartments differ from rooms in that they are separately ventilated and have watertight doors for ingress and egress. In any casualty, the first steps in combating that casualty are to secure the effected compartment by shutting the watertight door and the ventilation valves feeding that compartment. Next on the list of importance would be securing any unnecessary evolution taking place in the compartment. Breaking out the damage control equipment would follow in importance. Lastly, the watch standers should don telecommunication equipment to provide a status of the casualty to the controlling station.

Perhaps the biggest difference in casualty response between fire and flooding is that with flooding, the crew remains in the compartment to secure the flooding; whereas, for fire, the crew initially may flee the effected compartment to don breathing apparatus prior to re-entering to combat the fire. Flooding may sink the ship, so remaining to fight the flooding is of paramount importance. Fire, on the other hand, emits smoke that displaces the air within the ship, resulting in a situation, if not isolated, that could incapacitate the crew. Underwater, there is only so much air within the ship's interior.

Normal breathing atmosphere will contain between 16-21% oxygen. If the oxygen level drops appreciably below 16%, the crew will begin to lose consciousness. Monitoring oxygen level is done continuously with electronic equipment. When the oxygen level falls to near 16%, oxygen is fed into the ship atmosphere from on board oxygen tanks. An oxygen producing system that breaks up seawater into hydrogen and oxygen replenishes the oxygen in the oxygen tanks. If the oxygen level approaches 21%, the ship's air is re-circulated with outside air. This requires the ship to approach the surface and extend one of its snorkel masts to allow outside air to be drawn into the ship and mixed with the ship's internal air, thereby reducing the oxygen level within the ship.

Surfacing

Since this at-sea exercise was primarily a day-operation for testing the crew's preparedness, once the scheduled exercises are complete, the ship transits back to the dive area and prepares to surface. Once again, during the transit to the dive (surfacing) area, the crew busies themselves with checking valve line-ups for surface operations.

Surfacing is a little more difficult than diving because of the greater probability of encountering a vessel. Surface vessels greatly outnumber submerged vessels in every port area of the world. Ports are vessel magnets. With that in mind, the ship's crew dedicates a number of watch standers to tracking surface targets. Sometimes, in busy ports, it is not uncommon to be tracking as many as thirty vessels. Tracking refers to monitoring a vessel's course, distance and speed. As previously mentioned, vessels traveling away from the surface area are given lesser attention-priority than those vessels approaching the surface area.

How does a submarine surface? Interestingly, the accomplishment is quite simple. The submarine makes itself positively buoyant, and the ocean's pressure lifts the submarine to the surface. There are two methods a submarine may obtain positive buoyancy. One, the main ballast tanks vent valves can be shut and high-pressure air can be injected into the ballast tanks, displacing seawater and creating the positive buoyancy required for surfacing. This is called "blowing to the surface." Second, the submarine's variable ballast tanks (water tanks connected to the trim system) can be pumped, via the trim pump, to remove water weight from the submarine, creating a positive buoyancy that would cause the ship to rise to the surface. This is called "pumping to the surface." "Blowing to the surface" is far more common than "pumping to the surface."

In the dive (surface) area, the ship will proceed to periscope depth, as the crew finalizes the preparations for surfacing. Once the prescribed location for surfacing is reached, the commanding officer will bring the ship to periscope depth and scan the intended surface area with the periscope. Periscope depth refers to that depth in which the periscope can be extended above the surface of the water. For most classes of submarines, periscope depth is less than one hundred feet from the ship's keel. At periscope depth, the main objective is to verify the number and location of the surface contacts identified by sonar. It is very important to visually verify these vessels. One of the most common causes of collisions between submarines and surface vessels is omitting to evaluate thoroughly all the surface contacts in the intended surface area. This is important, because surfacing does not always immediately follow a periscope check of the area. Sometime evolutions, required for performance standards, precede surfacing. In those instances, some time may elapse between the final periscope check and the actual surfacing. Therefore, it is important that an accurate and predictable assessment of the surface vessels' movements above be obtained.

The most common collision occurs with fishing trawlers that for some reason alter course randomly. When fishing trawlers are present, extra care has to be taken in monitoring their direction and speed. On more than one occasion, a trawler has changed course one hundred and eighty degrees, dropped nets and steered onto a collision course with a submarine. Often, the trawler crew cannot even speak English and are unaware of designated submarine operations areas. They chose to enter unknowingly into a submarine operations area, because they had a feeling that the fishing would be good there. Catching a submarine in their purse seine net confirms their suspicions. Unfortunately, when the ocean laps over the gunwale of their vessel, they realize how overzealous their feelings were. Most trawlers meet their demise in these encounters. Interestingly, the trawler crews first identify the netted creature as a huge whale. Only the survivors from the encounter will learn that they netted a submarine.

The surfacing procedure requires the submarine to position itself within the assigned area. Depending on the pre-scheduled evolutions, the submarine may elect to surface immediately or await the completion of those evolutions. By immediately, the submarine performs a complete area check of surface contacts. All contacts are relayed to the commanding officer on a chart. Once the surface contacts are acknowledged, the commanding officer raises the periscope and performs a least two three-hundred-and-sixty-degree sweeps of the area, identifying the surface contacts on the chart. The commanding officer stops the periscope on each surface contact to verify its range from the submarine. Once all the contacts are identified, and it is determined that none will intercept the submarine while surfacing, the periscope is lowered. Once the periscope is securely housed, the commanding officer issues the order to surface.

The order to surface is repeated three times followed by the blasts from the submarine air horn, or claxon, three times: ouga, ouga, ouga. The difference between the dive and the surface order is the number of times the order is sounded: two for dive, and three for surface. Following the order to surface, the commanding officer generally will order the main ballast tank vents shut and the ballast tanks filled with high-pressure air. The actual order is: Blow Main Ballast Tanks.

The entire crew can hear the high-pressure air enter the main ballast tanks. It is a loud noise that reverberates throughout the ship. As the high-pressure air displaces the seawater in the main ballast tanks, each member of the crew can feel the ship begin to rise to the surface. Despite the depth from which the main ballast tanks were blown, the rise of the ship suddenly is broken when the ship broaches the surface. It is a strange feeling within the ship during a broaching. The ship seems to bob and then sway to one side. The bobbing is more distinctive in a rougher sea state. When you are sitting down, the "sway to one side" effect is more pronounced, because you will physically move to that side on your seat. If you are standing, you just need to adjust your legs in order to acquire your sea legs again.

Since submarines surface outside the breakwater, the first few minutes on the surface are spent getting your sea legs. If the sea state is rough, then getting your sea legs requires a bit more time. Walking inside a submarine on the surface can be a treat as well. With a rough sea state, you simply bounce along the walls of the corridors and passageways, stopping from time to time to allow gravity from the ship climbing a wave to loosen its effect upon you.

Once on the surface, the commanding officer issues the order to "Prepare for Surface." The order sends the crew scrambling about below decks locking valves in position and performing surface valve line-ups. Certain valves have to be locked into position on the surface less their operation inadvertently could sink the ship. Once on the surface, a submarine crew enjoys staying there for a while.

As the submarine approaches the breakwater, the commanding officer will set the maneuvering watch, sending the topside watches onto the main deck. The topside watches will don life vests and attach umbilical cords to them in order to anchor themselves down on the deck girders. Despite all these precautions, one of the most performed drills by the commanding officer and his understudy officers of the deck is the man overboard drill. Essentially, the man overboard drill requires the officer commanding the ship to be able to perform a figure eight pattern with the ship whenever a crewman announces that someone has fallen overboard. The figure eight enables the ship to return along the approach the ship was originally on when the man fell overboard. Accordingly, it is important for the announcement of the man overboard casualty to indicate into which side: Port or Starboard, the man fell over.

Port and Starboard are ship's lateral directions. Roughly, they are equivalent to the left and the right side of a person. This holds true as long as the person is compared to the vessel. The trouble arises when a person aboard a vessel is moving towards the vessel's aft end. In that situation, though the person's left and right sides remain the same, the ship's left and right sides have likewise remained the same. In this case, the person's left side, rather than facing the Port side of the vessel, would be facing the Starboard side. General rule: the Port side is the side on the left when a person is facing the front or bow of the ship.

The terms Port and Starboard were created in the days when sailing ships used the stars for navigation. The Starboard side of the ship was the side where the navigator estimated the ship's position by calculating the ship's relative movement with respect to the stars. This was done on a plank or board. Hence, the name star-board came into being.

The term Port came from that side of the ship that was preferred for mooring alongside in a port. That side generally contained more of the moving equipment: i.e., derricks, swivels, ropes and pulleys, as well as the gangplank for ingress and egress.

Port and Starboard have colors associated with them as well. Red indicates the Port side, whereas, Green indicates the Starboard side. Nightlights lit during maneuvering at night are colored Red and Green to distinguish the two sides of the ship, enabling other vessels to steer clear.

Red has taken on more significance than Green in navigation. Channels entering a harbor are marked with channel buoys that are generally colored Red or Green. The Golden Rule in entering any channel is: Red, Right, Returning. It cautions returning vessels to remain on the right side of the Red buoy. To find yourself on the left side of a Red buoy means you are soon to be aground. The safe-transit within a channel is marked between the Red and the Green buoys.

There is a vast expanse of ocean out there, but there are few safe harbors. Those few safe harbors often cannot be seen from the ocean, because sand banks or little peninsulas shelter them. Therefore, it is important to be able to distinguish their opening from the rest of the landmass. Red buoys announce a harbor. There will be two buoys marking a channel. The color of the other buoy may vary around North America. Be sure to steer to the right of the Red channel entry buoy. If both buoys should be Red then steer between them.

Passengers often have a favorite side of the ship in which to berth. In the days of sailing ships, I suppose the Port side made access to the gangplank more available. Today, since ships can moor to either side, it does not seem to make that much difference. Nonetheless, I prefer Starboard. Starboard allows me to fantasize about being a navigator, shooting the stars with a sextant.

Starboard has adventuresome connotations affixed to it. When afloat, adventure seems to motivate me. The sense of the unknown in the giant expanse of ocean excites me. To me, it is akin to traveling to the stars. Being assigned to a submarine, the crew is never told of their specific operation until they are underway and submerged. The sense of the unknown enticed me on every deployment. That sense of the unknown, I have interpreted as Starboard. We sailed, submerged, into the vast expanse of stars. It never bothered me where we were going or where we ended up, as long as we were afloat.

Once the breakwater is cleared, the sailing becomes smoother, almost as calm as being on a raft in pond. Noting the channel markers, the submarine steers right of the Red buoy and allows the navigation aids to direct its maneuvering into the harbor area. Most of the navigation aids after the initial two channel markers are white with black stripes. Identifying those black and white markers comforts us that we are in the bosom of the harbor. Like a mother folding her arms gently around her babe, the submarine is embraced tenderly to the pier.

Channel navigation has an added perk for the topside watches in that the banks of the channel often are dotted with well-wishers. Long channels seem to attract a multitude of onlookers when a nuclear submarine transits. For the civilian population, the only time a nuclear submarine can be seen is when it transits through a channel. For popular submarine bases, the site of a submarine in the channel is no big deal. However, for the ports where submarine calls are less frequent and random, the news of a submarine sighted entering the channel spreads like wildfire. Soon the channel banks are teeming with onlookers. Overseas, it has occurred on more than one occasion that schools have let their students depart early to witness a submarine making a port of call in their harbor.

Jules Verne's *Twenty Thousand Leagues Under The Sea* probably more than any other form of propaganda fueled the thirst for the thrills of undersea life. From today's modern scuba diver to the actual submariners themselves, Jules Verne stands as their White Goddess, enticing them into the seas. The sight of a submarine entering port propels one's imagination into the wondrous realms of undersea life. Seeing a submarine for the first time calls up visions of a giant squid wrapping its tentacles around its hull. Awe seems to be the first reaction from those newcomers on the channel banks. Then, they smile as Jules Verne's imagination overcomes them with, as they say: "...the glory that was Greece and the grandeur that was Rome." Before their eyes lies a chariot of the seas carrying home their mortal gods. The road to Rome for a returning general was never sweeter. A submarine in the channel is just a bigger chariot. Before their eyes lies the culmination of all their culture, philosophy and science wrapped in the toughest material of their industry, manned by the brightest of their offspring, armed with an unimaginable deterrence, skilled by the best of their war-masters and more determined than all the gods of the ancients. Hercules would have knelt before them. For a few precious moments, onlookers can capture the grandeur of their accomplishment. It will be a scene that will live long in their memory. The onlookers will boast, as many did of champion knights of the joust, with advantages. The submarine is second to none when it comes to lethal combat. The nuclear submarine is the most deadly war-machine ever created. All the sports' champions of all time measure little when compared to the accuracy, dedication, determination and skill of a nuclear submarine. Unquestionable victory is assured.

As the ship enters the harbor area, the crowds gathered on the channel banks wave in the distance. The harbor tugs busy themselves with proper alignment of the submarine to the pier. Line handling skills interchange between the tugboat crew and the topside watches. To tugboat crews, submarines are surface vessels with very, very deep drafts. Tugboats like to snuggle alongside a submarine a little aft of amidships in order to better steer the submarine into the pier. Line handlers from the naval base will await the submarine as it approaches the pier. Once the submarine is in close proximity to the pier, the tugboat will halt its progress toward the pier and allow the line handles on the pier and submarine to exchange mooring lines. Once the pier and submarine have exchanged and tied up their lines, the tugboat will ease the submarine into the pier. The pier and submarine line handlers will tighten the mooring lines ever so taught with each movement of the submarine closer to the pier until the submarine is lashed to the pier.

When the gangplank is lowered into place, the ship's non-nuclear crewmen will disembark. The nuclear crewmen will remain aboard to shutdown the steam plant and bring on shore electrical power. Once the shutdown watches are set, the non-duty-section nuclear crewmen will meander off the boat toward Andie's. It is not exactly a hero's welcome, but it is cold beer.

CHAPTER 2

Liberty in Agana, Guam

After the engineering crew had shutdown the reactor, a few of us old timers decided to go into Agana rather then meander over to Andie's for beer and pizza. By old timers, we refer to submarine crewmen above the age of twenty-five with more than two and a half years aboard the fleet boat. Submarine crews are young by the standards of any other industry.

The young dolphins are between nineteen and twenty-four years of age. During those years, the young crewmen spend most of their on board time qualifying their watch stations and this class of submarine. The average qualification time for first timers takes about two years overall. The submarine's availability schedule greatly effects qualification time. For an at-sea watch station qualification, the submarine needs to be in an at-sea environment. Hence, long periods in-port will hamper at-sea qualifications. Rankings for young crewmen range from seaman (E-3) through second class petty officer (E-5).

The next grouping of submariners runs from ages twenty-five to about age thirty, depending upon rank achieved. Ranking in this group runs from senior second class petty officer (E-5) to first class petty officer (E-6). This grouping has qualified their senior watch station and this class of submarine and spent over three years aboard. This is the group that makes the submarine run smoothly. In relationship to the complement of the entire crew, this grouping represents the vast majority of personnel aboard. With a crew of some one hundred and twenty personnel, it is not uncommon for as many as seventy-five crewmen to be in this category. The young bucks account for an average of fifteen to twenty crewmen. Another twelve to fifteen crewmen comprise the chief petty officer group (E-7 through E-9) while another twelve to fifteen embrace the commissioned officer complement (O-1 through O-5). Therefore, the mean age of a submarine crewman is about twenty-five years old and holds the rank of second class petty officer (E-5). A nuclear submarine with the capability to exterminate millions of people essentially is entrusted into the hands of twenty-five year olds. This is a remarkable achievement for any industrialized country. Interestingly, the number of crewmen above the age of forty easily can be counted on the fingers of one hand.

Compared with other industries, the youth of the nuclear submarine force is unmatched. Foremen in most engineering environments are at least in their forties before they are allowed to make critical decisions. The United States Navy entrusts the fate of the world to twenty-five year olds. It is not surprising that when these twenty-five year olds leave the naval service, they have the potential to be able to advance quite rapidly up the ladders of civilian industry. Senior positions in civilian nuclear power and related industries are replete with these former crewmen. Being a former nuclear submarine crewman can become a shortcut to success in any industry.

It is not uncommon for a former twenty-five-year-old, submarine crewman with a high school education to earn a bachelor's degree in engineering and become a consultant to the very companies that sell nuclear and submarine hardware to the military. Some of these twenty-five year olds have even gone on to acquire master's degrees and become members of the corporate profile of America's largest naval engineering firms. One could say that the spawning ground for America's engineering hierarchy breeds aboard her nuclear submarines. Nuclear submarine experience, with its immersion in inter-engineering, disciplinary experience, is second to none for enhancing the engineering acumen.

Charlie's

The choice of the evening is a place called Charlie's in the heart of Agana, Guam. Charlie's attracts the older sailors. After retirement, a former chief petty officer from the non-nuclear, surface fleet decided to remain on Guam and purchased the establishment. Although a former surface fleet sailor owns Charlie's, older submariners frequent the establishment more than surface fleet sailors.

The former chief petty officer remained on Guam not so much to operate a nightclub as in order to cash in on the planned military expansion in the Mariana Islands. Prior to his retirement, the former chief petty officer worked at the Surface Squadron offices and got wind of the plans to establish a huge, forward-deployed base on Tinian and Saipan.

Tinian and Saipan are two of the major islands in the Mariana Islands, now referred to as the Commonwealth of the Northern Mariana Islands (CNMI). The intent was to create a huge base on both islands in which an aircraft carrier could turn around in the area between Tinian and Saipan. Additionally, a nuclear submarine could enter the port submerged to avoid detection from foreign surveillance vessels.

Guam has been separated from the CNMI and incorporated into the United States protectorate system. Currently, Guam has the distinction of being a United States territory, much like Hawaii was during World War II. Guam is not very far geographically from Tinian or Saipan. A short, less than half-hour flight connects Guam with Tinian and Saipan. The possession of a US passport authorizes entry into the CNMI without difficulty.

Since Saipan and Tinian, at the time, lacked nightlife entertainment, the former chief petty officer opted to open Charlie's to cash in on the overflow from the huge military complex. Furthermore, it was no secret that Saipan was considered the fallback base in the event the United States would lose its privileges to forward deployed bases on the Philippine Islands. The former chief petty officer felt his retirement investment would be secure. It was a good bet, given the turbulent political climate of the times.

The central location of Charlie's in the heart of Agana, Guam was difficult to beat. Regrettably, the former chief's lack of entertainment experience reduced his clientele to the old timers, rather than the high-spending, low ranks. Old timers are notorious for ordering a beer and milking it for hours while they relate sea stories.

Another detrimental factor was Charlie's inability to attract the young, single females working in overseas assignments on Guam. These females fell into two groups: young female military personnel and schoolteachers. In the evening, the young female military personnel, for the most part, remained on the main naval or air base and frequented the military clubs. If they did venture off base, they did so in rented vehicles in which they toured Guam during the daytime.

The schoolteachers, fresh graduates from Mainland USA universities, spent their evenings at the Guam nightclubs that offered entertainment commensurate with what pleased them in the United States. They preferred live bands that played contemporary music. They enjoyed being alive, dancing and partying. They tended to be a little rambunctious. Since they were far from home, letting their hair down, so to speak, was acceptable. Band members touring the Guam hotels took advantage of the thrill-seeking nature of these fresh schoolteachers. Students from the University of Guam were likewise opportunistic. Lastly, young sailors who were politically correct could score with these schoolteachers when the competition was favorable. You could say the schoolteachers utilized a pecking order: band members, university students then sailors. The term "slumming for sailors" had meaning in Agana for schoolteachers.

Fortunately, anyone who frequented Charlie's avoided interaction with schoolteachers. Charlie's was a military establishment that promoted the ideals of naval service and a life of dedication. The language spoken in Charlie's was distinctly naval. Walls were bulkheads. The floor was a deck. The ceiling was an overhead. Patrons were shipmates. The bathroom was a head. In Charlie's, you were still aboard ship. No transition was required to acclimatize to the environment. Military ranks were often used in discussion. Charlie's was home for the military.

In description, Charlie's looked more like a car sales office with its large, three-quarter length windows on three of its four walls. The owner merely affixed shades to provide some seclusion from the street traffic for the patrons. If it were not for the four pool tables and eight-seat bar, Charlie's easily could be mistaken for a car dealership showroom or a restaurant. Lighting was inconsistent with beverage sales. Unlike the dim-lit establishments of the other nightclubs in Agana, Charlie's was always well lit. Hence, the environment discouraged heavy alcohol consumption. Furthermore, heavy alcohol selection was limited. As I can recall, liquor selection was limited to Crown Royal, Old Turkey and Black Label. Charlie's predominantly served draft beer. Most patrons kept with draft beer that was served in a frosted mug. For a quiet night of beer sipping, Charlie's was unmatched and highly recommended by the old timers. Fights never broke out there. The owner, military police and Guam police were on good terms with one another. Charlie's was a sanctuary for the military in the civilian sector of Guam.

This evening, Charlie's is nearly empty. There are a few old salts slobbering over some ancient sea tale at the bar. The pool tables are not being used. Some honky-tonk sound squeals from the juxbox. There are four of us tonight, so we settle in around one of the pool tables. We are all first class petty officers, so there is no rank apprehension. Actually, three of us matriculated from the same nuclear power prototype training facility. We have known each other for over three years. The fourth of the group is a non-nuclear trained person. Jokingly, we refer to him as the coner.

Coner is an affectionate term used to describe a non-nuclear trained, submarine crewman that spends his on watch time in the forward part of the submarine. Those watch standers from the after part of the ship are referred to as Nukes. Nuke is short for nuclear trained crewmember.

We are all single. The times seem to encourage being single. With the protest movement swinging from the Vietnam War to the new environmental consciousness, it seems the civilian population has lured many prospective, young females into a hate-frenzy against military personnel. Nuclear submariners usually avoid the "protest" gals anyway. Their excessive drug usage detracts from any serious intentions one might fantasize about them.

Tonight, we can run the pool tables and sip draft beer. The best pool player is Hansen. Hansen is an electrician from one of the Dakotas. On first sight of him, you would swear he just disembarked a longboat. His features are very Nordic: tall—over 6', rugged like a lumberjack, blonde and blue-eyed. And, he can play some pool. He can call double-bank-shots with ease. Fortunately, we play 8-ball, a game that breeds in lucky shots. The rest of us have difficulty even handling a pool cue.

Boris is the next best pool player. He is a Russian-American from upstate New York. As I recall, he is from some no-name area in the middle of the Adirondacks. From his appearance, he could easily be mistaken for someone from the lower part of Eastern Europe where the Turks intermingled. His thick, jet-black hair makes everyone question his ancestry. He looks Mongol rather than White Russian. Standing the shortest of our group, he makes up in height with his tongue that never seems to stop flapping. By naval rating, he is a nuclear machinist, the dirtiest and roughest of the nuclear jobs. Boris always appears sweaty, and grease seems to cling to his on board work uniform.

Dorf, the next member of the group, is the poorest pool player. His ability for the game decreases exponentially with each draft beer he consumes. No matter how good he is doing in the beginning of a set of games, one need just allow him time to gargle down three draft beer mugs, and losing is all he will witness the rest of the evening, unless he falls asleep waiting his turn to play. Dorf is German-American from somewhere in Ohio. Given his thin appearance, one might mistake him for a death camp survivor. He must have a tapeworm, because he eats more than the rest of us at each meal, and he certainly consumes more beer than any of us. Jokingly, we often refer to him as a walking beer filter. I cannot imagine him making the age of forty-five without being a permanent member of Alcoholics Anonymous.

Lastly, I take the stage, hailing from a French-American background. My shape and stature links the other three quite nicely. We seem to fit as a foursome.

It takes Hansen a few beers to lose his concentration enough to allow the rest of us to compete with him at 8-ball. For the first four or five sets, we stand around watching him run the table. Other than our expression of awe at his artistry with a cue stick, we merely sip draft beers to overcome our boredom. Sometimes, while we wait for Hansen to miscue, our conversation wanders off into venturing into one of the other nightclubs on the strip to checkout some of the college gals. This night is no different. Hansen's talent to drive us into boredom brings on such enticing thoughts.

Right across the boulevard from Charlie's is the more chic nightclub, Equator. Equator attracts the college students and the foreign-employed schoolteachers from the Mainland USA. It is actually a smaller club than Charlie's. If superimposed upon the floor plan of Charlie's, Equator would create an L-shaped pattern. Equator's entranceway resembles the long length of the "L". It consists, at best, of a one-person walkway with the bar lining one entire side of the "L", and a few four-seat tables line the other side of the "L". At the base of the "L", the establishment opens up into raised dais for a band area, a number of four-seat tables with chairs and a small hardwood dance floor. On weekends the more popular island bands are featured.

Equator is quiet all day. The difference in walk-in traffic between Charlie's and the Equator during the daylight hours is negligible with advantage slipping towards Charlie's. As nightfall descends upon Agana, Equator begins to attract more clientele. The current contemporary music played at the Equator attracts a much younger crowd. By 9:30 PM on Fridays and Saturdays, Equator is teeming with young adults. Popular tunes jet out from within the Equator whenever the front door opens, alluring sympathetic ears within. Equator will remain packed until just before closing time at 2:00 AM. This evening is no different.

Boris cannot restrain himself from moving to the tunes emanating from the Equator. He seems to go into a solo-dancing frenzy whenever one of his favorite tunes is played. The remainder of our group seems unaffected by the sounds from the Equator. One good thing is that Boris' pool play worsens with the music. To our delight, it gives Dorf and I a better chance at winning a game. Dorf actually encourages Boris to listen attentively to the Equator music. There is a sense of victory for Dorf whenever Boris misses an easy pool shot. As for Boris, the importance of the pool game all but vanishes, as he moves to the tunes.

By about midnight, the Equator has cast its charm on both Boris and Hansen, and they plead for the group to go over and check out the band. Reluctantly, Dorf and I agree to tag along. Dorf and I feel uncomfortable with the college crowd. College students are naïve about the military and seem to feel threatened by our presence. Given their numbers, it is not hard to imagine a situation turning violent, as they nag and insult us over imaginary faults of the military, propagandized by the drug-addicted and misguided leaders of the protest movement.

We finish our pool game with Dorf winning. I believe Hansen and Boris lost the game intentionally to encourage Dorf to accompany them into the Equator.

We tally up our bar bill and pool fees and make our way across the boulevard to the Equator. It is not much of a walk, but we do have to wait for the only streetlight in Agana to change in order for us to cross the street. That is right! There is only one streetlight in Agana. Since the boulevard is the main vehicular artery on the island, it takes a while for the light to change to allow cross traffic and pedestrians to cross the street. You have to be alert for the change, because it is a hair trigger change. By the time you have ventured three steps into crossing the boulevard, the light will turn yellow. Unless you run, it is unlikely that you will be able to reach the other side of the boulevard, before the streetlight allows normal traffic flow to recommence. There is no time to be tipsy, if you intend to cross the boulevard in Agana.

It is still early for us, so the trip across the boulevard is successful. As we approach the entrance to the Equator we plot our strategy. It is agreed that we will walk directly into the base of the "L" portion of the establishment and find a table. We agree not to be distracted by the bar or the tables in the length of the "L". Those tables generally are reserved for the wilder, more anti-military students from the university. We need to avoid them, completely. Unfortunately, the anti-military students are offspring of the more affluent families residing on Guam. If trouble should erupt, the local police will tend to favor the students, irrespective of the situation. The military is always guilty in these altercations. We get arrested while the students carry-on unchallenged. It will be an all-eyes-forward walk from the entrance to the rear of the establishment. We remind each other of the hazards of entering this place, often, before Boris opens the front door.

Equator

Like automatons, we walk single file pass the bar into the seating area next to the dance floor. Boris, the Romeo of the group, does not fail to notice a group of gals enjoying themselves at one of the tables across from the bar. As soon we locate a vacant four-seat table, Boris cannot wait to inform us of the gals. To Boris, the Equator is a target rich environment for females. I suppose any area containing a few young females would acquire that designation for submariners deployed overseas. Nonetheless, Boris spends the entire time we wait for our first round of beers to assess approach scenarios in order to meet the girls. Interestingly, the girls are unaccompanied. Even the local guys seem to give them a wide berth. Perhaps, they are waiting for their boyfriends. Perhaps, they are regulars and prefer to be left alone. Worse yet, they might be lesbians. Whatever the reason, Boris is determined to make a play to meet them.

As our beers arrive, delivered by a college age Guamanian with a soft smile, two of the target girls leave their table in order to dance to a popular tune. They cheer the band as they stand up. Obviously, the band is playing one of their favorite dance songs. As fate would have it, both girls walk right pass our table and exchange smiles with Boris. Boris is certain of his fortune this evening. As soon as the girls begin dancing, Boris takes one sip from his beer…for courage no doubt…and gets up to join them. His approach is smooth. He just eases in between them and begins dancing. The girls giggle at one another and allow him to join them. More amazingly, Boris turns out to be a good dancer. He knows the current dance moves really well. We all wonder how he got the time to learn them. We are as surprised as the girls. From the expressions forming on the girls' faces, they enjoy his dancing and his company. Boris broke the ice with them. Soon, they are chatting away as they dance. When the dance finishes, the shorter of the two girls invites Boris to join them at their table. Although, we do not hear the invite, the wide smile on Boris' face communicates success.

Hansen cheers Boris by tapping his beer bottle on Boris' to acknowledge the accomplishment. Boris leans over as he grabs his beer bottle and whispers to us that he will be right back to get us. There are five girls and four of us, but Boris is certain they will invite us to join them. He corrects our initial assumption that the girls were coeds. He informs us that they are elementary schoolteachers on overseas assignment. What is more, they are relatively new to Guam and the nightlife. And, they like sailors.

Boris departs to join the girls and make a plea for our company. In the meantime, the three of us debate which girl we would like. Hansen likes the chubby blonde. Dorf seems to prefer the slender brunette. She is a looker, too. I am unsure of which girl Boris plans to romance, but since he danced with two of them, we decide to allow him to choose one of those two. That leaves a slender blonde for me. She looks OK. She has long, light-blond hair that extends down her back to a point just below her shoulders. She smokes and seems reserved. The conversation the girls are enjoying does not interest her. Most of the time, she gazes up at the ceiling or at the empty walls. The music the band plays seems to keep her attention. I do not think she knows these other girls very well.

The three of us appraise Boris' romancing. He certainly seems to have a silk tongue. Like a gypsy rogue selling wares in a bazaar, Boris seems to marvel the girls with his small talk. Soon, two of the girls are making room for us and pleading for some unused chairs from the tables around them. We are in. Boris made it. When the extra chairs are assembled, Boris excuses himself and comes over for us. The girls acquired four chairs, yet there are just three of us. Apparently, one of the girls is waiting for someone.

The communication with Boris is short: "Guys, grab your beers. The girls are waiting." Boris does not have to repeat himself. We are already on our way. When we arrive, the girls suggest another arrangement. The chubby blonde prefers to sit next to Dorf, whereas, the slender brunette expresses a fondness for Hansen. The smoker blonde and I are left to make our own introductions. She seems to be like me, willing to take whoever is left over. As I take the seat next to her, she lights up another cigarette. It is one of those popular, chic women's brands with huge filters. She is nervous. Well, so am I. It has been a while since I have been with someone. Somehow, I get the impression that she has not been with someone in a while either. Stranger matches have occurred, I suppose. Nonetheless, there is promise tonight for the two of us. It is obvious that we do not repulse one another.

Being in a nightclub like the Equator is unusual for me. Most of the clientele have a different political perspective than I do. I hear bits and pieces of their conversations as I move about inside these types of clubs. They favor clean air, yet they seem to chain smoke. They want to be free of nuclear materials, yet they scream very loud as soon as the weather becomes too hot or too cold. Most of the time they are referring to nuclear weapons, but for some reason, they boycott nuclear power plants.

Interestingly, the state that seems to object the loudest over nuclear power is Hawaii, yet that state has more nuclear power plants per unit area then any other state. Hawaii has even outlawed nuclear power. That is a strange position for a state that welcomes some twenty-plus nuclear powered submarines to homeport at Pearl Harbor within a few miles of over seventy-five percent of the state's population.

Nightclubs like the Equator do not welcome military. They welcome their money as long as the military just sits and drinks and does not bother anyone. It is the same in all the American ports affiliated with the United States. The macabre specter of Vietnam remains attached to every person in uniform. Some people make you feel welcome; however, every military person knows that welcome evaporates quickly at the first sign of resentment. This is especially true with the gals. They are very sensitive as to how the guys they grew up with, or work with, view them. The locals have this ownership attitude over their herd of women. The military can come to the nightclubs to drink, but that is as far as it goes. I am sensing that right now, as I sit next to this blonde.

We strike up a friendly conversation. Her name is Carol. She grew up in Northern California. The only time she went to a big city was when she flew to Guam. Her parents took her to the airport in San Francisco. From her mannerisms, the only sense of big city about her is her smoking. The rest is rural America. She told me her older sister started her smoking. Her mother smokes as well but tried to discourage her and her sister from forming the habit. She giggles as she says her mother failed. Her giggle resembles those I smiled at in New Hampshire when farm girls were exposed to animal husbandry for the first time. Carol could have fit right in with the girls I knew in New Hampshire. I guess there is a common connection among all rural gals.

My interests in Carol diminish as the evening chat wears on. She can smoke three cigarettes in the time I take to sip one beer. She will be dead before she reaches the age of forty. I am not slow with the beers either. She must be terribly nervous in my company. I might be the first guy she has sat with in a nightclub, since she has been in Guam. She seems nice enough, but I find myself on the fence leaning more toward leaving than continuing the evening with her. What keeps me around is that the other guys are hitting it off real well. Dorf has stars in his eyes. I smile at the thought that he might even propose to the girl that is with him. One thing is for certain. She is the best girl I have ever seen with him. He should make every effort to get to know her.

Boris and Hansen are too obvious in their intention to just bed their girls. Fortunately for them, the girls seem to have the same inclination. It will not be long before Boris and Hansen leave with the girls. Their lively conversation has kept the table alive all evening. I hate to imagine what will remain after they leave. They are doing so good that it almost becomes a compulsory act to follow suit. Dorf, I can tell, will follow them. As for me, I really do not know.

Suddenly, one of the girls orders another round of drinks and recommends that we take the party to their apartment. Boris and Hansen cannot answer quickly enough with an enthusiastic affirmative. Dorf just sits there with a smile on his face that could not be outdone if he were just told he was admitted to heaven. Carol upon hearing the offer just rests her hand on my thigh gently. It is amazing how a gal can make one simple gesture and have it speak volumes about her aspirations. I just smile at Carol and nod ever so slightly.

Through the next round of drinks, Carol does not speak to me at all. She immerses herself in the conversation going on at the table. Interestingly, she stops smoking. A sense of cool relaxation comes over her. I suspect that this is the way she is all the time. My presence made her self-conscious; however, now that things are settled, she returns to her normal charming personality. And, I admit, she is much more appealing when at ease than when she is chain smoking.

The conversation for most of us at the table settles down. It is like we have known each other for some time. As for me, I find myself drifting away from the conversation into a strange area of reflection. What am I doing here? Do I really want to spend the night with this Northern California gal or not? It would be nice. It has been months since I had been with someone. I do enjoy inhaling the fragrance of her perfume. I like the way her hair flows down her sides. It is especially appealing as it drapes over her shoulders. When she moves her head from side to side, I like the way her hair follows like a gold, silk scarf. She is pretty. My lower charkas are coming alive as well to ascertain my attractiveness to Carol.

Finishing up the drinks, the girls busy themselves with the arrangements to cart all of us to their place. Since the five girls all came in one car, room will become a premium. The fifth girl decides to remain in the club with her boyfriend who will take her back later. After some deliberation, it is decided that Boris and Hansen will travel with their girls in the girls' automobile. Dorf and I, with our gals, will take a taxi. The problem of four couples is troublesome. If there were just three couples, then all parties could travel in the girls' car. That thought pushes me back over the fence. I announce that it would not be wise for me to go along, since I need to get up early. My announcement only startles Carol. The rest of the group seems to seize on the opportunity, and all three pairs make their way out of the nightclub.

Watching the others leave, Carol asks me again if I would not like to reconsider. She offers to pay the cab fare. I decline. If I thought there might be some future for us, I would reconsider. However, I just do not like gals who smoke. I know I would not be good company for her.

Carol and her girlfriend agree to go back together with the other gal's boyfriend when he gets off work. Apparently, he is associated with the band. I order another round of drinks for us when the other gal's boyfriend sits down at our table. It is the least I can do. The remaining thirty minutes or so, we chat about their lives. As it turns out, the two gals attended the same teacher's college in Northern California. They chose that college because of its excellent overseas placement program. The girls confide in me that all they wanted to do was travel. The girl that left with Boris worked a lot overseas with the Red Cross. She is the one that persuaded the others to embark on a career of work/travel experience. Interestingly, their preferences resembled mine in the Navy. In difference, they get a three year assignment to one overseas post, whereas, I can see many different ports during my deployments. The girls intend to overcome their travel-short-coming by catching weekend flights to surrounding areas. From Guam, they believe, the Republic of Palau and the Federated States of Micronesia should keep them occupied for the three years.

Being a sort of history buff, I make a list of interesting sites to see in those two Pacific Island countries. Palau has the spectacular reefs near Kyangel and the war remains from the invasion of Peleliu. The Federated States of Micronesia is broken up into four major island groupings: Yap, Chuuk, Ponape and Kosare. Chuuk (formerly called Truk) prides itself on its underwater sites from World War II remains. Ponape has the ancient site of Namadol. Yap and Kosare have excellent deep-sea fishing opportunities. The other gal's boyfriend attests to the diving experience in the waters adjacent to Chuuk. He has been on Guam a bit longer and has taken advantage of some of the sites.

Some of the band members begin to join us at the table. One member orders a round for all of us. I decline and begin to bid my *adieus*. Despite pleadings from the group for me to stay, I decide against it. Carol manages to stand as I am getting up to leave and kisses me on the side of the lips. I can smell the tobacco in her breath and taste the tobacco on her lips. She is a pretty girl, but I just cannot stand the taste of tobacco. She holds me firmly, but I convey with my eyes that I will not change my mind. I thank her for spending some time with me, turn and walk out of the Equator.

Fortunately, the popularity of the Equator attracts a number of taxi drivers to sit and wait for fares just outside the establishment. In no time, I am in a cab and on my way to the Apra. After the Equator is out of sight, the cab driver hints that he can provide me with a girl, if I am interested. Once again, I decline. I suppose single military guys leaving a hot nightclub, after midnight, present targets of opportunity for the prostitution trade on Guam. This night, I just could not see visiting a whorehouse after just turning down a sure thing from a nice gal.

The Way Back to the Boat

The drive from the Equator to the base is not that far, but with essentially one-lane of traffic on either side of the road, any accident or rubbernecking slows the travel time. Tonight is not an exception. We have a fender bender at about the midway point. As we sit in traffic, the taxi driver and I strike up a conversation. He is ex-Air Force and was stationed at the big airbase on the far tip of the island. He spent six years here doing bombing runs into North Vietnam, before he decided on leaving the service. I inquired as to why he left after six years. He replied that he had difficulty adjusting to the fact that without a college degree he would remain a junior enlisted person for most of his career.

The military nowadays requires an undergraduate degree in order to advance into a line commissioning status. I suppose it is a fair requirement. Obtaining an undergraduate degree does display that the individual can stay focused for four years on a particular goal. Also, it ascertains that the individual was exposed to the better aspects of civilian life. It is sort of like a Roman consul's experience. Before the Roman Senate would appoint a consul, they would have the individual come to Rome and experience all its grandeur. That way, when the consul was far away in his consulate area, he would have the comfort of the Rome experience to remind him to attend to his duties. College life, I suppose, stands in for that experience nowadays.

Nevertheless, the taxi driver was unwilling to accept the disparities. To him, how could a kid right out of college and officer candidate school be awarded better privileges than someone with over five years of combat mission experience in the Air Force? He was not too keen on the fact that he took five years to make E-4, whereas, the college kid made 0-1 in less than six months and receives double an E-4's salary. It does seem unfair on the surface.

Early in my career, I wrestled with a similar concern. What I discovered was that an officer is selected in order to sustain a system of leadership that will ultimately produce a military genius with the character and courage required to lead the nation in a time of crisis. Now, to achieve this goal, the officer corps has to be competitive. And, it is. At every grade increase, the officer corps sheds some of its numbers. These dropouts can be individuals that would, in enlisted status, be able to continue a full career. But, because they chose the officer corps, they will be discharged before they are eligible for any retirement. Unfortunately, for the most part, their dismissal from the military will not be because they performed poorly, but because they performed, in the opinion of their supervisors, less than others in their grade. Sometimes very good officers have to be let go, because their performance did not meet the standard at the time. One look at the Naval Academy acceptance standards is prime example.

For some ten years, the target grade for sure acceptance into the Naval Academy was 1100 on the performance aptitude test. Then, some movie like *Top Gun* comes along and enthralls an entire generation of high school students with the desire to become Navy jet pilots. Suddenly, in the next few years, because of the increased number of applications from very qualified candidates, the acceptance criteria jumps to 1200 and begins to rival the Ivy League for candidates. What happens to the Naval Academy applicants who scored between 1100 and 1199? They were just as qualified as the applicants who successfully were admitted in the ten prior years, and I think, it is safe to say that would be as successful as the individuals who will apply after the "Top Gun Era" has elapsed. But, what happens to them? They get passed over. Their application is rejected. If they desire the Naval Service, they will be required to attend a regular college with a Naval Reserve Officer Training Cadet Program (NROTC) or enlist in the Navy and work their way toward commissioning, as they serve their country. Sometimes, it is a tough deal to be an officer.

The taxi driver and I continued chatting about his job in the Air Force all the way back to the base. I could tell from the conversation that he missed the Air Force. Had he not reflected on the disparities, he would have made a career of it. As it is, he left after six years. Another down point for him was the ending of the Vietnam Conflict. He saw his military operational specialty (MOS) being downsized. That meant he would remain an E-4 for many years until the upper ranks began retiring. He assured me that once someone achieves the grade of E-5 in the Air Force, the individual makes a career of it. He further commented that to have any chance of making E-5 in the Air Force he would need to remain in an overseas assignment, like Guam, for at least five more years. He chuckled when he said that he made more money from tips as a cabby than as an E-4 working long hours.

The taxi driver was disillusioned, as were many enlisted military personnel at that time. In the military, he was underpaid and disliked by the civilians. Outside the military, he was paid reasonably well, and he was popular with the local gals. He made some great connections in Guam and planned to capitalize on them in the future. He envisioned himself running a nightclub, eventually. To him, success and happiness awaited him there. I wished him luck, as I disembarked the cab and tipped him. He smiled and drove off. I watched his cab as it climbed back onto the main highway and disappeared into the night.

As I walked toward the piers of the base, I reminded myself that I had chosen to stay the course. In reflection, I believe the taxi cab driver resented his decision, but he was too proud to admit it. How much esteem can you muster up driving a cab and hawking sailors for prostitutes? Maybe he decided to remain on Guam, because he could not face going back home to the United States and starting over from scratch. I felt sorry for him, but somewhere deep inside me I was saying "I'm glad it's not me."

This time of night, the path back to the boat is quite dark. Since this base is relatively new, no street lighting has been installed. The path consists of a newly-pressed, sandy road. The used portion of the road is distinguished by worn in dirt in which smaller pebbles, almost like a thick, cohesive powder, have risen to the top, making them easier to travel upon. The newer portion of the road still retains a mixture of small and larger rocks that make walking difficult. In the dark, having your shoe tip stumble against a large rock could cause you to fall. The walk back in the dark is fraught with opportunities for mishaps. A pace resembling meandering is recommended.

From the entrance gate to the boat, only the dim lights from the piers are visible. It is about a three-quarter mile stretch to the pier area. Andie's is off to the right. From the sounds coming from within Andie's, it was a slow night that is just about closing. I decide against stopping in for one last beer. I have had my fill of alcohol this evening. Besides, the humidity will cause me to sweat enough as it is on the walk back.

It is not especially humid tonight. A slight breeze coming from over the mountains to the left of the piers seem to provide just enough cooling to restrain a torrent of perspiration. Thank God for that breeze.

The overhead canopy of the night sky is speckled with stars. The moon is in its last quarter, essentially not enhancing visibility at all. There is an eerie feeling waking into a dark area. During thunderstorms in my hometown, I would dread having to ambulate around the inside of my home looking for candles. Your eyes become meaningless. Often, mimicking a blind man, you extend your hands as probes to detect walls or furniture. It is almost the same experience on this path tonight. Though there are no expected walls or other obstacles to encounter, forward motion is navigated by the feel of the texture of the road beneath your feet. As long as you feel a rocky, unstable substance beneath your soles, you are on the right track. Any sudden sensation of soft gravel or grass indicates that you have departed the path and are wandering about the fields of the base. It is really that bad.

The base itself was constructed on the shore of a deserted inland bay of the Apra channel. There was nothing here before the Navy Seabees began clearing the area. It was not even used for fishing by the locals.

Taxi drivers operating in areas of Guam outside the confines of Agana have no knowledge of the base's existence. Climbing into one of their cabs is an experience. They simply fumble around like blind men trying to locate an opening in the fence line to drop off their passengers. The base has no street markers to indicate its existence. From the main highway at night, there are no visible lightened areas to indicate anything like a base was on the property. The manning of the marine guard shack near the entrance area discontinues after sunset. The base is a mystery.

Unfortunately, most forward deployed bases for submarines are like this one. I recall those in the Pacific Northwest of the United States and Canada. Those bases truly were isolated. There was one in particular that was not even listed on any map. The submarine would approach the base via an inland channel, also unnamed, that seemed to be always curtained by a dense fog. Without radar for navigation, running aground would be assured. The submarine would enter the base area by emerging from a cloud of fog. For someone ashore, it must have appeared to be like something from one of those ancient Greek plays in which a sea god or serpent suddenly appeared out of the firmament.

Once moored at the lone pier on this base, only one building was erected on the shore. It contained soda and candy dispensers with a plastic-table and—chair, relaxation area in which to make long distance phone calls. Every four hours or so, a military van pulled up to the pier to deliver mail and exchange passengers. There was nothing else there. The pier at this isolated base was designed as a night over spot for submarines testing their torpedo operations.

This evening, the closer I get to the submarine tender the more the lighting from the piers illuminates the sandy road I am on. That is a relief. Being able to see the road below my feet enables me to move faster and surer. It also relieves my concern about stepping on a brown snake. Brown snakes over-infest the island. There are so many brown snakes on Guam that the meal of choice of these snakes—birds—has been totally eradicated from the island. There are no bird sounds on Guam at all. At night, the lack of bird life is obvious from the roar of the insect population. Now that the birds have been devoured, brown snakes are biting the human population at a rate of over fifty snakes bites a month. Walking an unlit dirt road at night alone merely invites a snake encounter. Tonight, as I emerge onto the piers, I breathe a sigh of relief that I made it without incident. From this point, I merely walk from pier light to pier light, using the lighted area under the pier lights to make my way to the gangplank of my vessel. I feel safe in so doing, because brown snakes prefer dark areas for ambush.

The feel of the cold metal of the gangplank against my thigh reminds me of the smoking-blonde's hand. The metal's coldness amplifies how warm her hand felt and how inviting her gesture comforted me. I could be exhausting myself in her embrace right now rather than perspiring from the night's humidity on a lonely pier. That is the choice I made. Sometimes, I wonder if I would have remembered that blonde more if I had bedded her. For some unknown reason, not bedding her fills me with fond memories just the same. How strange life is? Whether you do something or not captivates your imagination. Some would argue that not taking advantage makes you regret more than taking advantage sates your appetite. If that is true, then no doubt my submarine life will be filled with a plethora of regrets.

CHAPTER 3

Underway On Deployment

Getting up early after a long night has to be the worst feeling in the world. I almost forgot that my section had the reactor startup. It is a good thing that the ship provides wake up calls for 4:00 AM; otherwise, I doubt I would ever make an early morning inspection round of the engineering spaces, much less a reactor startup.

Berthing resembles a dark cave, almost like a catacomb. Only the faint red lights, affixed along the deck, illuminate the berthing area at night and while the ship is at sea. Every time I have had to wake someone in berthing, I felt an uneasy feeling about entering the area. At eye-level, the compartment is dark. Only the feeling of the bunk drapes enables you to navigate through the passages. To check your position, you look down at the deck to determine what frame you are near. Unlike in the wilderness or out in the open sea where you look up to check the stars or some tall reference structure in the distance, in berthing you look down. As a safety precaution, it is wise to carry a red-lens flashlight to assist you in the event you find yourself hopelessly lost. I can imagine the young sailor who woke me this morning must have experienced these same apprehensions.

Since I sleep in the top of three bunks, I have to be awake before I attempt to slide down gently from the upper bunk. It is a strange feeling getting out of a top bunk. I guess you could say that it resembles dismounting a tall horse in which you grab the saddle horn for dear life and allow your body to ease down the trunk the horse. Probably a better example would be sliding down a very steep, grassy hill. You hug the hill, drag your hands along the surface to reduce your falling speed and allow gravity to pull you down to the base.

First stop, after donning your shower shoes is the shower. Submarines have phone booth size shower stalls. You learn quickly to allow the water to run a while before entering; else, the sudden spray of icy water shocks your body. Fabricated from stainless steel, the walls of the shiny shower stalls are cold as well. Allowing the water to heat up lowers the shower wall temperature. Stainless steel does not keep temperature well.

Shower times are short. Most submarine showers last only a few minutes. The stalls are small, so the water from the flow nozzle immerses your body immediately. A little lathering and anti-dandruff shampoo is all you need. Besides, another ten sailors may be waiting to use the shower after you. You have to be fast.

Second stop is to don your at-sea attire that consists of a single jumpsuit like uniform resembling a flimsy flight suit called a poopysuit. The poopysuit was chosen for its fire retardant capabilities. Furthermore, it is flexible and lightweight, and the material it is made of does not shed much during washing or drying. Hence, it does not contribute to the refuse that accumulates on board the ship while on patrol. Scientifically speaking, the poopysuit is state of the art attire for long, undersea deployments.

Once attired, a short stop off in the crew's mess for a cup of coffee and then it is off to the engineering spaces to startup the reactor and steam plant. It is too early for breakfast. Once the reactor plant is started up, watch reliefs can be alternated to enable the startup crew to have breakfast.

The startup crew begins to filter into the crew's mess. As we draw our coffee, we discuss the assignment. Any crewmen in qualification status that require any practical factors for a startup are assigned to a specific watch stander. Practical factors refer to actual performance evolutions that a new crewmember is required to perform, or observe, prior to qualification for a particular watch station. Irrespective of the watch station, every watch station requires a prospective watch stander to observe, at least, one reactor startup from that watch station. Every reactor startup will have at least one new crewman assigned to observe the evolution somewhere in the engineering spaces. Affectionately, the observing watch standers are referred to as "trainees."

For nuclear submarine reactor plants around a dozen watch standers are required to complete the evolution safely. The watch standers range from extremely experienced, or supervisors, to the new crewmembers standing their entry-level qualification watch station. Control of the reactor startup is vested with the supervisory watch standers. The lesser watch stations just follow their lead.

Although, the connotations associated with a phrase like "Nuclear reactor startup" seem unfathomable, the procedure itself is quite simple. The amount of knowledge required to understand the reasons behind the simple, reactor startup, procedural steps is immense and requires a few years of experience and study in order to master. However, once mastered, the procedure becomes second nature.

Reactor Startup

This early morning startup is no different than any other. The age and prior use of the reactor might dictate certain minor changes; otherwise, the startup will be conducted with the same routine.

By 4:30 AM, the watch standers have manned their stations, careful so as not to spill their coffee. Coffee transportation becomes an art form for those watch standers in the lower spaces. Being able to lower a filled coffee cup, without spilling a drop, down a vertical metal ladder is a feat. After one deployment, most submariners have mastered the art. Trust me, no one ever drops a porcelain coffee cup onto a metal deck. To do so would be to watch the cup explode into hundreds of little pieces, requiring an intense clean up of the effected space all day. If a cup should fall and shatter into a lower lever watch station, then the cup's pieces would be scattered all over the bilge area under the deck plates. Extracting each of those pieces would be a job and a half. It would be a job for which few would volunteer. The bilges are known for their accumulation of foul water and unsightly debris with alien characteristics.

After each watch station reports that they are manned for the startup, the commissioned officer, overseeing the evolution, confers with the senior watch standers and then orders the startup commenced. The senior watch standers acknowledge the order and proceed to their assigned spaces.

Starting up a nuclear power plant is much like boiling water. First, you have to energize the hot plate/grill beneath the pot. Second, you carefully watch the water in the pot begin to boil. Third, once you observe large bubbles forming, you can edge the lid off the pot and allow some of the steam from the bubbles to escape in order to control the rate of boiling.

For a nuclear power plant, the nuclear reactor replaces the hot plate. The pot is your steam-generating device. Piping systems are connected to the pot in order to be able to use the steam produced to drive turbines. Some turbines are connected to electrical generators that supply the ship's electrical machinery. Other turbines are connected to the ship's propulsion train in order to move the vessel through the water. The basic configuration of a nuclear-powered, steam plant is quite simple. The advantage of nuclear power is that once you have installed the nuclear reactor, you have a guaranteed energy source for your pot for some seven years. That is seven years without refueling or electrical bills.

For this reactor startup, I am assigned to supervise the procedure from the reactor control spaces. I order the reactor control technician to commence the procedure…

After about an hour and a half, we have steam to the turbines. The startup is complete, and we ask for watch reliefs, so we can catch the tail end of breakfast. Surprisingly, the watch reliefs arrive quickly. A short turnover is conducted in order to enable the reliefs to become acquainted with the nuclear power plant's conditions. Right after our counterparts have accepted responsibility for the watch, they give us a head up on the treat for breakfast: creamed beef on toast, affectionately referred to as "shit on a shingle." I decide to stick with my usual scrambled eggs with toast and bacon.

Knowing the ship will be underway shortly after breakfast discourages any idea of braving the sumptuous entrée. Besides, "shit on a shingle" has too close a resemblance to human expectorate from seasickness. When the ship shifts colors in preparation for getting underway, I become concerned with seasickness. I do not need to tempt it.

Departing for Patrol

Shortly after breakfast, the maneuvering watch is stationed in preparation for getting underway. Given my susceptibility to seasickness at the beginning of patrols, I am left off the watch bill. Instead, I am assigned to the battle stations watch bill that gets called up many more times than the maneuvering watch during an underway period.

I am quick to respond to the call of the maneuvering watch, insuring that I am in my bunk, prone, before I feel the ship unmoor. I find it strange that usually I am sound asleep before the submarine clears the breakwater. The rocking of the round-bottomed submarine, as it negotiates the waves, comforts me into sleep. What wakes me is the sudden change in inner-submarine air pressure as the hull openings are all secured and the ship submerges beneath the waves. If I have not roused shortly after the submarine achieves periscope depth following the dive, the eerie shrieks from the submarine hull as the ship accommodates for the compressive and temperature stresses upon the upper hull areas from the immersion in cold water and increasing depth will wake me to full consciousness.

On the surface, the submarine's upper hull is exposed to bright sunlight in the tropics. The hull's metal tends to expand when heated. At patrol depth, the upper hull is immersed in cold water many degrees different from the surface air temperature, and the water pressure increases with increased depth. The change in temperature and pressure occurs swiftly. Since the two stresses, though compressive, apply in different directions upon and within the metal, the hull, in its attempt to accommodate, shrieks as the metallic layers within the hull slip into their new positions in order to relieve the two stresses.

The shriek is quite distinctive. It is almost as if the ship's hull is being torn apart, or at least a newcomer to the submarine would think so. Submariners often tease, or terrorize, new crewmen by attaching a thin string to each bulkhead (wall) and allow the new crewman to observe the string bend as the submarine increases its depth. In the World War II fleet boats, it was rumored that such a string could almost touch the deck from the submarine's accommodation to the deep depths by compressing its hull. Fortunately, we have stronger and tougher steels fabricated into the hulls now. However, the string still bends enough in the depths to slow a newcomer's breath and force his eyes to bulge open. The thought of being exposed to an implosion terrorizes the imagination.

After the shrieking stops, I disembark my bunk and begin preparing for my upcoming watch. The shrieking does not endure long; however, no matter how short it is everyone is glad when it is over. Submarines are guaranteed to endure so many such stresses. In the older vessels, the shrieking has a greater psychological effect, because one actually never knows how much submergence the submarine already experienced. Could this be the one that takes the hull beyond the warranty? The rule in submarining is to insure your surfaces match your submergences.

On my first watch, the submarine will transit to our initial operational area. Essentially, that means we will be answering Full bells for most of the trip. The power plant will be operated at elevated conditions. Most support machinery will be operating near maximum performance capability. This condition requires extremely vigilant monitoring by the watch standers. I am a supervisor, so I am constantly touring the engineering spaces in order to oversee the performance of the watch standers.

In the days of the World War II fleet boats, full propulsion speed was reserved for surface operations. Nowadays, as a result of enhanced hull design, submarines travel faster submerged than they do on the surface. Underwater operations during World War II were limited by the ship's energy source: the battery. Batteries depleted quickly at elevated speeds. On the surface, a World War II fleet boat would run the diesel generator to charge the batteries and in order to support higher propulsion speeds. With the advent of nuclear power, the submarine's energy source essentially is unlimited. There is no need to account for a relatively short-lived battery.

Since power plant conditions remain essentially constant during transits, those are good times to schedule long evolutions like battery charges. For the next few days, the submarine will maintain a certain speed, slowing down only to carryon necessary electronic surveillances. For most watch standers, the readings on their gauges and meters will remain essentially constant from one hour to the next and from one watch to the next. In this tempo, it has been said that watch station readings on machinery could be taken by simply copying down the previous hours readings. This is not allowed, of course. The purpose of taking the readings each hour is to be able to detect anomalies and track the development of trends. Every watch stander, no matter how insignificant, is well versed in the philosophy behind taking readings. There is no excuse for missing a reading.

Some readings are interrelated. An electrical operator sensing a slowly drifting frequency will alert the steam plant watch standers that a problem with vacuum control is developing. Steam plants use a vacuum as a pressure sink in order to attract high-pressure steam through the turbines. Hence, any slight increase in vacuum pressure would not encourage the high-pressure steam to race through the turbine blades, so to speak, resulting in the steam turbine slowing down.

Noticing these slight variations in readings is what makes the power plant run so smoothly and efficiently. Each set of primary watch standers is augmented by a set of supervisory watch standers in order to double-check the readings. In the event the primary watch stander, usually a novice or less experienced submariner, misses a trend developing in his readings, the supervisory watch stander will catch it. Identifying trends goes a long way to minimizing problems and allows the steam plant to run at optimum performance when required.

Transit runs are important for testing the power plant's performance at elevated conditions. Elevated conditions accentuate trends that might fall under the threshold of surveillance at low operating conditions. Running the power plant at elevated speeds en route to the operational area allows the submarine crew to iron out all the wrinkles in the power plant before the submarine gets on station. If troubles arise, the crew has time to repair them before the submarine goes full operational. It turns out to be a very effective and efficient system of surveillance.

Since there are few evolutions during the transit to our operational area, some of our spare time gets consumed chatting in the cooler areas of the engineering spaces. There is seldom a topic of conversation that runs from one on watch period to the next. At-sea we are without the daily news. Our news comes to us via Teletype messages. Only the more pressing international issues seem to get attention. And, it is not like we can pick up a phone and call someone. We are isolated, truly.

As a result, conversations seem to focus on the past events in port. The bravado and cocksmanship of the crew, with advantages, captures most of the conversations. Since Boris is in my watch section, I never can get away from the tales of his sexual prowess. As for me, the topic is silent. I employ the best evasive tactics imaginable in order to avoid such conversations. Maybe it was the way I was raised in the company of more women than men. I prefer to keep those few tender moments, truly few, to myself. The other crewmen, it seems, were raised in the company of men. They seem to have no sense of sanctity for those moments in their lives that they will cherish long after their military service is over. To me, those moments are best kept to oneself. To relate them would be to diminish their importance.

That blonde in the Equator nightclub will be in my memories forever. Although, I chose to abandon a night of entertainment with her, I will always return to that moment of decision and ask, "Should I have gone with her?" Andrew Marvell's poem *To His Coy Mistress* will second-guess me for the rest of my life. She was lovely. I am sure she was, because Boris never stops chiding me for not taking her home. But, I could not. There were things about her that prevented me from arousing to her charms. Someone like Boris who considers a woman as a port in any storm would never understand. How could I ever relate to him? He practically wears a bandoleer of condoms around his neck whenever he leaves the ship.

Perhaps, when I am in my retirement years, I will regret some of my choices and laud those who acted upon their instincts of the moment. Somehow, I sense to overindulge in wantonness diminishes satisfaction. If all one does is to move through life from one easy woman to the next, I would find that boredom would accentuate each period in between those women. And, I have seen that in many of the sailors who partake in the offerings of the Orient. Their minds seem empty in those periods away from women. They resemble drug addicts in those moments just prior to withdrawal symptoms beginning to appear. I find it sad. Conversations are exhausting for them. They prefer to just sit and contemplate. They are not reliving the excitement of the past evening. They just sit there, nursing their coffee. Somehow, I can sense their bodies working overtime to replenish their semen levels so they can be ready for another performance that evening. Thank God for duty days to allow their bodies time to recuperate.

Actually, it is boring to listen to all the cocksmanship tales. Somehow, my crewmen, overflowing with a desire to spill the excitement they experienced the night before, leave me desirous of tranquility. There is a peacefulness to the sound of running machinery underwater. Often, I will seek out that sanctuary, as the crewmen try to outdo one another's sea tales.

One thing for sure, port women keep the fleets afloat. If there were no port women, sailors would not have anything to talk about and no excitement for which to aspire. They would abandon their ships out of boredom and go back to their farms in the deep interior of the nation. It is amazing what makes someone go to sea. Going to sea is not natural. We are land creatures. Going underwater is even more unnatural. So, why do we do it? I suppose that somehow we have been lead to believe that it is exciting.

From inside the submarine's hull, there is little difference between the transit and the operational area. The ocean environment seems to be the same. Sometimes, if the operational area is in the far North Pacific, the water temperature sensed coming inside the ship is much colder. Besides that, there are few differences, and those are negligible. The Pacific Ocean is the Pacific Ocean no matter in which part you are submerged.

Once in the operational area, the speed of the ship is reduced. We are now on patrol, as if we were a sentry guarding the outer perimeter of a fence line. Just like a sentry, we move along the boundary, alert, silent and slowly. Once we reach one of the outer limits of the boundary, we change course and either follow the boundary's perimeter or reverse course and move back along the outer perimeter that we just traversed. Essentially, the submarine is an enormous sentry made of state-of-the-art materials and equipment.

The outer perimeter is America's first line of defense. Nuclear submariners are considered first-line combat troops. Though none of us carries a firearm, the submarine contains the most horrible arsenal ever conceived by man. In fifteen minutes, any time of the day or night, we can deploy these weapons of mass destruction to any location in the Pacific Theater. Our accuracy is unimaginable. We could hit a sidewalk, hot dog stand in the center of any metropolitan area. Now, that is a hot sausage order for a sentry.

When you consider sharp shooting badges are awarded for scoring so many rounds in the center portion of a target at a distance of one hundred yards, our accuracy at distances exceeding one thousand miles is beyond the imagination.

But, the American defense industry can materialize the impossible. And, our accuracy approaches the impossible.

When you consider a few decades ago, sending a rocket outside the earth's atmosphere was considered a great feat. And, that meant just sending the rocket straight up. It did not even have to hit anything. You were successful, if you just shot the rifle, so to speak, and the projectile traveled a certain minimum distance. And, we had done that before. Cannonballs were a similar feat. Of course, they reached a limit around three miles. Three miles became such a limit to the projection of firepower that it was canonized as the outer limit of a nation's sea boundary...the Three Mile Limit...and still remains as the international sea boundary, today. So, firing a projectile to a predetermined distance or beyond was not an unimaginable feat by the time rockets were considered. Yet, we had a problem with it.

Twenty years later, our distance problem has been surpassed and perfected with an unimaginable accuracy component. As far as technology is concerned, it is a paramount feat of engineering. On the side of humanity, however, it has produced the potential for Armageddon. All the beauty accompanying the technological accomplishment is matched with the ugliness of the specter of mass destruction. The sending end of every finely calibrated rocket is countered by Hiroshima-and Nagasaki-like landscapes on the receiving end. A fleet ballistic missile nuclear submarine on patrol contains the contrasts between beauty and death. For all the beauty, there exists all the potential death. Like an ancient, black, Roman mask with the face of love on one side and the face of death on the other, the silent, black, nuclear submarine, undersea on patrol, represents the latest artistic expression of that concept. Maybe, in life, the lure of beauty eventually leads to death. Or, said another way, the paths to destruction are lined with good intentions. The marvelous of a nuclear submarine on patrol dances with death.

In the Operations Area

One feels the ship's speed reduce as the operations area is entered. Like the distancing of an echo, the collapsing reverberation in the ship's hull and machinery from the transit speed gently massages the contents of the submarine. Noise level decreases as the auxiliary loads needed to support the transit speed are deenergized. The operational area accepts us like an inviting womb.

For the next thirty-days or so the submarine will ease about in this area, alert, silent and waiting. Like the cocked hammer of a magnum revolver, the submarine waits for the order to discharge. Professionalism overcomes the crew's social attitudes. Even off-watch, the crew takes on the air that we are engaged in serious business. Like a snake shedding its outer skin, the crew metamorphoses into militant automatons. The jovial camaraderie of the in-port, maneuvering and transit periods of this deployment is discarded. We are now on station. In fifteen minutes, we could destroy the world. It is hard to imagine anything more serious than that.

Shortly after entering the operations area, the commanding officer orders "Man Battle Stations Missile." Interestingly, on a nuclear fleet ballistic submarine, we distinguish between Battle Stations Torpedo and Battle Stations Missile. Both orders require similar watch stations; however, Battle Stations Missile calls on the entire missile launch watch stations to man. Battle Stations Torpedo is a more immediate defensive posture and resembles the regular battle stations announced on surface ships.

On non-ballistic missile submarines, or fast attacks, only one battle station is called: simply, "Battle Stations." That is intended to be Battle Stations Torpedo. A submarine's main defensive weapons are torpedoes. Nuclear submarines have no deck guns and no intention to surface in order to shwashbuckle it, so to speak, with the enemy.

Upon hearing the order to "Man Battle Stations Missile," the crew quickly makes their way to their assigned watch stations. Those crewmembers already on watch await their replacements before they can proceed to their assigned stations. A golden rule in submarine watch standing, or for that matter any naval watch standing, is never to leave your post until you are properly relieved. Hence, if you are on watch in the bow compartment and your battle stations post is in the control room, you must await the battle stations watch stander assigned to your current watch station to arrive and receive your turnover prior to going to your battle stations control room assigned post. Generally speaking, this wait and turnover usually causes the delay in manning for battle stations. Whatever the delay, fifteen minutes from the issuance of the order to man battle stations missile, the crew is prepared to launch missiles. Remarkable as it may seem, over one hundred men are at their assigned posts, and missiles are ready for launch in fifteen minutes or less. We are never late! From a philosophical perspective, this is one assignment in which everyone in the world wishes we were late. We always will disappoint them.

Missile launching occurs underwater. As a missile departs, seawater enters the void created by the missile. Interestingly, the composition of a missile and its associated housing space equates quite nicely with the density of the incoming seawater. There is a slight difference that needs to be compensated. For that, the ship's trim system activates an associated system referred to as "hovering" that automatically adjusts the compensation. The hovering system works quickly. By the time the next missile is ready to depart, the hovering system has compensated for the imbalance caused by the departed missile and adjusted the ship's trim. This is a marvelous feat of engineering.

A departing missile propels its way to the surface of the ocean. Upon broaching the surface, the missile's navigation system activates and aligns the missile to the intended trajectory. The missile physically rotates and adjusts its cone to the desired flight path. From an observatory, it is an amazing maneuver to watch. It is as if a huge, invisible scientist grasped the missile with his hand and set it in the right direction. From that moment on, the missile just follows the preset flight path.

Some thousands of miles from where the missile broached the surface of the ocean, the cone section of the missile opens to release a number of independent warheads. Depending on the number and location of the targets, any number of warheads can be released. If a series of targets are selected, one missile can release warheads to destroy each of those targets as it passes over an imaginary ejection point somewhere in the atmosphere. Many high priority targets, like military facilities and ports, can be destroyed by one missile employing a multiple target warhead. Expanding this concept to a few missiles, equipped with multiple warheads, could easily eliminate all the high priority targets in a medium size country.

From the point of impact of a nuclear weapon, called "ground zero," an area with a radius of some five miles would be devastated, completely. Imagine a city the size of New York City impacted by a series of warheads at prescribed locations for maximum effect. One can visualize the entire metropolis reduced to ruble by one missile equipped with multiple warheads. It is just a matter of ejecting the warheads in an overlapping blast-pattern to produce the maximum destruction. That is how simple it is. With ten multiple-warhead missiles, the entire Eastern Seaboard of the United States could be reduced to a refuse site. Civilization, as we know it, bequeathed to the junkyard rats. Armageddon lies dormant in the missile compartments of the American fleet ballistic missile submarine force.

The payload of a fleet ballistic missile submarine could render Europe ineffective. The payload from two nuclear ballistic submarines could send Europe back into the Stone Age. The United States has some twenty or so fleet ballistic missile submarines on patrol at any one time. I guess the nuclear-blast-effect masterminds disapproved of the survival of even the junkyard rats. Apparently, Darwin's notion of survival of the fittest needed to be erased from the end game scenario.

All the while that thoughts like these flow though our minds, we sit before control panels monitoring parameters or walk the decks in the bowels of the submarine doing likewise. Besides random conversation, a cup of hot coffee comforts us, as the submarine bores a hole in the ocean depths. Like a worm following some innate instinct, the submarine probes its way through the depths. Far below the surface, the submarine practices for a "dance with Inana" (frenzied behavior in battle).

We often theorize about how one of our missiles would look to a fishing trawler crew on the surface above, as it suddenly broke the peaceful setting of a calm sea. The sudden appearance of an airborne whale would, at first, dazzle the trawler crew. The antics of the missile's rotation in the air, much like that of a humpback whale as it leaps out of the ocean, would awe them. However, the sudden realization that their return to port, laden with their catch, would be meaningless would send them into despair.

The sight of an inter-continental ballistic missile broaching the surface would mean the end of civilization. The thrill of the trawler's at-sea expertise would be diminishing as the sight of the inter-continental ballistic missile faded. Everything the trawler crew held sacred would be fading. Being a fisherman would take on new meaning. A profession, once relegated to the periphery of the ocean industry, would now take upon prominence as the world's food supply disappeared. All land foods would be contaminated. The sea would hold the only bounty for those who were unlucky enough to survive the interchange of nuclear blasts. That is a heavy burden to bear for a lonely trawler crew. Undersea, we pity them.

I suppose the sight of an inter-continental ballistic missile breaking the surface would be worse for pleasure boat passengers. Where they are going will be gone. Where they departed from will be gone. Since the pleasure boat is little equipped for anything but pleasure, one can imagine their last days before the fuel and on board stores run out. It would be dangerous to pull into any port. They would be beset by a horde of would-be stowaways. So many people would try to board that the pleasure boat could capsize. Eventually, the pleasure boat crew would acquiesce into simply being adrift, allowing the currents of the great ocean to take them to whatever destination fortune dictates. It would become a sad death.

We did well on manning for Battle Stations Missile. We will not require additional drill time. That is good. There is nothing as unpleasant as continuous drills to get the crew up to speed on manning their stations. We have an older crew.

Many of these men have been together for a few years now. They know what is expected of them. It is always the new crewmembers that are late for assignments. It just takes a while for them to get settled in. This run, we have an experienced crew.

We are in the North Pacific, a few hundred miles off the coast of Asia. The inlet temperature of the water is cold. It is not so cold as to form fog in the lower bays of the engine room, but it is cold. One pleasant experience is to sit on the larger pipes and feel the refreshing coolness upon your buttocks and hips, as seawater enters the ship. It is almost like the feeling mountain climbers acquire when they rest on boulders in excess of a mile above sea level. There is a sense of accomplishment conveyed in the sensation. Few people experience that.

There is nothing spectacular about this patrol. We silently bore holes in the ocean within a prescribed path. We maintain the same ship's speed unless we change depth for navigational purposes. For the next thirty days or so, we will operate in this manner. Day after day, we dine, sip coffee, stand watches and sleep. There will be no trips to MacDonald's...no discos...no drive in movie theaters...no women...no cars...we are alone asea. Since we are a large submersible, fish life will not approach us. To them, we are a huge, hungry predator invading their biosphere. We are truly alone and silent.

The first watch passes without incident. Watch turnovers are routine. For the most part, merely the mention of new running equipment to our watch reliefs is all that is required. All the rest is the same. Time is counted by the shifting of machinery...making the rounds taking the hourly logs readings...and refilling the coffee pot. Time, in port, that could be used to chase women...buy new stereo equipment...scuba dive...attend sporting events...drops quietly like the sand from an hourglass. We sit idle and silent in an isolate area of the North Pacific, listening to the strange mix created by the sound of pumps, ventilation fans, motors and generators.

Some crewmen take correspondence courses to pass the time. It is an advantageous choice. Those aspiring for a Bachelor's degree in order to acquire a commission in the naval service can earn college credits. Others read the latest novels. The novels of James Clavelle are popular, as some of the ports the submarine may visit are described in his books.

Off-watch, card games are popular as well with the crew. Poker seems to attract the senior enlisted members. Bridge is popular in the wardroom. For some reason, the chiefs do not play cards that much, unless they join in on the poker games with the senior enlisted members. They play backgammon. It seems that anytime one enters the Chiefs' Quarters a backgammon board will be open on their main table. Other popular games include: hearts, spades and rummy, although, these games are usually played by the junior enlisted personnel.

Over thirty days of our lives will be spent away from civilization, submerged. Those thirty days will never be able to be relived. They are lost. Few people, other than dangerous prisoners, understand how time is wasted in isolation. Each of these crewmen could be doing something else far more enjoyable than sitting in the bowels of a sewer pipe in the depths of the North Pacific. Yet, they are here. They are here not because they were sentenced. They are here because they chose to be. They are here because they are willing to sacrifice their time...the pleasures of their lives...for their country's way of life. There are no medals for this. There are no parades. There are even few thank yous. Rewards remain silent.

Soviet Submarine Encounter

On the third day in the operations area, the word is passed over the announcing system that we will be rigging for silent running. We have received a message from Squadron that a Soviet submarine will cruise through our area.

Unlike the Army, submarines are not assigned to regiments or battalions. Our chain of command begins with Squadron. Squadron reports to Fleet. The chain of command is very short. There are not that many submarines to make a big thing out of it.

Silent running refers to taking steps to minimize noise emitted from the ship into the ocean environment. The crew does continuous monitoring of the ship's equipment noise levels in order to identify which pieces of machinery run the quietest.

Submarines are designed for reliability in that each major piece of equipment is installed with an alternate. The major piece of equipment and its alternate are differentiated by nomenclature. One is referred to as the Starboard piece, and the other is referred to as the Port piece of equipment. Routine practice dictates that we alternate running the Starboard and Port pieces of equipment with each change of the watch. However, when silent running is enforced, the more silent piece of equipment is run.

Another implementation during silent running is to have all unnecessary crewmen in their bunks. This eliminates any noise from random, social and work accidents. To further keep the noise level down, social activities are reduced to a minimum. The evening movies are secured. Chow is reduced to an easy-to-make cold cut selection. The announcing system and the regular, automatic, telephone-ring service are deenergized, redirecting all telephone communication to a sound powered system. Extra watch standers are relieved and sent to their bunks.

Without a doubt if that Soviet submarine detected our presence, it would spend an exorbitant amount of time trying to track us. They would relay our presence to their high command, and other submarines would be dispatched to our location. We must remain undetected.

It is not really that hard to remain undetected. Most transiting submarines are traveling at high bells. The noise emanated from their hulls masks the surrounding noise level. In order for another submarine to detect us, if not by colliding into us, would be to be pre-alert to our presence and enter our area slowly and quietly. It is a big ocean. It is easy to slip by anyone submerged, if you are silent. Besides, at high bells, our sensors would easily detect a submerged vehicle long before they ever got close enough to suspect our presence. Once we detected their presence approaching, we would maneuver evasively and maintain silent running until they cleared our sensors. We can hear for many miles in all directions. We could even descend into the depths and just hover until they passed over us. On a fleet ballistic missile submarine, this maneuver is affectionately referred to as "The Chicken of the Sea Maneuver."

At most, we will be at silent running conditions for a few days. Usually, it is just for a matter of one or two watches. The closeness and the Soviet submarine's rate of speed will determine the extent of our evasiveness. Soviet submarines seldom come close enough to cause us any real concern. They usually pass through our areas like a high-speed freight train late for an arrival. They are rushing to get to some inconspicuous operational area, like ours, somewhere else in the ocean where they will maneuver around looking for a submarine. Apparently, their intelligence command has identified a potential target area somewhere south of our location where their submarine has been ordered to search. They will not be looking for us in this operational area. Sometimes, we wish they would, so we could add some excitement into our time out here in the depths.

The off-going watch informs me that the Soviet Submarine will pass closest to us on my watch. I double-check the silent running alignment with the off-going watch stander. All is in order. We should be silent. The off-going watch and I chuckle at the thought that the Soviet submarine would even get close to us at all. Usually, encounters with Soviet submarines are measured in miles. Our sensors are all that will hear the Soviet submarine. Nonetheless, we prepare for that sudden and unpredictable change of course that is the hallmark of the Soviet undersea fleet.

Our attack submarines experience Soviet submarine unpredictability first hand. Unlike our operations, attack submarines have no "Chicken of the Sea Maneuver." They are assigned to seek out enemy submarines. Once a Soviet submarine is detected, our attack submarines tail them and monitor their maneuvers. Since Soviet submarines do not have the luxury of our advanced, technical sonar, they resort to drastic maneuvers in order to conduct surveillance of their operational area. Our fleet refers to one such maneuver, affectionately, as "Crazy Ivan."

When a Soviet submarine suspects the presence of a submarine tailing them, they turn 180 degrees (reverse directions) and travel down the same path that they just sailed at full propulsion. If a submarine is tailing them, the chances are that they will collide. The American Navy might find recruitment difficult for submarines, if they advertised that our submarines employed such a tactic. Unfortunately, the Soviets have different recruitment guidelines.

About midway through the watch, I am informed that the Soviet submarine is passing by us at some twenty-plus miles off our starboard bow. My first thoughts are "Why bother to rig for silent running?" We could be raising roosters inside our hull and be quiet enough for that distance. Fact is sound travels far in water. Someone striking a hammer against the hull could be heard quite a ways away, if someone were listening for us. Precaution eliminates any accidental hammering.

As the Soviet submarine is passing, I refill my coffee cup and continue my rounds of the spaces. As I encounter each watch stander, I update them on the location of the Soviet submarine. We are all somewhat tense. Really, this may be the only action we encounter this entire deployment. Think of it, one "Chicken of the Sea Maneuver," and we are done. It is not exactly commensurate with the excitement of the submarine war patrols of World War II. But, if ordered to fire our missiles, our one action would outdo all the conflicts of World War II in less than an hour. I suppose we should rejoice in the fact that our missions are peaceful.

Toward the end of the watch, the word is passed to secure from silent running. The Soviet submarine has departed our operations area. For the remainder of the watch I coordinate returning the machinery lineup to a normal rotation.

An early watch relief wanders back to our spaces to announce that trail markers are the main entrée for dinner. Now, there is a gut bomb meal to anticipate. Trail marker is the affectionate submarine slang for Salisbury steak. I laugh at the announcement, but I do appreciate the cuisine our chefs prepare. We eat really well in the submarine force. This entrée is prepared with brown gravy and onions. To round off the other food groups, the side dishes included French fries and mixed vegetables. Of course, those with a penchant to complain about any meal will demand A-1 steak sauce in order to mask the taste of the entrée. Salisbury steak does not need any masking, but it keeps the peanut gallery quiet to offer them some form of liquid potion with "magical" powers. It is often the case that those who complain the most have never really experienced fine dining. To them, a MacDonald's burger with fries and a coke is the ultimate in high cuisine. Toss in a chocolate malt, and they are sated. I wonder where these complainers would be if they were forced to eat the Army field rations: MREs. On hearing of the Army's affectionate name for their field rations: "Meals Rejected by Ethiopians" should apprise anyone of their succulent content.

Dining in Crew's Mess

The crew's mess resembles a crowded, industrial dining cubicle. Five, oval, metallic tables fill up the entire area. The passage area between the tables does not provide enough space for two crewmen to pass abreast. Table surfaces resemble lacquered linoleum popular in industrial areas. Metal benches, doubling as canned and dry food storage lockers, furnish the seating on the longer side of the tables. The shorter sides offer one pop-up, metallic seat. The normal seating is designed for six crewmen; however, as situations necessitate, the two, short-end, pop-up seats can be used to seat eight crewmen per table. With five tables, thirty to forty crewmen can be seated per setting. Since the oncoming watch consists of some thirty watch standers, the six-table setting is ideal.

Stainless steel is used to fabricate the tables and the benches in crew's mess. Given the moist environment of submarine operations, a metal with anti-corrosive characteristics is important. Adding slight amounts of chromium and nickel to iron creates the right resistance to corrosion. Additionally, one of the side features of stainless steel is its shiny appearance that bestows a MacDonald's like cleanliness to the mess area. Stainless steel is easy to clean, as well.

At this setting, the crew mumbles about their affection with trail markers. At first, to new comers, the comments disturb the dining ambiance. But, after a few meals, one just settles in, oblivious of the drivel in the background, and enjoys the dining experience.

Trail markers are not small by any stretch of the imagination. They resemble the size of little footballs given away as side prizes at county fairs.

Trail markers earn their reputation as gut bombs. After you devour one, you are ready to nap. When served with French fries and gravy, they truly drive you into slumber.

This evening's meal is no different. Since we are second call, or off-going-watch, our trail markers were made earlier. The one I forked from the serving bowl actually bounced in my plate, after it slipped off the tongs of my fork. A low, sluggish, thud sound accompanied the trail marker, as it struck my plate. I could imagine this creature nestling into my stomach for the entire deployment. Lots of catsup was applied to the trial marker in order to make it moist enough to intake. Unfortunately, the second-call trial markers are drier than those at first call, requiring ample marination in condiments. Another insight into devouring a second-call trial marker is to slice it up into tiny pieces. The tinier the better is preferred. Larger pieces tend to spend too much time in the esophagus, rendering a crewman incapable of voicing his disgust with the entrée. We cannot have that!

Actually, trial markers are not as bad as I am making them out to be. However, they do attract a plethora of negative comments from the crew. In caparison, has anyone ever ordered a trail marker at a restaurant? I would say not. That is because trail markers are not served outside the military. Apparently, civilians get wiser, after they have experienced a stretch in the military.

As we chow down, the other members at the table, when they are not trying to out-fork one another for a trail marker, seem captivated by the recent football scores that the ship just received. Since we hail from different parts of the country, we have different favorite teams. Two teams that seem to attract the most fanfare are the Pittsburgh Steelers and the Oakland Raiders. Maybe, it is because the two teams have an abundance of the color black on their uniforms. Those two teams seem to portray the manliness of the sport of football; whereas, some teams like the Dallas Cowboys seems to acquire more notoriety from their cheerleaders than their football prowess. Trial markers go hand-in-hand with the Steelers and the Raiders. Rough food for rough teams.

At sea, the crew does not get to see any football games. We are too deep to receive any of those types of radio-communication frequencies. Many a season has completely passed us by. All we receive is the scores, and those scores are received sporadically. If the Squadron radio communicator is an avid sport's fan, the submarines, asea, will get weekly updates on the games. If the Squadron radio communicator is not a sport's fan, maybe we get a few scores once a month. The crew can tell when an officer has edited the general message traffic. Sports like golf and tennis fill out more of the message space assigned to sports than the contact games.

Actually, in observing the crewmen boasting of the Oakland Raiders while they devour their trail markers, the lack of sauce on their entrée is noticeable. It is difficult to swallow dry portions of a trail marker, but if you are a hearty Raider fan, you can swallow anything. Interestingly, the Dallas Cowboy fans marinate their trial markers in catsup or brown gravy. Perhaps, the Cowboy cheerleaders seduce them to crave additional moisture.

We end the meal with scoops of ice cream from the Dairy Queen-like ice cream dispenser in the crew's mess. This ice cream tastes as good as any from Dairy Queen. We have similar ice cream cones as those offered by Dairy Queen, and we can swirl the ice cream as high as we desire above the cone. Fattening, it absolutely is, but we work hard enough to burn it off on watch. Besides, you sleep real well on a full stomach. You snore a bit, but you sleep like a babe. I prefer my ice cream in a bowl, so I can add toppings, like butterscotch, and lots of nuts. Eating like this after a watch makes me feel like I accomplished something. To me, good eating is a reward. Of course, that perspective might account for all the added weight I have accumulated. If the ship ever sinks, and I survive, then, at least, I will float well. On another positive note, the added hydrogenous material will improve my body's resistance to harmful radiation.

We bid our adieus to our tablemates and wander on back to our bunks. Sleeping is easy. I just slip out of my at-sea coveralls, or poopysuit, and ease into my bunk. Once inside my bunk, I draw the curtail in order to provide me some privacy, turn on my bunk light and say hello to my now-separated family that I have posted in pictures on my bunk walls. I have a young son that just managed to rollover on his belly before I left on deployment. By the time I return, he will be walking. I will miss an important period of his childhood development. That is one of the silent sacrifices not promoted on the glory of submarine life, or navy life in general, that anyone ever mentions. My eyes water a little as I reflect on my absence from my family. I pat the picture of my young son tenderly, as if he were asleep beside me in my bunk. I even create an imaginary space at the head of my bunk where I imagine he is resting. Soon the effects of the trail markers and ice cream overtake me, and I succumb into slumber.

CHAPTER 4

Port Visit Hong Kong Island

We have arrived at that point in the patrol in which we are allowed a port visit. For this run, Hong Kong has been assigned to us for a four-day mooring. We have to sit in the Pearl Estuary tied up to one of our surface ships in order to have enough electrical power to enable the crew to take day liberties onto Hong Kong Island.

Hong Kong Island resides close to the perimeter of Mainland China. In order to sail there, the submarine must surface and navigate through a series of island networks. Entering the Pearl Estuary is not as easy as entering a US Mainland port, or even Pearl Harbor. The continental shelf builds up gradually in East Asia. It is not the straight drop off experienced along the North Atlantic seaboard of the East Coast of the United States. Consequently, a submarine cannot come close to most Asian ports submerged. The submarine must surface a good distance away in order to avoid running aground in the shallow depths of the shelf.

The approach to Hong Kong is dotted with little islands. Some of these islands are closer qualified as rocks that just seem to protrude out of the ocean. In the days of sailing ships, absent any form of sonar or radar, these protruding rocks marked the tombstones of many a cargo vessel. Luckily today, we can detect these anomalies from afar and avoid them.

Our patrol has been patterned to have our submarine exit the operational area a few hundred miles from the point required for surfacing in order to approach Hong Kong. Hence, we have about a day, sailing time, in between our operational commitments and preparations for entering the Pearl Estuary. The commanding officer utilizes the time wisely to clean up the ship and perform a few needed drills.

Cleaning up the ship in naval terms is referred to as "field day." Field day for our submarine occurs prior to entering port and usually on Friday mornings while on patrol. Four hours of solid cleaning are allocated to get the ship spic and span. All hands get involved in the clean up. Unlike surface ships in which only the junior enlisted personnel clean, submarines involve all enlisted personnel and some junior officers. In the engineering spaces, it is not uncommon to see senior enlisted personnel in the bilges, scrubbing away at the hull.

The organization of cleanup in the surface navy is based on having an abundance of junior enlisted personnel of the rank of E-3 and below. Since the mean rank on board a submarine is second class petty officer, or E-5, cleanups involve all enlisted personnel to insure there are enough hands to do the job satisfactorily. We cleanup submerged in order to maintain a workforce able enough to do the job. After surfacing, some cleanup continues, but the maneuvering watch standers handle that assignment as time permits. Since the trek into Honk Kong will take an entire workday, cleaning up is a way to pass the time when the watch standers are not taking log readings or monitoring their spaces. And, it keeps the watch standers' minds off seasickness that will incapacitate a number of the crewmen during a long maneuvering watch.

Currently, Hong Kong Island remains a British Colony. It has been that way since the truce of the Arrow War in 1841. In the form of a war reparation, China agreed to lease Hong Kong Island to the British until 1997. In 1997, the island will return to China. It should be quite an affair to follow. Capitalism of Hong Kong will be reunited with communism of Mainland China. The Mainland Chinese have assured the world that the island of Hong Kong will retain its capitalistic character for fifty years after the turnover. Few Hong Kongese believe that rhetoric, but what can they do? Fate has dealt against them.

We have a few years yet before the turnover. Naturally, the appearance of American servicemen in the streets of Hong Kong offers opportunities for young female Hong Kongese desirous of leaving the island colony prior to the turnover. Liberty on the island furnishes some "instant romance" settings in which young ladies profess their eternal love for a sailor. Of course, we are aware of their motivation. How you play your cards determines your ability to score. It is a much different setting with the ladies in Hong Kong than in any US Mainland city where the American women could care less for you. Here, in Hong Kong, American males are in demand. The ladies here do not snub their noses at you, because you are a US military person. It is a different feeling being appreciated. And, we submariners like it.

The familiar three blast of the claxon announce the submarine's intention to surface. Soon, the long maneuvering watch will commence. Some ten or so hours from now, we will be mooring in the Pearl Estuary. In the meantime, I will get in my bunk to avoid seasickness. I feel sorry for the maneuvering watch standers. Some watch relief will be provided for meals and toiletry breaks, however, for the next ten hours, they will be on station. The control room operators will be the most taxed, as they will be navigating on the surface through an arduous passage. They will need to remain alert the entire period in order to ensure that we do not run aground or collide with another vessel.

I only have witnessed the control room once during a surface-maneuvering transient. Position indications constantly blare over the intercommunications system. Sonar, radar, periscope and lookout positions flood into the control room. How the plotters kept track of the contacts and land bearings truly is amazing? I can just imagine what air traffic controllers have to endure.

The approach to Hong Kong Island is riddled with hazards of all types. Wooden Chinese junks without any running lights suddenly appear without warning. Many of the control room operators claim that these unlit junks are smugglers trying to evade coastal patrols. Cargo vessels, with so much rust on them one doubts that they have undergone any sea-worthiness inspection in decades, often appear in the wake of submarine unannounced. The worst thing about cargo vessels is that they have few hands topside to detect other vessels. Their radar often is defective or inoperative. Collisions with these vessels are quite possible. Our watch standers must be vigilant to detect these night creepers. If a submarine should collide with one of them, the junks, or rust buckets, would sink immediately. It would be unlikely to be able to determine who they were. If they were smugglers, any of their crew who survived would deny any association with them. Hong Kong is a strange place where seamen sign on for service aboard ships with identities that they would never disclose even to their families. The cargo on these floating disasters stretches the imagination: heroin, human traffic and guns are the most prevalent. Any of these items, if discovered by the Chinese authorities, would exact capital punishment.

Trade in illegal commodities, including heroin, has been ongoing in these waters for centuries. Regrettably, the British commercial enterprises were the first to introduce heroin. Although heroin was never mentioned in the settlement documents of the era, almost every conflict between the Chinese authorities and the British military involved a dispute over the heroin trade. Britain had nothing legitimate to trade with China and was desirous of much that China had to offer. So, the enterprising, commercial British agents developed triangular trade between Bombay, India, London, England and Canton, China. The British vessels carried spices and silks from China to London in return for heroin grown in Bombay. The British just did not have enough gold and silver to purchase the Chinese goods and had nothing in their home country that the Chinese desired. So, they improvised. The great trading houses of Hong Kong dealt in heroin. Of course, this was never publicized. Heaven forbid the negative effect it would have tolled on the Christian community of London. I wonder how the British explained the heavily loaded, cargo vessels from China entering their ports as compared to the lightly loaded vessels departing their ports to China. Someone must have suspected! Even Hong Kong Island was created as a British port as a result of a heroin dispute. There must have been some tongue-in-cheek situations when the British Royalty knighted some of these British traders who achieved commercial success in China.

We must be passing through a channel between some islands. The ship has begun to rock from Port to Starboard and back. Usually, channel currents cause the ship to behave in such a manner. Submarines are round bottom boats, absent an extended keel to stabilize them like sailboats, so they tend to heave every which way to the wishes of the ocean surface. Old sailing ships did not experience this problem, because they were equipped with an extended keel. Current day sailboat designs are reminiscent of the underbellies of the old sailing ships.

As long as the submarine does not run perpendicular to a channel current, the ride into Hong Kong harbor (Victoria Harbour) should be pleasant. This is not monsoon season, so the winds will not be a factor. In the old sailing days, trips out of Hong Kong back to Europe required one to follow the winds. That meant above all things to be knowledgeable of when the monsoon season arrived. Nowadays, independent of wind power, most navigators find it difficult spelling the word monsoon.

Another feature that makes submarines so different from the old sailing vessels that pried these waters a century or so ago is the location of the crew during the transient. In the old sailing days, the crew was topside and some members of the crew were dispatched to the lookout post atop the masts of the vessel. In submarines, with the exception of the Commanding Officer, the Officer of the Deck and two lookouts stationed in the fairwater, the remaining members of the crew are below decks, unable to see the ocean around them. Submarines rely mostly on instrumentation to navigate through inner-island waters.

The fairwater refers to the extended tower that rises above the top deck of the submarine. In some Hollywood depictions of World War II submarines on patrol the phrase "Conning Tower" was used to describe the fairwater. Fairwater is the correct designation. In most classes of submarines, the control room resides, below decks, directly below the fairwater.

Running on the surface at night is dangerous for a submarine operation in waters frequented by cargo vessels. Submarines lie low in the water and offer a small silhouette to oncoming vessels. Being low in the water also means our running lights are low and can easily be mistaken for reflections from other vessels. When you add that dangerous pair to the fact that cargo vessels have few watch standers topside during transients, it makes for a lethal combination. Submarines must be very alert in the vicinity of cargo ships. The unpredictability of cargo ship maneuvers is another legend that troubles submarine watch standers. A coastal runner will make sudden turns to make at-sea deliveries to Chinese junks a few hundreds yards off the coast of an island. Few Chinese junks have any running lights to alert anyone of their presence. The coastal runner types of junks do not present any running lights at night, because they have reason to remain undetected. When someone mentions smuggling, these waters of the South China Sea are notorious for the trade.

In the old sailing days, the main trade was heroin. Today, unfortunately, human trafficking has replaced heroin in these waters. The term for an at-sea human trafficker is "Snake's Head." Like a snake weaving its way down the river, the human traffickers weave their illicit cargo delicately from port to port. If the human traffickers fear being apprehended, they will dump their human cargo into the South China Sea. Unlike their slave trade counterparts in the Americas, the Chinese traffickers dump their human cargo in 40-foot containers into the sea. If captured and convicted of human trafficking, the penalty is execution in China. Hence, a "them or us" scenario unfolds on the deck of a cargo ship engaged in human trafficking. The waters are deep enough along the approach to Hong Kong Island to deter Chinese authorities to waste money salvaging 40-foot containers. "Them" is the selection of every human trafficker!

As the submarine rolls to Starboard, we sense ourselves passing through another channel current. Since there are many islands dotting the approach to Hong Kong, we expect to experience a number of these rolls.

It must have been quite scenic in the old sailing days with only starlight to illuminate the voyage between the islands. Nowadays, there are channel makers blinking everywhere. Huge searchlights often accompany the channel markers when an important vessel is entering the channel. Although, these lights are nothing compared to the strobe effect of the neon lights of Hong Kong's skyscrapers.

Hong Kong radiates like a huge jewel illuminating the estuary at night. Most of the neon signs are in English; however, Chinese and Japanese can be discerned.

These neon signs can be read from any point in the estuary, or for that matter, from quite a distance out to sea. Some of the neon signs seem to extend down an entire face of a huge skyscraper. Most strobe as well, while others displays different pictures to communicate an advertisement. Hong Kong is a marvel to witness from the estuary.

Money and commerce are what the neon signs convey to any visitor. Despite the third world character of Mainland China, Hong Kong rises up above the water to announce the promise of the area. Hong Kong, though a mere island, represents Chinese commerce to the world. It is through Hong Kong that China trades with the rest of the world. Hong Kong acts as a tollbooth, exacting a levy, on all trade entering and leaving China. This is not a bad financial position for a small island. Interestingly, this is the key to the British financial genius of the earlier centuries: to acquire strategic locations with which to foster trade for a fee. The Hong Kong commercial enterprise was a duplication of the British technique used in Calcutta to harness India and in Singapore to harness the Malay Peninsula.

Today, the influence of the British is diminishing like the sun setting on the horizon. In this part of the world, actually in a few decades, British influence in the Pearl Estuary will all but cease. In mid-1997, the British flag will be lowered for the last time over Hong Kong Island. Britain will be missed. Trade flourished so well under her supervision. I pray that these waters remain open to trade.

All too often in Chinese history, piracy rampaged these waters and essentially halted any meaningful amount of trade. Waterways within these many islands soon become a haven for waterborne bandits as soon as the local authorities lose their sense of vigilance. Right now, the increase in the number of coastal junks predicts an era of piracy approaching.

The roving watch informs me that the senior engine room watch stander needs a relief. I will relieve him. He has been on watch for some time now. It will be a short relief. He may need to make a toiletry call.

The engine room contains one urinal; however, there are no facilities aft for more demanding bodily functions. Hence, when nature calls in that manner, off-watch personnel are summoned to provide relief. All watch standers understand this duty, because we have experienced those uncomfortable cramps ourselves on one occasion or another. I hurry to don my poopysuit and rush back aft. I pray he has not waited until he has been forced to cross his legs to refrain from discharging.

Thank the Lord I got to the engineering spaces quickly. The supervisory watch was about to relieve in a plastic bucket. I could just imagine being tasked with having to carry the bucket forward to empty it into one of the latrines then having the dreaded task of cleaning out the bucket for reuse in cleaning during the next field day.

From the watch stander's grimace, I can tell he is under pressure to turn the watch over to me as expediently as possible. There are some new evolutions ongoing, so the turn over takes some time. I hope he can restrain himself long enough to apprise me of all the conditions. Some five minutes pass by as we turn over. His breath is irregular from the downward pressure that he is applying to his buttocks to keep them closed. He eventually succeeds in turning over the watch. As he departs the engineering spaces, I watch him as he gingerly walks forward. He looks like someone trying to hold a corncob in his anus while he walks. Poor guy! It must be excruciating each time he pauses in the passageway. He waited too long to ask for a relief.

I make way around the engine room checking the watch standers' logs and monitoring the gauges of the running machinery. We are answering a standard propulsion bell, so most of the machinery is running in the slower modes of operation. As I walk under a ventilation duct, a rush of cool air greets me. The ventilation fans are on high speed. The humidity of this island waterway must be seeping into the submarine. Either that, or we have a few new steam leaks to detect and repair once we are in port.

Steam leaks are common. They arise from gaskets in the steam valves wearing out. Most are simple repairs. Since we will be in port, we can attend to them then. However, if we have a few steam leaks, we will need to identify them while we are steaming. Identification is simple: just place a mirror around a steam valve, if water droplets begin to form on the mirror surface, there is steam leaking from the valve gasket. When we shutdown the steam plant, we can change the gasket.

If we were at sea and required to repair a steam leak from a valve, we would isolate steam to that valve and two valves up and downstream of the affected valve in order to change the gasket. This method of repair is called "Two Valve" protection.

Two valves are chosen to isolate the affected steam valve in the event that one of the isolation valves leak by. The added valve protection is needed, because steam is water elevated to saturation temperature of some two hundred and twelve degrees Fahrenheit or more. A sailor could be scalded if exposed to steam at that temperature. I instruct the engine room watch standers to commence looking for steam leaks. They grab their special, metallic extension devices with a mirror attached and commence circulating the outer surfaces of the steam valves.

I bet we have at least one steam leak causing the humidity in the engine room to rise.

While the engine room watch standers are busy looking for steam leaks, I continue monitoring the running the machinery. Another problem we encounter while running on the surface is maintaining adequate seawater flow to cool our condensers. The condensers act as heat sinks for the steam turning our turbine blades. If condenser pressure should rise, the turbine would slow down. Since the turbines control the electrical frequency within the submarine, it is of paramount importance to insure they are running at normal speed. On the surface, checking condenser pressure requires major attention. If the condenser pressure is in fact rising, we could be experiencing a clogged seawater valve strainer. All seawater valves are protected by a strainer, so that large objects will not be sucked into the ship by the seawater pumps and foul the valves. If a strainer clogging is suspected, I recommend a seawater system realignment to enable me to close the effected, inboard seawater valve. Once the valve is closed, I can attach a high-pressure air hose to a fitting located between the outboard, seawater hull valve and the strainer then blow high-pressure air through the strainer to unclog it. That procedure has never failed to unclog a seawater strainer.

As I bend down to check Port condenser pressure, I feel a tap on my shoulder. It is the returning supervisory watch. He is smiling. We turnover quickly, and I am on my way forward.

Entering the Pearl Estuary

As I enter the crew's mess, I notice that the periscope camera has been patched into the TV. Some of the crew is gathering in the mess to observe the ship's approach to Hong Kong Island. It is still dark topside, but the lights from the shore-based, navigational aids and stars illuminate the approach enough to be able to discern certain landmarks. In the distance, a small bright light lurks amongst the darkness. The light is barely noticeable, but everyone in the mess knows that it is the light from Hong Kong Island.

Islands in the distance to sailors do not look like islands. They look like a group of upside down brooms. As you approach the upside down brooms, the islands seem to rise up from the water. The curvature of the earth's surface provides that effect. Lighting has the same effect. Hong Kong Island lies below the ship's horizon right now. Like a precious flower unfolding its petals, Hong Kong Island will reveal itself, as we get nearer.

The waters seem calmer now. The submarine has settled comfortably into the waves, as if being cuddled like a babe in the arms of an affectionate mother. The rocking and rolling has dampened to a point where it is barely perceptible that the submarine is waterborne at all. Actually, I have just acquired my sea legs. My body's equilibrium has adjusted to the surface anomalies. Seasickness will not bother me now.

I stop at the dispenser to pour myself a cup of fresh coffee. As I pour, I can overhear comments from the crew, identifying certain landmarks along the approach. I can tell that these crewmembers have experienced this trip to Hong Kong Island before. It is good to be able to remember sites from past visitations. A flood of memories pours into my mind, as well, of places that I have visited a second time. I recall with advantages how well I appreciated them. As for Hong Kong, I cannot wait to visit the China Fleet Club again. Last time, I bought a few precious silks. This time I will purchase enough Chinese silk to make a dress for my separated wife, or a future girlfriend. I believe five yards should do it. It will be best if I get one five-yard length of each color of silk the China Fleet Club offers. The price for Chinese silk is dirt-cheap here. In the United States, I would pay ten times as much for pure Chinese silk, if I could find a place that would sell it.

One of the crewmen screams at the sight of the bright light on the horizon as the periscope camera scans by it. The bright light has enlarged. We are getting closer. This time, the bright light seems to strobe. As I recall, the taller skyscrapers near the waterfront on Hong Kong Island flash advertisements along the upper portion of their facades. The strobe effect that we are witnessing must be emanating from one of those skyscrapers. It is dazzling to witness though. It resembles a strange spacecraft in the distance preparing to emerge from the ocean and hover over us. In the old sailing days, I can imagine the types of tales that would have been told about such sightings.

Given the excitement of the crew, I will join them a while just to share in their apprehension, as they watch Hong Kong Island emerge on the horizon. Hot coffee and the company of submarine sailors make a touching and memorable setting to witness one of life's at sea adventures.

It seems that the larger the bright light on the horizon becomes the communication traffic increases proportionately. One of the members of the crew walks up to the TV in order to turn down the volume, so we can appreciate the emergence of the bright light amongst the plethora of communication. The periscope seems to be scanning more purposefully amongst four contacts crossing our approach path. All the contacts are cargo ships heavily laden with stores. As with all cargo ships encountered during night, surface operations, caution is the order.

The periscope scan will stop on one vessel then quickly scan to the next. The vessels are close. We can discern their country of registration flags. The closest cargo vessel, a top-of-the-line merchant, hoists a French flag. The next in line is carrying a Panamanian flag. The Panamanian flag often identifies a convenience registration to avoid strict waterborne regulations of their true country of origin or a tax evasion decision. Panama offers ship registries at extremely accommodating prices and taxes with few compliance regulations for the sea worthiness of the vessel. The affectionate saying that a raft could acquire Panamanian certification is not far from the truth.

The third vessel in distance from our bow displays a Saudi Arabian flag. Now, this vessel is loaded with overseas workers and very well equipped. Although the Saudis have very strict compliance regulations, they outfit their vessels accordingly. Luxury can be found on a Saudi vessel. Last in line from our bow is a large, rusty looking cargo vessel that seems overloaded with containers. One giant wave could topple its cargo of stacked containers. This vessel exhibits a Malaysian flag. Undoubtedly, it is bound for Singapore or Kuala Lumpur. If one were to guess, one of those containers might be holding human cargo from Mainland China. If the vessel's first docking is Singapore, the Chinese human cargo could easily slip ashore and blend in with the community. The dirty appearance of the vessel suggests that more than routine cargo is stored aboard.

Seeing these cargo ships afloat like ducks in a shooting gallery reminds the submarine crew how fortunate they are. If war were to break out, these cargo vessels would not last the hour in the sights of our periscope. There is no way that these targets could escape a submarine on the prowl. They are too slow and unmaneuverable. The only destination they would be sailing is to the ocean floor.

Air streams from a foghorn emanate from the closest vessel. Apparently, the cargo ship has recognized us low in the water. We are uncertain, if he blew his horn out of shock or with intention to communicate that he is passing us on our Port side. We pray that he has noticed us from a distance. Otherwise, we might have real difficulty as we come abreast of the other three cargo vessels. Our horn responds to the French vessel. We should pass one another without difficulty. Thank God, if the French vessel were to turn into our Port side, the collision would buckle our hull and scuttle us. With the exception of a dented bow, the top-of-the-line, French vessel would be unscathed. Ramming a submarine is a sure way to sink her.

By now the strobe effect from the bright light on the horizon is emitting different colors. We are getting closer to the Pearl Estuary. From the expanded scanning being performed by the periscope operator, it appears that the approach is widening. This could be the entrance into the backwater of the estuary. A little further into the approach path, we should be able to make out some of the advertisements being flashed on the top of the facades of Hong Kong Island's skyscrapers. If my memory serves me correctly, the first advertisement that we will see is for Coke Cola in Japanese script. The building hawking that advertisement overlooks Fenwick Pier in the Wan Chai District of Hong Kong. We will moor alongside a US surface ship not far from the Fenwick Pier landing area. I have to laugh. It really should be a beer sign that appears first. We are too old to appreciate fully a Coke Cola sign. It should be a *Tsintao* beer sign. *Tsintao* is the name of the local beer. I believe it is brewed in Shanghai.

By now, the advertisement that has created so much anxiety in the crew is visible. My memory was correct. It is Coke Cola in Japanese. Most of the Fenwick Pier area is visible now. Our escort, a US Navy Frigate, is waiting for us to moor alongside her not far from Fenwick Pier. Our submarine will be moored in the estuary, as we were told; however, it will be only a short water taxi ride to the pier.

During my last trip to Hong Kong, our submarine was tied up alongside a Destroyer Escort. The water taxi service from the Destroyer Escort to Fenwick Pier was less than ten minutes. The distance between what seems to be our mooring and Fenwick Pier should provide for a shorter water taxi ride.

The water is very calm in the estuary, despite the myriad of junks passing us in every which direction. Hong Kong resembles a large treasure chest filed with precious gems glittering away, enticing us to reach out for them. I find it unfathomable that any submarine sailor will choose to remain aboard during this port visit. Hong Kong is just too alluring. For those of the crew who have read John Clavelle's *Taipan* or *Noble House*, the temptation will be much too great to explore the island and site those landmarks described in the novels. For those of us who have been to Hong Kong before, the nightlife of the Wan Chai District more than fills us with anticipation. Promises of romance were never so vivid, as they are in Hong Kong for sailors. Truly, the movie *Sand Pebbles* serves an inspiration fueling the minds of the crew of what awaits them ashore.

A tugboat comes out to greet us from Fenwick Pier. It does not resemble the junk-type craft that just manages to stay afloat about us. This vessel is as equipped as any in the harbors in the United States. It does not take long for the tug to tie up alongside us and begin to direct us toward the Port side of the Frigate. As our submarine approaches the Frigate, the tug aligns us with our Starboard side abreast of the Frigate's Port side. Large rubber cushioning devises are draped along the Port side of the Frigate that act as separators providing a safe distance between the hull of the Frigate and submarine. The large cushions are called "camels."

Soon, heevies are tossed upon our topside. Heevies are essentially a clothesline cord with a baseball size ball at one end. The Frigate sailors toss the heevie, as if they were tossing out a drop line for pond fishing. The ball end of the heevie bounces on our topside where our crewmen gather them in. Attached to other end of the heevie is a mooring line. The Frigate crew and our topside line handlers feed the rest of the heevie and the lassoed mooring line from the Frigate to our topside. Once the mooring line is aboard our submarine, our topside line handlers attach the eye of the mooring line firmly around our deck cleats. Five mooring lines are passed over to us in this fashion. Lines one, four and five are handled to attach our submarine to the Frigates corresponding cleats: one, four and five. Line two and three are crossed such that, the Frigate's line two is attached around our cleat number three; whereas, the Frigate's line three is attached to our cleat number two. This arrangement firmly attaches the submarine to the Frigate.

Once the mooring is secure. Shore power cables are fed from the Frigate, via the heevie-method previously described, to the submarine. Receiving shore power from another US Navy war vessel is different from received from a tender or pier facility. The cables, rather than being nicely encased in a large amphenol, are fed to us separately. This requires the electrical crewmen to match cables individually and connect them accordingly. Once matched and connected, the cables are wrapped in a preordained sequence of insulation material. Since each individual little cable will carry some one hundred amperes, we cannot have that electricity running up and down the topside of the submarine electrocuting people. To say the least, this is a time consuming evolution that requires perfection to keep everyone safe. And, it consumes a lot of electrical tape.

As the electricians struggle away wrapping the shore power cables in electrical tape, the first liberty launch en route to Fenwick Pier ties up alongside the Frigate. According to the schedule, the launch will arrive every thirty minutes to transport liberty parties to Hong Kong Island. It is a good schedule. The launch is a good-size wooden vessel with a high-powered engine. Safely, some thirty passengers can be transported per trip in the launch. A canvas canopy deflects the water spray from the high-speed transit away from the passengers. Given the speed of the other crafts afloat in the estuary, the launch blends right in. It seems that water speed is the primary concern to passengers in the estuary. The faster the craft, the more popular it becomes.

The electricians pause to watch the launch, fully loaded with sailors from the Frigate and the submarine, as it pulls away from the Frigate and heads toward Fenwick Pier. It is as if you could read the minds of the electricians. They knew they would experience these situations where their crewmembers departed for liberty hours before they could. It is sad though to watch others enjoying the evening while you toil away.

The launch moves so effortlessly on the water. The electricians wish their job of bringing on shore power could be accomplished in the same effortless manner. There is a peacefulness that comes from watching a launch glide over the water. In a sense, that peacefulness comforts the electricians, as they continue to wrap the electric cables.

Another experience of note is how the submariners on the launch intentionally do not look the electricians in the eye. The liberty party is aware of the sacrifices of the electricians and the other nuclear-trained crewmen. The reaction from the liberty party is almost akin to an infantryman leaving a fallen comrade behind on the field of battle. A sense of guilt overcomes anyone who leaves his comrades behind. This situation is no different. The electricians, aware of the guilt, likewise do not look the departing launch personnel in the eye. It is kind of a way of saying: "It's OK." It will be OK. In a few hours, those electricians going ashore eventually will meet up with the liberty party departing right now. The only difference may be the amount of alcohol the two groups have consumed. When they do rendezvous later this evening, nothing will be mentioned about the one group departing early. It is something that remains silent amongst submariners.

I suppose that there are many assignments that carry similar negative interchanges; i.e., those chosen to engage in battle versus those selected to remain in reserve. Whatever the situation, it always seems to remain unspoken. Luck of the draw favors one over the other, despite the fact that the entire group was there for the same purpose. It is that way amongst submariners as well. Fortunately, this time it is just a liberty run. There will be the unfortunate circumstances as well. For those circumstances, everyone prefers to await, in silence, the outcome of the wheel of fate.

It will be late before the electricians are free to go ashore. Many decide to rest in this evening. A few are adamant about liberty. Fortunately, Hong Kong Island never sleeps. The music of the nightclubs throbs away until 5:00 AM each and every morning. At 5:00 AM, the nightclubs do not actually close. They simply turn off the music, turn on the lights and allow the clean up crew to sweep down the establishment. By 6:00 AM, the lights are dimmed, and the nightclub is pulsing away again.

The smaller beer and wine bars will close around 2:00 AM. They do so not so much for regulations as from experience with the behavior of their patrons. Most patrons who frequent the beer and wine clubs in the early evening will meander on over to the cabaret clubs after 2:00 AM for dancing, live music and/or dining. Entertainment actually never stops in Hong Kong. The island seems preoccupied with living it up. Perhaps, it has something to do with what lies buried in every Hong Kongese's mind that the good times will end abruptly, soon enough, when the Mainland Chinese reassert their will over the island. It is like knowing when and where you will die. Every moment up to that point needs to be cherished and lived to the fullest. Every resident of Hong Kong understands that.

One of the disadvantages of being moored in the middle of the Pearl Estuary is the humidity. Even though it is early evening, the humidity still causes your clothes to stick to your skin. Although not as bad as Apra Harbor, Guam, it still encourages immersion in air conditioning.

Liberty in Hong Kong

I have decided to go ashore this evening. We shutdown the engineering spaces and set our interpretation of cold-iron watches. The most probably launch for me and a few friends to catch is the one coming at 10:00 PM. In the nuclear submarine force, you get accustomed to these late hours of departure on liberty. It is the same everywhere. The Nukes are last to leave the ship.

About 9:30 PM, I manage to get some time in the water closet (sub-sailor for shower). In reality, the shower stall is not much larger than a closet. With my extra-large frame, I have to concentrate whenever I need to turn around inside the shower. It is my shoulder span that just about touches the opposite walls of the shower stall. Dropping my bar of soap produces a real feat in contortionism for me to recoup it.

A few minutes before 10:00 PM, two friends and I cross the gangplank onto the Frigate's main deck. The launch ties up to the Frigate, so we are obliged to render honors to the Frigate Quarterdeck prior to disembarking on liberty. Being a surface ship, the Quarterdeck watch standers enforce military decorum quite seriously. Although they admire submariners, they concede no slack to anyone trying to go ashore in inappropriate attire or demeanor. We have to be on our toes. There is always one surface sailor whose ambition in life is to master the regulations manual. In the more fanatical types, it is a calling akin to a devotion to religious life.

This evening, the Quarterdeck watch is a relaxed person. He seems secure in the understanding of his duties. That is a good sign, because it is the junior petty officers and junior line officers that feel insecure in their watch standing abilities that will give you a hard time. I suppose they justify their existence in the Navy by intimidating sailors with their knowledge of the regulations manual. We pass through the Frigate's Quarterdeck unscathed.

There are few of us on the launch. The pilot has to call out for borders a few times, before he decides that this trip will have a lot of vacancies. My two friends and I take a seat to the rear of the vessel well under the canopy. Experience aboard these crafts has taught us that the front seats absorb any ocean spray that the bow kicks up. Though the surface of the water on the estuary is calm tonight, it only takes the wake of a passing junk to cause the bow of the launch to dip into a wave and toss water onto the launch. Unfortunately, a few of the Frigate sailors, on their first ride in a launch, learn this lesson the hard way, as the bow digs into a couple of good wake waves. Everyone, seated in the rear of the launch, just smiles as the Frigate sailors in the front curse the launch pilot. With this humidity, the cold estuary water will cool them down a little.

Soon the launch slows and glides up next to Fenwick Pier. It is not much of a pier with a width a little more than the span of three diving boards set side by side. The pier is constructed a few feet below a solid cement structure that acts as the entrance to the Wan Chai District. We disembark the launch and walk the wooden pier until we come to a set of cement steps that lead us to the top of the cement structure. Once atop the cement structure, we are stunned by the sudden appearance of a main highway just below us. The cement structure must double as a seawall.

The group disembarking the launch makes their way to a walkway that crosses over the main highway below. We walk cautiously over the walkway, as all sorts of upper class automobiles whiz by us below. If the automobiles are any indication of the wealth of the inhabitants of Hong Kong, Hong Kongeses are quite wealthy. This liberty port will be a little different from the others we have visited. Here, we are surrounded by affluence. We are not used to being amongst the lowest class in foreign ports. This will take some adjustment.

Lights, lights, lights, everywhere, there are lights. Hong Kong sparkles like the night sky on the Fourth of July in Washington, DC. There are more alternating lights here than on the strip in Las Vegas, or at least, it seems that way. In Las Vegas, English-speaking people can distinguish the flashing messages from the lights. Here in Hong Kong, there are too many languages flashed on the billboards. The Chinese characters are the worst. Most Chinese have difficulty reading them.

After the initial neon light shock, our group decides to meander on down the main thoroughfare of the Wan Chai District. We pass world-recognized tailor shops. All closed at this hour. Music from the main disco pumps away as we walk by. We are tempted, but it is too early for rowdy entertainment just yet. We decide instead on a quieter beer and wine bar known to merchant sailors as the "Panda."

The Panda attracts the more affluent, upper rank merchant seamen. It is a quiet place. The music is more in line with a relaxed setting. The beer selection might well be the most extensive in the world. Connoisseur beer drinkers frequent this place. As we enter, we notice that there are no pool tables or any other recreational type equipment in the establishment. Four luxurious booths line the sidewall opposite the long bar. The restroom area shares most of the far wall with a wide-screen TV monitor. We select stools at the bar.

As we are getting settled into our stools, the bartender asks for our choices of beer. You cannot just request a beer in here. Being naïve, we all ask for an American beer, Olympia. Sure enough, the bartender produces three ice cold Olys.

Upon hearing our request, the other persons, seated at the bar, begin to chuckle. We find it strange but begin sipping our drinks. There is even a strange smile on the bartender's face as well. He even mentions that we must be new to Hong Kong. We inquire why he thinks so. Then, we realize why American beers are available in Hong Kong. They contain formaldehyde for preservation. Yikes, that means we can expect a dose of dragon-ass tomorrow.

Dragon-ass refers to the burning sensation that is felt in the anal tract as formaldehyde is excreted from the body. It is hard to avoid dragon-ass overseas, as most non-local beers are preserved with some amount of formaldehyde.

The bartender, sensing our sudden realization, offers us a selection of other foreign beers that do not contain as much formaldehyde. One selection is Extra Special Carlsberg Dark from Denmark. Now, there is a beer! Carlsberg Dark is popular around the world as a premier dark beer. Extra Special Carlsberg Dark means that it has greater than six percent alcohol. American beers are limited to six percent alcohol, and in some case limited to 3.2% alcohol, referred to as "3.2 beer." In Hong Kong, alcohol content in beers can be at any value. And, it generally is, randomly so! No two beers of the same brand seem to have the same alcohol content. The consumer has no idea how much alcohol he is consuming. In Hong Kong, he does not care.

It only takes a few rounds of the Extra Special for us to realize that we have consumed more alcohol than we had anticipated. The buzz distorting our perception is the first indication. Extra Special is a powerful beer. One of the merchant seamen informs us that in some parts of the world in order to be sold to the general public, Extra Special requires classification with the wines. We agree!

My two friends decide to wander over to the main disco. I have struck up an interest in the merchants' sea stories and decide to remain at the Panda for a few more drinks. I bid my two friends farewell and promise to join them later in the evening.

Merchant sailing has always inspired me. Unfortunately, I am an American and required to perform a compulsory, military obligation on a submarine. But, hearing the stories of the merchants seduces me into staying a while longer, cherishing their company.

Another Extra Special and some 60s music from the juxbox soothes the atmosphere in the club for me. B. J. Thomas' "*I just can't help believin'...*" commences, and my mind wanders back to my high school days when the world presented me with so much wonder and excitement. Back then I thought everything was possible. There seemed to be so much promise in the future. That was before Vietnam. I recall sipping RC cola on the porch of the corner store in my neighborhood and passing the time chatting about the latest baseball game. And, at times, we talked about girls. We did not talk too much about them, because in our neighborhood, the pickings were slim. Those we admired were off limits, whereas, those who seemed to bother us were not inspiring. We learned early about our limitations. The richer families went out of their way to discourage us from getting to know their daughters. Unfortunately, some of our group that got too close ended up in a reform school. We learned our place in society.

All of a sudden, the entrance door to the Panda opens. Enticing B. J. swoons "*...misty morning in her eye...*" as the most beautiful Chinese woman I have ever seen, even in magazines, walks into the club. She is not dressed in the regular Chinese attire. She has on blue jeans and a blouse. Her hair is arranged like that of a 60s, East Coast cheerleader. She has long bangs that part two cascading waterfalls of hair. As she moves, her hair bounces upon her shoulders. She smiles at the direction of the bar. Everyone inside notices her. She enters alone. As it turns out, she knows the bartender.

Incredible as this may be, she takes a barstool right next to mine. She just nods to acknowledge me and begins chatting in perfect English with the bartender. Her accent is slightly British but different. The bartender brings her a mixed drink. I cannot tell what it is. But, the bartender knows her preference for liquor.

Noticing my state of awe over this gorgeous creature, the bartender introduces her to me as Maria. We exchange hellos. B.J. Thomas was never so right "*...this time the girl has got to stay for more than just a day...*" God is she beautiful!

From her conversation with the bartender, she is an accountant with a stock brokerage in Hong Kong. It has some Chinese unpronounceable name. She is fluent in English, Cantonese Chinese and Portuguese. Apparently, her parents divorced when she was young, and she spends time with each parent. Her father lives in San Paulo, Brazil and owns a company on the island of Macao. Her mom was formerly from Canton in Mainland China but now resides in Hong Kong.

In the intermissions of her conversation with the bartender when he has to pour drinks, I mention how impressed I am with her English. She comments that she learned the language from traveling and some home-school-like teaching in Brazil. Since her father has clients in the United States, she gets to accompany him often and acts as his translator in the after hours engagements. Judging from her present attire, she does have an American look about her. She reminds me that she is an American, a South American. We both laugh. Indeed, there are many Americans; although, it is seldom the case that we allow the other countries in the Americas to share in our identity. With this beautiful creature, I graciously allow her to call herself an American.

As fortune has it, the bartender is called away to cheer for a rugby squad with his fellow merchantmen. Maria is left with me. She finds it very odd that a club filled with merchantmen would allow a submarine sailor to share conversation with them. She reminds me that gazelles would never permit a lion to share a resting pad with them. Maria is right. In another time and place, I would be sinking these fellows wholesale. But, then again, they did leave me with Maria. There is solace to be gained in that.

Maria and I chat away all by our lonesome. No one bothers us. The bartender checks every now and then to replenish our refreshments. He seems pleased that I am entertaining Maria. And, I am pleased, as well. She seems genuinely interested in me, or in my profession. I guess there are few opportunities to meet a submariner. Imagines of Jules Verne's *Captain Nemo* must fill her mind with excitement. Sensing her inquisitive nature, I relate my profession with advantages. Well, I leave out the sea monsters.

Suddenly, she shifts on her stool gently, touches my thigh with her hand and whispers to me that she needs to visit the little girls' room. Just as I acknowledge her whisper, "*You're just too good to be true...*" commences on the juxbox. She smiles at me in a special way, as she dismounts her barstool. For the first time, I realize, for certain, that she likes me. She even turns around once as she makes her way to the restroom to check if I am watching her. When she notices that I am watching her, she smiles even more enthusiastically. Her face seems to radiate and her romantic, Portuguese, facial features surface and enchant me.

After she enters the restroom, the bartender comes over to ask me how things are progressing. He does not even wait for my response. He just smiles at me and says, "She's a wonderful girl." I understand perfectly. Strange, a few words convey everything.

While Maria is in the restroom, I get a chance to evaluate the crowd captivated by the rugby game. Most of the merchantmen resemble former players of the game. Their appearance is rugged, and the way they grasp their beer mugs displays the mannerisms of hardworking individuals. I suppose most merchantmen are of that category. What is more is that these men do not have beer bellies. They are lean around the waist. To a man, they are all in better shape than me. And, they drink. My God, do they drink! Their beer mugs never seem to touch a solid surface. As for the game that they are watching, it reminds me of some hillbillies trying to abuse a hog. What they could possibly admire in this fiasco on the TV screen is beyond my comprehension?

The opening of the restroom door disturbs my disgust with the rugby game. Maria adjusts her waistband as she emerges. Her bluejeans do fit her snugly. She must be involved in some form of athletics in order to maintain such a great shape. Her gaze catches mine, and from her facial features she is pleased that I find such enjoyment in observing her body.

It is a short walk to her barstool. She remounts her stool and extends me a warm smile that I swear I will remember forever. A quick brush of her hair with her right hand, and she resumes our conversation. Two questions that she asks often are how long I will be staying in Hong Kong, and how soon will I be able to return. The shortness of my stay disappoints her. The fact that I am unable to project a rapid return upsets her as well. She reminds me that I am an American, and I should be able to return whenever I like. We spend some time discussing visa regulations. The gist of our conversation is that she wants to see me again, and often.

The rest of the evening we exchange stories about our lives. We are both in our late 20s. As it turns out, I am almost a year older. As we chat away, one thing I notice is that Maria manages to get her face closer and closer to mine with each new topic of conversation. Finally, with kind of a surprise move, she leans over gently and kisses my cheek. It is a short duration kiss. I barely feel the moisture of her lips. But, from that moment on, our eyes seem to lock onto one another.

The bartender interrupts to inform us that it will be last call once the rugby game is over. For whatever reason, I suspect he thinks I am watching and understand the game. Maria touches my hand with hers and invites me to walk her home. She says that she has a condo apartment not very far away. I completely forget about the launch back to the boat and agree. There is a sense in the way she invited me that makes me suspect I will be housed for the night.

Sure enough, the rugby game ends. Apparently, the winning side was the one not favored by the clientele in the club. They seem to be disgruntled, as they retake position at the bar. The manner in which they swig their mugs is telling as well. It is as if they could eat the mugs. I fear for a moment that they will start tossing the mugs against the walls and start a brawl. I can sense a little apprehension in Maria as well. I suggest to Maria that maybe we should start off to her condo early. She graciously agrees, and we bid our farewells to the bartender.

The chilly air of Hong Kong surprises me, as Maria and I step out into the street. She comes close to me and allows me to place my left arm around her. In my arm, we begin to walk into the center of Hong Kong. As we walk, Maria points out sites of interests. She seems to have a story for each little shop along the way. Some of the stories are quite interesting. There is one about a tailor who sizes his overseas customers with the finest cloths. After the customers have purchased, he substitutes the items with lower quality fabrics and ships them to their designated addresses overseas. Since the correct fabric is identified on the customs label, the recipient is none the wiser. Even if the customer does object, the customs label settles the dispute. I have to chuckle at the tailor's ingenuity and courage. Maria insists that he often gets repeat customers.

We pass a restaurant with live eels sucking against the glass of the storefront. Maria asks if I am hungry. I decline. She reminds me that we do not have to order eels. I still decline. God only knows what other creatures are squirming around in that place.

Soon, we reach an area, outfitted with old gaslights. She tells me it is a new residential area designed for professionals. After walking past a few buildings into the gas lighted area, Maria informs me that we have arrived at her building. The façade of the building is fabricated from dark marble. My guess is that the building comprises of some fifteen floors. Each apartment contains a balcony area with a metal table and two metal chairs. After she has given me some time to scope out her building, she asks if I would like to come up for some tea. She squeezes my arm and claims that she makes the best pot of tea in all of China. I could not care less whether or not she does make the best cup of tea in China. I smile and say, "I could use a cup of tea."

A black-painted, wrought iron fence separates the walkway we are standing on from the building's entrance. I turn my head away from the fence, as she types in her pass code. It is an old habit of mine from the submarine security environment. Soon after she touches the last number on the keypad, the gate clunks open. A slight push on the gate enables us to pass into the garden area of the condo complex. To the right of the entranceway is a small Japanese-style fountain. Its slow trickling flow encourages reflection. A series of mailboxes line the left side. The boughs of some strange trees form a canopy. In the shadow of the gaslights, the walkway resembles a comfortable cocoon. By the time we get halfway through the canopied walkway, Maria has settled comfortably under my shoulder. For the first time, I realize that she is about six inches shorter than me.

At the entrance to the building, Maria has to insert a key to penetrate yet another barrier. Security is of paramount importance in this complex. Once inside, we are refreshed by the building's air conditioning. Truly, it is a relief from the dampness of harbor area. Maria directs me to the elevators. They are very modern, paneled with the finest timbers. It takes no time to get to her floor. As we exit the elevator, my feet respond positively to thick carpeting. Each step massages my feet. Her apartment resides at the end of the hallway. Being an end unit, it offers a partial view of Hong Kong harbor.

In the United States, her unit would be described as a one-bedroom. Sliding doors constructed of thick paper with black-painted bamboo frames separate each room. The largest room is her kitchen/dining area. The dining table is actually an extension of the kitchen counter. Instead of having a four-seat dining table, she has installed a large computer desk. From her desk, she can look out over her balcony to a spectacular view of Hong Kong harbor. The bathroom area abuts the far kitchen wall. Beyond the bathroom area resides the one bedroom. From my quick calculation, the entire apartment comprises maybe some eight hundred square feet.

Maria offers me a seat at the lunch counter, as she prepares some tea. She runs through the floor plan in the apartment. One room I had not noticed was a den area to the far end of the bedroom. She keeps her athletic equipment in there. It also doubles as a storage area. As she moves about her large kitchen, from refrigerator to oven to garbage disposal, I am amazed at her organization. Every little space in the kitchen has something appended. Her counter contains a toaster oven, microwave and regular, two-slice toaster. Without question, one person could survive here quite nicely.

As the tea is heating, Maria excuses herself and goes into the bedroom. Soon, the kitchen area is filled with the sound of soft instrumental music. Maria returns wearing a comfortable, one-piece, paper-thin, island dress, secured by a string loop around the neckline. As she dims the lights, the entire kitchen area transforms into an incredibly cozy area. What a way to enjoy a cup of tea!

A hissing sound from the teapot disturbs my sensual contemplation. Maria asks if I prefer cream in my tea. I respond that I have never tried cream in tea. She teases me with some first time dare. I decline.

After my first sip of her tea, I realize just how good she does make it. I comment to her on its taste. I do so not to flatter her but genuinely to praise her talent. She slides her kitchen stool near mine, and we sip tea together making small talk. For some reason, I am somewhat reluctant to make a move on her. She senses my uneasiness and spends most of the next half hour or so persuading me. It really does not take that much persuasion. By the time my teacup is empty, the aroma of Maria's perfume has captivated me. The soft, silky feel of the texture of her lounging attire on my hands tingles every sensor in my nervous system. Maria body feels as soothing as an immersion in a warm bath. That first, tender kiss on the lips propels me into her embrace. The softness of her breasts against my chest awakens the desire within me. Soon, I am being lead to her bedroom. I do not even sense the floor beneath me. It is as if we floated into her room. At the edge of her bed, she unloosens the securing string of her dress, tugs a little on the neckline towards her shoulder and releases the string. A short shake of her head and hips to each side allows her dress to slide down her body and bundle up around her feet. She smiles at me, as she raises her hands into her hair and steps out of the bundle around her feet. I embrace her around her waist, and my mouth comes alive on her breasts. She moans her approval, as she drapes her arms over my shoulders. Soon, her hands are undressing me. First my shirt then my pants are removed in the most efficient of manners.

Before I can continue my adoration of her breasts, she begins mouthing my chest and neck. In my embrace, I feel her knees bend, and her body weight shift toward the bed. It is not long before we are off balance and tumble onto the bed. She is a beautiful woman. I thank God I am alive tonight. I thank God He has kept me alive long enough to partake in this pleasure. She feels so wonderful wrapped around me, as I move appropriately within her moisture.

A harbor bird awakes me, as he touches down on Maria's balcony ledge. I watch the bird awhile. He notices me observing him and decides to relocate to another perch. It cannot be more than 5:00 AM. Although it is nighttime, the lights and sounds from the harbor maintain a glow around the surrounding areas. I check Maria lying next to me. She is in a peaceful sleep. I move slowly and ever so gently so as not to disturb her, as I exit her bed. There is an easy chair located near the sliding glass door leading onto her balcony. I settle myself into it and gaze out over the harbor. Her apartment has a spectacular view of the entire estuary. I could sit here forever and watch the estuary traffic come and go.

The air conditioning chills me as I sit. Under her blankets, my body oozed with perspiration; first as a result of my pleasure with Maria, second from my body's effort to equalize its chemistry and third from the weight of the blankets. I notice a few bath towels stacked on a hamper just ahead of me. I reach over and grasp one to cover me. It is fluffy and thick, just the right kind of material to keep me warm. In covering my torso with her bath towel and adjusting myself in the easy chair, I cannot help sensing her dried moisture clinging to my body. When fluid, it brought me so much pleasure. I should have showered after I exhausted her, but I chose not to. I wanted to have her clinging to me when I returned to the submarine. Port women always have been good to me. Although I may only meet them once in my life, their memory lingers on in me forever. Maria will remain with me in this way. Each time in the future that I adjust myself in an easy chair, the sensation of her moisture clinging to me will return to fill me with excitement and desire, and I will recall and cherish the time I spent with Maria.

Maria rolls on her other side in the bed. Her movements break my concentration. For a moment, I thought she might awake. She did not. I turn my gaze back to the estuary. My mind follows one junk after another, as they navigate the obstacle course of random moorings. It is amazing to watch today, but on reflection I realize that similar vessels were making the same runs for centuries. Heaven forbid, it might even have been for millennia. It is as if I can comprehend five thousand years of Chinese history in this one evening with my Princess of the Middle of Kingdom. What a wonderful experience!

Most of the sailors aboard those junks in the estuary are not much different from me. They work all day doing similar, but less technical, chores. They find some time to relax in the evening. They might even have a favored liberty port where they can experience the same kinds of pleasure as I have. They just operate on a different social level. But, pleasure and appreciation for life are measured similarly. It probably has been that way for millennia in China. I am not so different from the Chinese. What matters is how we enjoy our time. I truly can say that I would not swap this evening for all the evenings I have experienced over the last few years. This evening was special.

The night shows signs of weakening. Hints of daylight start to appear. The birds seem excited like they are expecting a big event. I guess to them, daylight is everything. To me, it signals my eventual return to Fenwick Pier and the launch that will take me back to the submarine. I have enjoyed the peacefulness of these early morning hours, as I watched the traffic on the estuary and contemplated life in general. Truly, I was in need of some quality time spent in that area of the mind.

Small moans from Maria disturb my concentration. She turns to one side then the other on the bed. Finally, she realizes that I am not lying next to her. She wakes quickly. At first she is surprised, but then she calms when she notices me in her easy chair. After she has rubbed the hair out from in front of her face, she asks if I slept well. I did. She manages to rise to a sitting position and asks me how I like my coffee. One thing I have learned about port women: if they have enjoyed your company overnight, then first thing in the morning they cannot wait to feed you. I guess I measured up to her expectations last evening. Sailors usually do.

Despite sleep still clinging to her face, Maria manages to get up and walk toward the kitchen. At first, her standing seems unsteady, but after a few steps, she awakens her legs and walks smoothly. I have to admit. She looks as wonderful in the morning as she did last night. I was not persuaded by my consumption of Extra Specials. This woman is truly beautiful. I pray that I see her again.

Before she starts the coffee, she slides into a colorful bathrobe. I am taken by the gorgeous butterfly design embedded upon the robe. To me, Maria is a gorgeous butterfly. The bathrobe is so perfect for her. As I enjoy the moment looking at the butterfly, Maria scoops some cold water from the sink into her hair in order to manage it back into the waterfall design that makes her so desirable. I feel myself awaken, as she prepares the coffee maker. God, I adore this woman.

After pouring the water into the coffee dispenser, she asks if I will be available today. She mentions some sites around the island that she would like to show me. With regrets, I inform her that I have the duty today aboard the submarine. I will need to be getting back soon. The sparkle in her eyes seems to fade, as she hears me say the words "going back" to the ship. Before the focus of her eyes lowers to the floor, I mention that I will be free tomorrow, and she can show me around the island, then. As her eyes rise to meet mine, the approving smile on her face conveys everything. Yes, she will pick me up at the pier. I tell her I will not be available until noontime, and she understands. Smiling, she excuses herself and scoots into the bathroom.

While the coffee percolates, I go over my recent good fortune and continue to enjoy the scenery on the estuary. It is amazing how daylight makes the estuary fill up with traffic. How the junks avoid one another resembles the spinning dances of the West Asian fakers. Congested living conditions must hone the senses of distance.

Maria emerges from the bathroom humming a romantic tune. I do not recognize it. Before I can inquire as to its name, Maria informs me that the coffee is ready. She tells me to freshen up while she pours me a cup and makes some breakfast. As I pass her on my way to the bathroom, she pinches my right waist.

That is another sign of affection in Asia. She really does like me. In the bathroom, I choose a submarine shower so as not to wash off the remnants of her moisture. I want to cherish her upon me a while. A little soap and water under the armpits, abdomen and facial area does the trick. I emerge from the bathroom to find Maria standing in front of the door offering me a cup of coffee. After I take the coffee cup from her hand, she holds my free hand with her free hand and guides me to the counter where she has prepared some toast with strawberry jam and a few slices of cantaloupe. She invites me to sit, and we spend the next forty-five minutes making small talk. The way she mouths the strawberry coated toasts awakens me. Between the small talk, my mind struggles to keep down thoughts of mounting her again before I depart for the boat. What a wonderful morning!

The time comes when I have to be getting back to the boat. For a sailor, that time always comes. By now, you would think that I would have adapted to it, but I have not. She offers to walk me back, but I decline. I tell her that I get all mushy in goodbyes. She reminds me that I will see her again tomorrow, so it should be fine. I still decline. I tell her I need to clear my mind before I embark upon the launch. She says she understands, but I know she does not. During the walk to the elevator, she persuades me to allow her to accompany me to the boundary of her entrance gate. She says she will not let me out the gate unless I allow her that last moment. I acquiesce.

The trip down the elevator is filled with long passionate embraces. It makes her smile to feel me awaken against her body. She is wonderful. How can I just leave her like this? Life should be easier. I should be allowed to abandon the routine of my social position in order to follow my passions. Career puts too many social restrictions upon us. I guess, in the end, my career is more important than my passions. I have to chuckle when I realize that I prefer a black submarine, mooring in the middle of the estuary filled with diesel fumes, sanitary tank exhausts and loud machinery noise to the comforts of her embrace. I must be insane to leave this woman. But, I will.

At the front gate, we embrace one last time, exchange performance pleasantries until I turn slowly and walk toward Fenwick Pier. Maria remains at the gate entrance and watches me until I am out of sight. I turn a few times to wave to her. She waves back. There are tears in her eyes. Though the tears sadden me, they also convey her fond emotions. I have experienced too many farewells. It comes with being a sailor.

As I walk passed a few of the sites Maria told me about on her way to her place last evening, my mind fills with thoughts of her. Even the eels seem to be mouthing goodbye to me, as they suckle up to the restaurant's windowpane. This morning, the eels do not seem to exhibit that squirmy repulsiveness I attributed to them last evening. Today, they seem gentle, like park squirrels. I even nod as I pass them in acknowledgment of them seeing me off. In a sense, I thank them.

Fenwick Pier appears as I turn a corner after a tailor shop. I see my submarine sitting pretty like an autumn duck on a pond. I have returned. Soon, last night will be a distant memory. Like many port women before her, Maria will take a fond place in my recollections. It is best for me that way. I will remember her with fondness, before she could affect a change in any part of my person. It seems that I prefer port women, because they never actually get to confront me and force me to change my aspirations or habits. Chances are, if I got to know Maria too well, she would urge me into some advanced education field to better myself for the time when I depart the submarine service. I am not ready for that. I am not ready for change. I like who I am. I am comfortable with who I am. Maria, on the other hand, would not accept me as I am. She sees the potential in me. She would want to develop that potential and mold me into someone she admires. It would not be someone I care to be. Maria scares me.

As the launch approaches, my mind is filled with anxiety over Maria. I realize that I can never see her again. She will want me to become someone I am not. Worse yet, she will want me to be someone I desire not to be. Well, I shared her charms last evening. I do not dare share anymore, less I be transformed into a plastic person of her aspirations. She would change me, too. That is the kind of person she is. She could never accept me as simply a submarine sailor. Is it not odd that I will never see this woman again, because she wants to better my life? Then again, that is the reason I spend my time with port women rather than settle down with anyone. I get to be, and remain, me for better or worse.

The coxswain announces boarding time for the launch. I make my way to the rear of the launch, well protected from the ocean spray. The coxswain opens the throttle, and the launch proceeds to the frigate. Goodbye Maria, and thank you!

CHAPTER 5

Battle Group Sanitation

The traffic on the estuary seems never to stop. It is early morning around 5:00 AM, and everywhere we see junks going this way and junks going that way. I suppose they are in a hurry to get where they are going. To me, they could just sit idle a while, enjoy the scenery and contemplate. But, they do not. They just keep chugging away.

We are up early to divorce from shore power. We get underway today. The cool, morning air on the estuary is refreshing. Some of my electricians wear windbreakers to keep warm. Almost all of them came topside with a cup of hot coffee. Mornings should be like this, sipping coffee and admiring the way the ripples in the estuary lap the sides of our tough, black, steel sanctuary.

Our four-day stay in Hong Kong is over. Besides the evening with the port woman, I managed to slip away to the China Fleet Club to purchase some Chinese silk, an ivory chess set and some jewelry. I enjoy shopping in Hong Kong. Even if I would never use the stuff I buy, I would purchase it because this is the only location in the world that I could possibly buy it. Take the ivory chess set. I could never envision myself going all the way to Central Africa to purchase ivory from someone who dislodged it from an elephant that happened to die of natural causes. Then, I would need to hire a craftsman, skilled in using ivory as a medium, to carve a chess set. That would be impossible, given my lowly financial means.

The frigate crew is up early as well. We say little to each other. My electricians and the frigate's just go about their work disconnecting the cables. I guess the sadness of leaving such a wonderful port city has overcome them. As I watch them go through the rote motions of disconnecting, my thoughts take me to Maria.

I never showed up to meet her on that Wednesday morning. She probably waited a long time on the pier. I suppose I should have made some excuse and sent a messenger, but I did not. It is best this way. She was someone from an affluent family, and I was a lowly sailor. Sooner or later, pressure from her family would persuade her to abandon me. How much of my time would I have invested by the time that happened? It is an old, well-beaten path that I found myself on. Love between classes is doomed. Although I admit enjoying the moment, the future would have been wrought with unpleasantries. Why bother with having to endure any unpleasantry? Life is much more enjoyable when lived in simplicity.

My lead electrician informs me that the shore power cables are separated. He tells me the crew will stow them for at-sea operations. I glance at him and motion that I concur. He can tell that I have other things on my mind, so he leaves me to my thoughts. As the electricians begin to climb down the hatch, I take my last, long look at Hong Kong. It is a long glance around the harbor. Finally, I stop at Fenwick Pier and whisper "I'm sorry, Maria." I take my turn climbing down the hatch into the submarine. Each step, as I descend into the boat, seems to take an eternity. It is as if Hong Kong is tugging me topside. I have to go down the hatch.

Once my feet are on the first level deck, I do not look upward at the blue sky above the hatch opening. I just walk back toward the engineering spaces. By the time I reach the engine room watertight door, I have regained my identity as a nuclear submarine sailor. I am back in the bosom of the boat. For a while, the carefree atmosphere of the port city tempted me, but I endured, once again. Now, I am ready for another month or so asea in this huge metallic tube, boring holes in the ocean.

One of the officers asks me, as we pass in the engine room center passageway, if I am ready to go to sea. I respond with enthusiasm that I am. And, I am ready. If there is anything in this life that I am prepared for it is that I am ready for arduous sea duty in a submarine. Somehow, I believe my body was designed for this kind of life in the depths of the ocean. Jules Verne's tales of undersea life must have captivated me when I was kid. Nonetheless, I keep to myself as the crew prepares to get underway. I am so comfortable asea in a submarine. Why? How can anyone be comfortable in a sewer pipe away from his loved ones for months at a time without any contact with anyone? But, I am. Maybe my refusal to meet with Maria again had something to do with a way in which she might have threatened that comfort. That just might be it.

The sound of the tugboat backing down its engines reverberates through the hull of the submarine. It is a familiar sound associated with getting underway. The sound reminds me of the grunting emitted from a defensive football lineman gearing up to meet the oncoming rush of the offensive linemen. Soon, the topside sounds subside. The last mooring line must have been retrieved, and we are adrift in the estuary.

The submarine's announcing system blasts the word to man the full maneuvering watch. My ears sense the change in inner-boat pressure, as the six-inch-thick-steel, main access hatches are dogged shut. With the exception of the fairwater hatches, the submarine is sealed for at-sea operations. Since I am not assigned to the maneuvering watch, I make my way forward to the bunking area. The voyage on the surface leaving Hong Kong is as arduous as the one entering. As I move forward, I feel the familiar rolls, as the waves generated from the wakes of passing cargo vessels push against the hull of the submarine. Yes, we are underway again.

It is about mid-morning now. Visibility in the estuary is good. The periscope camera has been connected to the ship's internal TV system, so the crew can watch the ship maneuver through the estuary and island channels. Seeing the bright neon lights of Hong Kong fade into the background brings on a sense of sadness. I had a wonderful time during this port visit. Chances are that I will never be able to experience that again. Those chances diminish the fainter the bright neon lights of Hong Kong Island become. Hong Kong was good to me this time. I will miss her. As the waves lap up and dampen the piers of Hong Kong, I recall how Maria dampened and embraced me with her moisture. I will never forget that sensation that urged me into a rhythmic movement as her fragrances filled my nostrils with desire. I will miss her.

A sailor, yelling out the identity of a famous landmark, interrupts my pleasant and sensuous contemplation. I remember that landmark as well. It was one I used to get my bearing back to Fenwick Pier from Maria's condo. Interestingly, the sailor just thinks of the landmark as a historical site. As it turns out, it was a site mentioned in the novel *Taipan* that was deeded to the church so as not to cause animosity between rivaling taipans. The landmark meant so much more to me. Since it is an identifying landmark of Hong Kong, I suppose I will be reminded of its significance whenever I see a postcard from Hong Kong. Maria will haunt me forever.

Some of the channel currents are beginning to rock the boat. It is best I recline in the shelter of my bunk, before my breakfast suddenly decides to grace the floor. Sliding into my bunk, I place the earphones over my ears and allow the ship's entertainment system to lull me into sleep. I prefer the softer, romantic music to the popular rock & roll of the crew's preference. The first song is from the Carpenter's "*We've Only Just Begun.*" This song brings back wonderful memories of my earlier life in training for a career in nuclear power. There were girls associated with that song as well. Regrettably, none of them had just begun with me. We spent some time together, but the relationships were short and sweet. We all were going on our separate ways. Most of those girls were in training to become schoolteachers, whereas, we sailors were off to submarines. Very few made lifelong commitments. As the song plays on, I sense the hope that I never felt in the relationships with those would-be schoolteachers in the voice of the female singer. Maybe if I had listened to the song more closely in my earlier days, I might have found some hope in a relationship. The would-be schoolteachers were fine gals. They exemplified everything I would have desired in an eventual lifelong partner. But, I just used them for sex. That is all I wanted from them. And, I suspect, that is all they wanted from me. Unfortunately, I still have not outgrown the wanting.

I feel a nudging in my back from someone outside my bunk. It is the forward roving watch waking me for the oncoming watch. I must have dozed off, as I reminisced the friends I encountered during my training days. The berthing area is dark when one first awakes. Nevertheless, I slide down my bunk onto the deck below. The small red deck lights illuminate the way to the bathroom. Much like runway lights for an airplane landing at night, I make my way along them. The walk is smooth, so I suspect that sometime during my sleep the submarine must have dove.

Opening the door to the bathroom, my eyes squint in order to adjust to the white light. For some reason, the bathroom lights are the brightest on board. I guess the designers must have wanted the crew to see the commodes. They must have been strange fellows.

In the bathroom area, I am queried about my time in Hong Kong. To which, I provide a short response: "You know, same old stuff." The responding smiles indicate their suspicions that I had a good time. It is that way with all sailors. Well, at least the old sailors. Ports are our playgrounds. If you say little, it means you really enjoyed yourself. Nothing else needed to be said. Silence communicates volumes to submariners. The rest of the time in the bathroom, those present just go about their business preparing for the oncoming watch.

In the shower, I finally succumb and wash the area of my privates completely. As the water flows down the lower contours of my legs and into the drain in the deck below me, I sense Maria releasing her grip on me. Once again, I bid her farewell. I insure the shower water rinses me off completely. As I turn off the showerhead, I realize that I have cleansed the last of my meeting with Maria and Hong Kong. Now, refreshed and a new man, I towel dry, don my poopysuit and make my way to the crew's mess for Mid-rats.

The crew's mess resembles an overcrowded hog sty this evening. The oncoming watch standers are huddled around the tables bent over forking and grabbing at this entrée and that one just like starving hogs. The absence of hog grunting restrains me from hollering "soowee." I manage to maneuver my way through the hungry mob to the cold cut table where I quickly assemble a hoagie like sandwich. That and a cup of coffee is all I will need. Observing the feeding frenzy before me, I swear if the cooks just sloshed Mid-rats out on the deck, these half-crazed sailors would slurp it up without any reservation.

As I munch on my hoagie, one of the control room chiefs informs me that we are on our way to meet up with the Battle Group in the area. Without responding, the forward chief and I communicate with a quick eye contact that we have been given a sanitation assignment.

Sanitation refers to operations in which a submarine stealthily stalks the Battle Group to uncover any enemy submarines trying to gather intelligence, via underwater surveillance, about the vessels in the Group. Our submarine will first perform a perimeter check of the entire Battle Group to identify any enemy submarines following the Group. Once that is accomplished, our submarine will enter the area of the Battle Group from one of the distant corners and slowly sonar scan the underbelly of the entire Group. Usually when that task is accomplished, we are allowed to return to our mission. On some occasions, we are tasked with running ahead of the Battle Group to sanitize a port call for the Group.

The difficulty of sanitizing a Battle Group is that the flagship of the Group seldom alerts the subordinate vessels that one of their submarines is operating in the area. In a sense, our mission is also to evaluate the effectiveness of our surface ships' underwater detection capabilities. If none of the Battle Group's vessels detect us, then the flagship commander will have a few unkind words to pass down to his subordinates and their inept crews. Our prayer, of course, is to avoid detection less one of those subordinate commanders gets a hair-trigger and fires an underwater missile at us.

Finishing the last of my hoagie, I refresh my coffee and head back aft to assume the watch. As I make my way aft, my thoughts are filled with the fun and games upcoming in the next few days. My mind fills up with the need to locate all the required equipment we will need available back aft for this operation.

Stowing for sea will need to be double checked less some unattended wrench fall onto the deck and alert the Battle Group of our presence, or worse yet, alert an enemy submarine.

Upon relieving the watch, I make my initial rounds through the engineering spaces, directing the watch standers to double-check their spaces stowed for sea. Having the watch standers check for any loose gear hanging around from the in-port period will get the engineering spaces a long way down the road to silent running conditions when they become activated.

The engineering spaces' pumps are in fast speed. We are anticipating elevated propulsion bells this watch. That must mean that the Battle Group is an appreciable distance from our location. We will need to make up ground quickly in order to accomplish our mission. One good thing about being at elevated propulsion speed, it is unlikely we will be surprised by a period of ship's drills.

Before I can complete my initial tour, the word comes over the announcing system to increase speed to Ahead Full. Since most of the engineering spaces' pumps were in fast speed already, there is little additional noise emanating from the decks below. The power plant should remain in this status for the rest of the watch. Changes in propulsion speed will come when the ship comes up to periscope depth. For now, we are boring a hole in the South China Sea at Ahead Full. We should scare a lot of little fish today.

Speaking of little fish, I have often wondered how the undersea life interprets us. Given that we are so big and black compared to their daily predators, we must be seen as some kind of whale. Although we do not eat the fish, our propeller must chew up a considerable number of them that get entrained in the water flushing along our hull. The future response of the semi-chewed survivors must alert other little fish to keep clear of us. All other undersea life must be cautious as well, because we have never collided with a whale.

On the surface, dolphins enjoy riding in and upon our wake. They often follow us into ports. For one reason or another, dolphins must respect our presence. We have never run over one, and they get so very close to us when we are underway. To dolphins, we must resemble some huge undersea playground. They certainly seem to come to life upon our wakes when we are entering port.

One maneuver that always has amazed me is how dolphins manage to time crossing our bow. A dolphin will be "surfing" upon our Port wake and, for some reason, quickly dart across our bow onto our Starboard wake. The effortlessness and speed with which the dolphin accomplishes that crossing are absolutely awesome. The dolphin seems to be traveling faster than a spear gun could launch a dart. It happens like a slight of hand from a card shark. You realize the dolphin crossed the bow. You realize that you observed it, but you have no recollection of the exact movements of the dolphin's performance. Yet, there the dolphin rides upon the Starboard wake. Dolphin bow-crossing is an experience reserved for sailors.

The watch standers in the bowels of the engineering spaces are called the Lower Level Watches. It does sound better than the Bilge Cleaners, an activity they perform when they are not making their rounds and taking readings on their equipment. In a round bottom boat, all the fluid system leaks and vents drain to the bilge. It is an ongoing struggle to keep the bilges dry.

The ship has a pumping system installed that can take a suction on every bilge in every space. Liquid refuse collected from this pumping system can be directed overboard or collected in an on board, specially designated tank. When this tank nears its capacity with fluid, it can be pump overboard. The naval architects that design submarines literally think of everything. In a sense they have to, because underway submerged is the wrong time and place to discover the need for a special system, like bilge draining.

Like most of my other on-watch tours of the engineering spaces, I always find one of my lower level watch standers with his torso in the bilge area. This watch is no different. Apparently, some sticky debris, affectionately referred to as "mung," has taken a fancy to the underside of some small seawater piping. The watch stander is stretching as best he can to reach around the piping and dislodge the mung with an abrasive pad, affectionately referred to as a "greenie." A "greenie" consists of a rectangular piece of sponge with an abrasive green pad adhered to one of its sides. "Greenies" are quite handy for cleaning engine rooms. They fit nicely in your hand and interestingly have the shape of Golden Rectangles. Some of the more artistically-talented officers have chided that the Golden Rectangle shape is what makes "greenies" so desirable to the crew. I don't think so.

As I approach the watch stander with his torso entangled in the lower level piping, all I hear, in the form of muffled grunts, are true, at-sea expressions of appreciation for the intricate piping design of the submarine. I interrupt the busy watch stander; otherwise, I would be overcome with a symphony of such profound admiration in short delicacies of expression. Upon hearing my voice, the watch stander seems to slither out quickly from his position in between the seawater piping. As he stands to greet me, he commences to explain his purpose in the bilge. I halt his rendition quickly and nod in acknowledgment that I am aware of his duties.

Over the next few minutes, I go over his log readings and discuss the state of the stow for at-sea in his space. The logs are reflective of upper propulsion bell operation. There are no trends building, and he has no out of specification readings. All is well here. I commend the watch stander on his initiative to keep the bilge clean, return him his logs and continue my tour.

Since the propulsion plant is answering Ahead Full, I will need to make my rounds of the engineering spaces more often in order to insure that the equipment is operating properly. Also, I will need to be able to detect any developing trends quickly in order to make adjustments to the machinery. High propulsion orders carry additional requirements as well: Fluid systems need to be sampled more often in order to monitor their chemistry more closely. Pumps running at high speeds need to be alternated to insure they do not overheat and that they are run an equivalent amount of time as their counterparts for lifetime warranty considerations. The watch standers have to be attentive to any sudden changes in noise levels that could indicate some piece of machinery experiencing trouble or malfunctioning. Vigilance is the order of the day when answering high propulsion bells in the engineering spaces.

In the next lower level space on my tour, I find the watch stander drawing a chemistry sample from one of the fluid systems into a collection bottle. At upper propulsion bells, he is required to sample more often. Sometimes, under unusual conditions, the sampling is required every hour. Considering that to run all the tests required during each sampling takes up to twenty minutes, that leaves little time for anything else besides taking the required log readings of the running machinery and systems. This watch stander gets pretty involved when we answer upper propulsion bells. I notice he is busy, nod to him that I will leave him be and just review his logs.

Four log reading data sheets accompany this space. It will take me up to ten minutes just to review his readings. Each log reading data sheet contains about 25-35 readings per side of a page. Four pages translate into some two hundred readings to analyze for trends. There are many systems that weave in an out of this space, and each one is monitored. Temperature, pressure and vacuum are some of the parameters of the fluid and steam systems. Each reading is important, as it indicates a system condition. At the top of each vertical data column, the upper and lower limits of the reading are highlighted in red. In between the reading limits in red are the average operating band temperatures listed in light blue. Having these aids imprinted on the log data pages facilitates the oversight. It is merely a matter of looking over the column of hourly readings entered by the watch stander and comparing them to the red and light blue readings at the top of the column. Almost always, a questionable hourly reading taken by the watch stander that is out of specification with either the upper light blue or red limit bands is annotated in the Remarks section of the log.

My watch standing group is experienced and conscientious, so I seldom find an undetected, out-of-specification reading during my log reviews. However, the exceptions do occur. One such occurrence, I recall, went unnoticed for the entire previous watch. Apparently, one set of running machinery was alternated for another. Unbeknownst to the prior watch was that one of the monitoring gages on the previously running machinery was discovered inoperative by the watch stander on the watch prior to the previous watch. Regrettably, he failed to enter the malfunctioning gage into the Remarks section of the log data sheet, and it apparently skipped his mind to inform the oncoming watch of the discrepancy during the watch turnover. He did, however, notify the supervisor of the division responsible for the upkeep of the machinery in question, and he entered the gage in the Out of Commission Log as in need of repair or replacement.

Since I often check the Out of Commission Log during my pre-watch turnover to note any new machinery that has been listed, I was aware of the defective gage prior to when I made my inspection tour of the engineering spaces. Amazingly, when I looked at the log data sheet containing the gage in question, I was amazed to see the reading listed as operating at normal parameters. I knew the piece of machinery was shutdown over a watch ago. Sure enough, when I went over to double check the reading on the gage, it was reading precisely as it was recorded in the logs for some eight hours. I tapped on the glass cover of the gage. The pointer quivered then fell to the bottom of the indicating range of the gage. The needle was stuck. We needed to replace the gage.

When I brought this discrepancy to the attention of the watch stander, all he could say was "I thought the machine was running." The overall noise level in the space often drowns out machinery sounds from smaller equipment like this one. I advised the watch stander to place the back of his hand on the machinery. If the back of his hand feels warm or vibrates on the machinery, it means that it is running. He embarrassingly acknowledged.

The back of the hand is used to detect heated surfaces, because the sensory part of a hand is located on the inside portion. If the machinery in question was overheating, a watch stander could burn the inside of his hand by touching it. Although a similar fate would befall the backside of the hand, the hand's sensory organs would still be functional.

For the rest of the watch, I alternate making my rounds of the engineering spaces with periods of hot coffee sipping with the roving watches. Roving watches are not assigned to a specific space. They get to roam about the engineering spaces taking log readings on auxiliary equipment.

Towards the end of the watch, the low frequency level noise suddenly decreases in amplitude. Those noises emanate from the propulsion train, indicating that the engineering plant is answering lower propulsion bells. We must have made good time. Randomly, the noise levels throughout the engineering spaces begin to decrease, as one by one pumps are shifted to slow speed. The sudden overall decrease in noise level announces that we are on station to commence our perimeter check of the Battle Group. Surveillance is a silent operation in order to allow our sonar sensors to detect any outside radiated noise in the encircling sea space.

Being inside a metal tube with no windows means we will be feeling our way around the Battle Group on the expertise of our sonar specialists. All we can do in the engineering spaces to assist the effort is to ensure we are quiet. We need not activate silent running, but we need to have our machinery in slow speed to reduce the over-the-side radiated noise from our spaces. Reducing machinery speed in the engineering spaces should be sufficient to enable us to detect another submersible in the area.

A yawing sound from the hull indicates that we are diving in order to operate at a depth well below an enemy surveillance submarine. This will enable us to detect him easier. If we discover an enemy submarine, we are not allowed to sink it. This is still peacetime. For an engagement to occur, the enemy submarine would have to display an aggressive action towards our submarine or the Battle Group. Since the primary objective of surveillance is to gather information, it is unlikely that the enemy submarine would provoke us in any way. However, we are allowed to discourage an enemy submarine. Of course, our ship would not do it. The Battle Group's escort submarine would be assigned that responsibility. The escort submarine is a fast attack boat specifically designed for such encounters. Probably, the only thing the Battle Group would permit us to do is to sneak up behind the enemy submarine and rapidly cavitate our propeller to alert the submarine to our presence aft. That procedure is usually sufficient to scare him off. I guess it is the same for all underwater entities, a big fish making noise in your rear means trouble.

As I make my last rounds of the engineering spaces, I notice the seawater pressure entering the ship. Seawater pressure is an indication of depth. As a rule of thumb, each one hundred feet below sea level represents some forty pounds of pressure. Two hundred feet below sea level would translate on a seawater gage as some eighty pounds of pressure. We are deep. Surely, an enemy submersible would not suspect us to be at this depth. We truly are undetected and approaching on his blind side. At this depth we possibly could scan a full one-fourth of the arc around the Battle Group.

The oncoming watch finds me admiring the inlet seawater pressure gage. He comments on the depth, as well. We both agree that we will need to remind our watch standers to be alert for any seawater leaks. At this depth, even a small leak would fill the engineering spaces quickly with seawater. Under greater pressure, seawater would flow through a hole in the seawater piping more forcefully. The spray of the incoming water, as it collided with the piping runs in the engineering spaces, would mask its point of origin. Emergency procedures would need to be enforced in order to isolate the incoming water source. Regrettably, those procedures would send us hurtling toward the surface and negate our detection efforts of any enemy submersible in the area. Seeing our submarine leap out of the ocean would not impress the Battle Group commander either.

As I make my way forward, the smell of something greasy greets me at the main compartment's watertight door. From the scant scent of vinegar, I would guess it would be chicken fried steak or one of the oriental chicken entrees. Chicken fried steak, affectionately referred to as a UFO, is actually a steak. UFO on the grill refers to unidentified frying object. The acronym hints at the entrée's popularity.

To my surprise, I had forgotten it was breakfast time. Underwater, it is difficult to remember what time of day it is. You have to know the military time. The magnitude and the direction of the shadows cast by the sunlight are not available. Daytime and nighttime look the same under the florescent lights of the submarine.

The entrée is a form of chipped beef. It does not look or smell too repulsive; however, I will forego breakfast and just settle for a cup of hot coffee. Coffee anytime is a good choice. If I linger around the coffee urn long enough I might even succumb to the temptation to munch on a donut. The cooks make great donuts for breakfast. The crew calls them sub donuts, because we have never seen these donuts anywhere in the civilian world. They resemble a kind of a twisted cruller sprinkled with sugar. The texture is not soft and spongy. It is somewhat hard like that of aged donut hole. But, the sub donut softens quickly when dipped into hot coffee.

As I am pouring my cup of coffee, one of the chiefs ask if I want to join them in a game of cards. I decline. I have to update the machinery logs. During our stay in Hong Kong, my division would have placed a number of machinery history reminders in my in basket. This morning watch will be a good time to get caught up.

Machinery history refers to the running time and repairs conducted to the electrical machinery within the ship. Each piece of electrical machinery has a machinery history card. On that card, the monthly run time of the machinery is tracked, and any repairs conducted are annotated in the remarks section of the card. This way, at one glance, the history of that piece of machinery can be evaluated. Also, this is one of the areas the inspection teams peruse during the annual audits.

Another important reason for updating machinery history is to evaluate the performance of each piece of machinery over its lifetime. Audit teams from the naval contractors that build submarines will look over machinery history in order to determine the effectiveness of a piece of machinery for suitability and use in the new classes of submarines. If a piece of machinery breaks down often, then a new piece of machinery will be created to replace it. Design specification will be sent out to all the manufacturers to bid on a contract to develop a replacement piece of machinery. The system works wonders such that each new class of submarine improves on the system reliability of the prior classes.

The sugar-coated cruller attacks me, as I wrestle it forward with a cup of coffee to the administration room to update machinery history. As I suspected, when I enter the administration room, I am alone. It is hard to get anyone going on administration this soon after a port call. I do it to ensure I have the room all to myself.

The administration room is a small cubbyhole of a space choked full of engineering department records. Although wide enough for all the records, the actual walking around area is quite small. In some areas of the room, my shoulders almost touch the opposite-facing stacks of records. All the ship's system drawings are located here as well. However, those drawings have been reduced in size and placed on little cards that require an amplification device in order to read them. They can be reproduced from the amplification device somewhat like a Xerox machine operates.

I settle into a comfortable table near the entrance to the space, so I can allow for a spill area for my coffee and the donut. Fortunately, my in basket is within reaching distance of the table. I reach over and grab the stack of machinery notes from my division and begin filing through the records and updating. A routine of coffee sipping, donut munching and record updating is a good way to pass the morning underwater. Every now and then, a yawning from the hull reminds me of how deep we are, and that we are changing our depth in order to detect an enemy submersible.

A few trips to the coffee urn in crew's mess are all it takes to polish off the morning updating machinery history. Of course, I indulged in another sugar-coated cruller. I have to learn to limit my intake of sugar, or "white death" as the corpsman calls it. Sitting in an office devouring donuts is not the best exercise to keep in shape. The corpsman tells me I will begin to look like a cruller, if I continue this habit. He is right. I have to quit.

Unfortunately, as I am locking up the administration room, I hear the sound of plates being set on the dining tables of crew's mess. It is lunchtime already. The aroma of deep fried shrimp and French fries permeates the air. How can I possibly refuse? Well, I guess looking like a French fry could compete well with looking like a cruller.

Realizing that the chow line will form in the passageway next to the coffee urn, I decide to go over the crew's mess space to bypass the oncoming watch lining up for the noon meal. By the time I get around the chow line, they have commenced seating. I decide to freshen up in the berthing area first in order to allow the oncoming watch to get first call. Sure enough, as I enter the berthing area, the morning watch card game is still going strong. These guys are addicted to the game. I doubt they will even break for chow.

A little freshening up in the birdbath size sinks of the berthing area readies me for shrimp. Seems like all I do at sea is eat. You would think I was a bull grazing in the meadow of crew's mess. But, how can I pass up shrimp? If this ship ever sank, their offspring would be devouring me. I need to consume as many of their ancestors as I can to make things even or me one up on them.

As I exit the bathroom area, one of the card players succumbs to the smell of shrimp and decides to partake in the feeding frenzy with me. The other card players invite me to take his place, but I decline. I exit the berthing area to chidings of "chow hound." Call me what you may, I respond. I will never pass up on shrimp.

By now the first call has been served up and the oncoming watch is slowly vacating crew's mess. The former card player and I take up open seats in the mess and begin filling our plates with shrimp and French fries. As we devour our first shrimp, one of the forward crewmen seated at the table relates that the control room thinks we have detected a submersible shadowing the Battle Group. This revelation quiets the others seated at the table. Like chickens in a coup initially startled by a sound, the table talk rapidly escalates in a querying frenzy. Of course, the follow up actions are unknown to us. Most of us agree that our mission is over, and the escort sub will be called in to harass the submersible. Whatever the action, we all appreciably slow down eating our shrimp. Actually, we are nibbling now rather than are usually fast pace devouring.

Knowledge of an enemy sub in the area is cause for alarm. We are not a fast attack boat. We are ill-prepared to handle this sub. Detection is the limit of our capabilities. We need to be cautious, less this enemy sub decides to track us rather then the Battle Group. Truly, our sub is as valuable a target as the Battle Group, especially, when the Battle Group is sailing away from Mother Russia.

Scooping another portion of shrimp from the dispensing tray, I feel a lifting sensation in the pit of my abdomen. The ship is rising. By the time I am finished loading my plate with shrimp and start on selecting some French fries from the serving bowl, the dishes on the table begin to slide to Starboard then back to Port. We are near the surface, possibly at periscope depth. This maneuvering indicates that we will receive message traffic from the Battle Group. We anticipate that we will be directed to break off surveillance of the enemy submersible and continue on with our original mission.

Within ten minutes, we dive and sail on a heading ninety degrees from the track of the enemy submersible. We are breaking off. Goodbye to the Battle Group.

CHAPTER 6

Illegal Trafficking Surveillance Malacca Strait

We have been on station for a while now. The crew has forgotten all about their time ashore in Hong Kong. Actually, for that matter, they have forgotten about anything to do with being ashore anywhere. It is that way at sea. You get to leave all your land troubles behind. Unlike a sailboat where you have to brave the elements of the changing winds and sea currents, in a submarine everything is forgotten. You enter a new world of electronics and silence.

To some, it is akin to going to sleep for months at a time. Your time aboard is dreamlike. The things you do and the things you get to know remain in the dream. When you return to port, they are things that you remember, but you seldom, if ever, mention to anyone who has not shared the experience with you. Most people would never understand life at sea. It is so different than life ashore. Life at sea fades into that silent compartment of memory.

For one thing, your roaming space is drastically curtailed. The ship's hull frames the outer barrier of movement. On a submarine, that means one, maybe two, passageways back and forward. You literally walk those same passageways the entire time at sea. Think of trying to describe that to someone conditioned to explore the sites of a large city. Just think of utilizing only one street in your hometown for month after month. The monotony would overcome you. But, at sea, it does not. You walk it over and over without even a thought about it being wearisome. You just do it.

Think of eating in one small, crowded coffee shop every day, month after month, sitting with the same friends for each meal. And, at sea, it is not humdrum at all. Somehow the conversations at the table are as lively as any in the cafes in your hometown. You actually enjoy conversing with the same people meal after meal. And, there is scant news coming in from the outside to liven up the conversation. Somehow undersea life creates an atmosphere of appreciation for the basics of existence.

Deep down inside each submarine sailor there exists a sense of duty that seems to energize him with pride to overcome the arduousness of the assignment. Stepping back to overview a life in the submarine force, one cannot help asking how people live in these oversized sewer pipes. Yet, they do, and they seem quite proud of having done so. How do you explain that to anyone? Most people hear the word submarine, and they shudder at the thought of being held captive underwater in a metal tube. Yet, submariners never look at it that way. To them, it is a way of life as natural as any other. Perhaps, they were born to do it. They say deep-shaft coal miners similarly experience the confinement of their work. Of course, they get to return to the surface and their families every evening.

Patrol will be like this for another month or so. We will walk the same passageways to and from our watch stations. We will dine together, every meal, in the small crew's mess. We will shower in phone booths and sleep in bunks not much bigger than coffins. And, we will enjoy it.

Although this is cold war time, we are not authorized to shoot any torpedoes. But, the entire crew understands that we are hunters. Until we deliver our payload of intercontinental ballistic missiles, we evade everyone. However, once we have delivered, we turn into ravenous hunters. Perhaps, the confidence of the hunter is within us, and that is what enables us to overcome the current boredom. We fear no vessel afloat. And, once we have delivered our payload, no vessel afloat will remain so that we encounter.

The hunter's spirit empowers us: silent, steel sharks of the deep, polishing their teeth as they patrol. No matter what our rank may be in society ashore; at sea, we are the silent lions of the deep. We may take life, as we please.

The seawater injection temperature is getting warmer. We are traveling south toward the Equator. The boat has not been reacting to underwater current movements. Sailing has been quite smooth. We must be somewhere in the straits that pour into the Indian Ocean.

The straits leading into the Indian Ocean were popular lairs for the World War II American submarines. It is in these calm waters where the American submarine force dealt the Japanese navy an enormous loss of shipping. This area was a shooting gallery. Life expectancy for Japanese merchantmen was short en route to Singapore.

If I were to wager, I would say the submarine is navigating submerged in the Malacca Strait. These straits are deep and wide enough for submerged operations. Like thousands of merchant vessels over the past millennium, this strait is our conduit into and out of the Indian Ocean. It is the famed waterway to China and the return voyage of Marco Polo. History of the West conquering the East was written here.

Today too, we travel on a similar quest to insure the supremacy of the West over the East. Interestingly, the last Eastern armada to lay claim over these waters set sail from China in the early 15th Century. That was over 500 years ago. Unfortunately, the success of that armada, many historians claim, is what enabled European sailors, fifty years later, to access these waters unmolested by pirates. It would seem that had the Chinese been able to foretell the future, they would have been better off leaving these straits to the pirates and small time warlords of the era. Regrettably, the Chinese did not know the future and cleared these waterways for tributary trade to their Middle Kingdom. Trade flowed easily, after the armada had accomplished its mission. Then, within two centuries, warships came laden with troops. Chinese history took a drastic turn for the worse.

History bequeaths to mind its lessons. I wonder what form of evil we unleash by maintaining these waterways open for trade. They are the busiest trade routes in the world. Vulnerability to terrorism ranks high in this strait. In these waters, ships must travel slowly, and the surface condition is calm. Two-thirds of the world's acts of piracy are reported in these waters, as it is. The amount of piracy would not take very much to double. A laxity in surveillance would suffice. Soon, I do not doubt, the function of submarines will be to deter piracy. As each of these bordering nations become more and more unstable, the inhabitants will flee to these waterways for survival. They will renew the piracy trade of their ancestors, and, once again, the world will suffer from their exploits.

Yet, today, we navigate these waters in search of hostile submarines and surface combatants smuggling arms to insurgents in South Asia and Africa. The focus remains on stemming the tide of political instability in the region. More than any other region of the world, this region is known for its illegal export of humans. What we refer to is not a slave trade industry. It is a giant industry of smuggling people out of countries where they are being persecuted for their beliefs, political affiliation or culture. Hardly one country in this region does not suffer from internal strife that terrorizes its population into flight. We have not departed from the days of the warlords of the early 15th Century. They regenerate in discriminatory political policies that pit one sector of the society against another. The great ideas of social engineering have spawned these confrontations. It is unlikely that our generation, or the next two that will follow us, will experience any relief from this ideological madness. One thing is certain though. As long as warships, like ours, ply these waters, we can keep this madness contained.

In searching for enemy watercraft, we make good on our country's effort to contain these experiments in social engineering. If we fail, then the entire world will be plunged into a senseless slaughter for survival. When Americans critique the racial problems in their homeland, they have no reference as to how horrible these other tensions can become. The random killings in America's inner cities are insignificant to the hundreds of thousands of people killed in the countries that border these waterways. So many are murdered that counting them is fruitless. Others live in such depraved conditions that death is welcomed in the form of malnutrition, starvation, and a horde of other ills associated with overpopulation. Trying to grasps the immensity of the problem leads to another macabre conclusion that our mission here in these waterways actually might be to hasten the end of this suffering in the form of a missile launch.

It would be afternoon, right now, on the periscope stand. Visibility must be good. It has to be to avoid the myriad of surface vessels using this waterway. The small draft craft are of no avail. They will pass over us without any interference whatsoever. It is the deep draft, super tankers that trouble us. Their very deep drafts can ram us while we are at periscope depth. Given their enormous tonnage, our bulkheads would collapse easily upon contact.

These are the times when you pray the sonar watches and navigation plotters are alert. They need to announce any deep draft, approaching vessel. Avoidance is our only sanctuary from these sea monsters. Unfortunately, on any given day, there are many of them afloat. Those coming from the Strait of Hormuz are laden with oil and displaced deep in the water. Their destination is the port cities of the South China Sea. All of East Asia depends on the crude oil from South Asia. It is the life's blood of their civilizations.

When professors of economics discuss the world economy, they refer to the sea trade in these waters. These straits have produced the Pacific Age. The economic miracles of Asia began in these waters. Harnessing these straits produced unparalleled economic growth that led to a sea change where the Pacific Ocean replaced the Atlantic Ocean in world trade dominance.

Regrettably, these growing economies have little military power to project. They rely on the United States to patrol these waters and deter hostile intentions. So far, we seem up to it. We are the great world power that can project our will anywhere in the world. The days of the China Fleet river gunboat has been replaced with the deep ocean, Battle Group. The idea is the same; however, the projection of power is immensely more persuasive.

From a world imbalance position, it would appear that the United States has the grand plan in order. It is unlikely that any nation would confront the United

States openly in prior war-type scenarios. It is the sector plan that needs adjustment. Small renegade bands of miscreants can create confusion and dampen the free movement of trade. As a submarine, we stealthily can detect waterborne activity of this nature in the straits and coastal waters. Naturally, small, at-sea, raiding parties would avoid our surface warships, hence, the need for our presence, silent and submerged, in these waters.

One thing the world can count on is that there is always some demented ego spawning up somewhere that is hell bent on conquest of any kind. Times of strife where one part of country's population is dispossessed make tempting targets for exploitation by these demented egos. From black markets to human trafficking, the spawn of these creatures continues to flog the human spirit.

Our job is to detect any suspicious waterborne activity and make reports via our immediate command to the proper authorities. Once identified, the proper authorities will arrange to intercept the waterborne craft. Each port city along the route of the strait is equipped with waterborne, police fast boats. These vessels are extremely swift traveling watercraft, mounted with 50-caliber machine guns. Larger intercept watercraft carry 5-inch, rapid-fire, deck guns. The fast boat fleets of the port cities easily outgun those of the raiders. Containment, however, requires stealth surveillance: the submarine and the overhead satellite.

In the straits we are answering lower propulsion bells in order to detect any raider activity. Slow moving cargo vessels are a prime target items for the raiders, so we watch those vessels closely. That will be our assignment the entire time that we are in these waters. Fifty years ago, submarines traveled in wolf packs hunting targets of opportunity. Now, we travel alone in search of hunters.

Chow is over. It is about that time for me to nap before watch. I am not that tired, but if I do not at least try to close my eyes for a while, I will be struggling to stay awake on the evening watch.

The routine is the same: a quick shower, dry-off then into the bunk. I will put on the earphones and listen to soft music until the feeling of sleep overcomes me. Soft music seems to do it. Particularly, the music of the 60s inspires me. Sometimes, I can handle the stuff of the early 70s. But, there is nothing like the slow, romantic sounds of the early 60s to lull me into sleep.

Sure enough, a few songs into the oldies succumb me. The next thing I sense is the forward roving watch nudging my back and informing me that it is time for watch relief. That was quick, but I slept well. Now, it is just a matter of sliding out of my bunk, showering and meandering off to crew's mess for the evening meal. Didn't I just do this a few hours ago?

The entrée tonight is sub-burgers, a greasy UFO that seems to slip down your throat as soon as you open your mouth. Oh well, they are made in quantity with little quality control. One trick is to wrap them tightly in a dinner napkin to absorb as much grease as you can before plying them between the buns. It works for me. I have to laugh. Sometimes, the sub-burgers are so slippery that as you attempt to bite down on the bun, the burger slips out and scoots into someone else's plate. We cannot have that, now can we?

I suppose some French fries and a burger will do nicely. I will load mine up with slices of pickles, onions and tomatoes. It makes a huge stack, but it also serves to lock in the slippery sub-burger. Survival in the art of submarine dining takes special training.

Most of the crewmen at my table devour three or four sub-burgers prior to watch relief. To me, that many would equate to a huge gut bomb and tend to bring on sleepiness throughout the watch. One of these UFOs is enough for me. It is the evening watch, so we have to be attentive. It will be nightfall soon, so the sea surface, surveillance watches need to be particularly vigilant. We cannot afford to be drowsy. I remind those at the table loading up on sub-burgers of the dangers of overeating these grease bombs. Though they chuckle in response, they understand the importance of staying alert.

Watch turn over is swift. We are answering low propulsion bells for the surveillance effort. Unfortunately, despite our slow speed, the deep draft, cargo vessels still ply these waters. We may need to answer emergency bells, if a cargo vessel suddenly appears on a collision course with us. That is always a possibility. Danger lurks everywhere in the straits.

Since the bottom of the strait is not that far below us, we might not be able to lower our depth to allow a deep draft, cargo vessel to pass over us. We may need to maneuver in order to avoid him. Shallow depth is another hazard of the straits. Maneuverability is restricted as well less we steer into oncoming traffic lanes. At night, it will be even worse. Some of these illegitimate, cargo vessels fail to turn on their nightlights. Now, that would be all we would need to engage disaster is to be confronted by a deep draft, cargo vessel on collision course with us and to steer into the path of a night smuggler. Another reason that I eat lightly before coming on watches like this one is to reduce the chance of getting an upset stomach over the mounting anxiety for disaster.

Stealth surveillance is fine, but this is dangerous. These cargo vessels do not know that we are out here. They make so much noise that they could never hear us. They never post deck watches. One could say they almost run blind in these waters. Many of the vessels steer by autopilot and have a very junior officer in the wheelhouse. So, we have to be alert for them and stay out of their way. As rabbits learn to stay clear of cows in a meadow, we become similarly adept in avoidance. The evening watch promises excitement.

I start my first tour of the engineering spaces in the lower levels. As expected, the first lower level watch is completely in the bilge area cleaning up. It will be a slow watch, so the watch stander takes the opportunity to clean his spaces. Seeing him in the bilge, behind the piping runs, reminds me of spotting animals of prey in the deep brush. Their eyes give them away, as their bodies blend in well with the surrounding vegetation. It is the same way here. The watch stander's uniform blends in well with the bilge area.

When I notice that he recognizes me observing him, I ask him where his logs are located. He looks in the direction of the main seawater bay and conveys their location upon a pop riveted stand. Pop rivets are little aluminum-like buttons that can hold aluminum plates together in order to manufacture lockers, stands and other temporary storage items. Submarines are infested with pop rivet creations.

A review of this lower level's logs reveal systems operating normally. I would not expect to discover anything out of the ordinary while we are answering low propulsion bells. Seawater injection temperature is high in the allowed operating band. We will need to be cautious of fouling from marine growth. Operating at low propulsion bells means the ship is traveling slowly through the water. Since we are close to the surface, marine life, like algae, may cling to our seawater screens and multiply. If enough alga builds up on the screen, it could foul the seawater inlet, depriving us of cool seawater. Since we use seawater to remove the heat energy radiated from our machinery systems, loss of cool seawater will cause all our machinery to overheat. I mention this elevated reading to the watch stander in order for him to be alert for rising seawater temperatures. If it reaches the upper end of the allowable operating band, I tell him to call me, and we will flush the inlet strainer in order to dislodge the build up of any marine life.

Another distraction from operating in warm waters is that our air conditioning is not as efficient. Humidity tends to build up in the lower levels. I feel the perspiration on my body increase as I pass through the less ventilated areas of the lower levels. This phenomenon works on the watch standers as well, encouraging them to spend little time in the more humid areas. Often, in really warm waters, the watch standers will congregate under ventilation ducts for relief from the humidity of their spaces. If I were a naval engineer, based on the humidity problems encountered by our submarines in the tropical climates, I would conclude that our submarines were designed for operation in the North Atlantic. The submarines seem more adept to operations in frigid waters.

Making my way to the next lower level, I feel the gut bomb, sub-burger making me drowsy. Thank God, I only ate one of them. By the middle of the watch, I will need to keep my watch standers alert in this humidity. I am sure a few of them went for the world record of devouring those gut bombs. All I would need is to find one of these guys asleep on watch.

The upper levels are better ventilated than the lower levels, and they are equipped with far more ventilation outlets. Most of the action in the engineering spaces takes place in the upper levels, so those watch standers are always busy. I will not need to keep too close of an eye on them.

Starting to descend the ladder to the next lower level, I hear the pop riveted items in the immediate area begin to shake. We are answering a higher propulsion bell, and we are doing it quickly. We must be maneuvering quickly to avoid a surface craft. I stop my descent and walk briskly toward the propulsion train to observe its operation. As I pass the engine room engine order telegraph repeater, I notice the operator answering continued bell changes. They are all low bells. Those maneuvering the ship, in the control room, must be attempting to ease their way past a large surface vessel. Why don't they just answer a large bell and avoid the vessel altogether? This maneuvering is odd. Wait! We make these kinds of submerged maneuvers when we are coming alongside a vessel. We must be checking the cargo stored on the main deck of a surface vessel that caught our periscope operator's attention. This could be a suspected trafficking vessel.

The odd maneuvering continues for the rest of the watch. It seems as if our submarine is making circular passes around a cargo vessel. The control room must suspect something to make this much ado about this one vessel.

During the watch, the aft lower level watch reports that seawater system temperatures are increasing. I request permission to blow the strainer to clear any clogs or algae build up. My request is denied. That means we are engaged in a sensitive operation around this cargo vessel. I mention the potentially clogged, intake, seawater strainer to my watch relief. He can resolve the matter on his watch when conditions permit.

The cooks are serving Mid-rats, as I pass through crew's mess. I am not that hungry, but I seldom can pass up a slice of pepperoni pizza. The cooks make a delicious pizza. As I am sharing a slice of pizza with one of my mates, one of the off-going control room watch standers shares with us that the cargo vessel we are tracking is a suspected heroin trafficker.

Heroin is grown on the Thai-Myanmar border (Myanmar is former Burma), smuggled down the border route and into the shipping ports near Bangkok. In Bangkok, heroin takes a sea route, via the Malacca Strait, to Hong Kong where it is distributed worldwide. This trade dates back to the days of the British *taipans* in China.

Taipan in Cantonese literally means King of the Outhouse. *Lopan* is the preferred name: Shepherd or King of the Flock. However, the foreigners in China fell for a typical Chinese mental game and prided themselves with the title: King of the Outhouse. To which, the subjugated Chinese graciously agreed to allow them that title of distinction. Obviously, the foreigners believed the title *taipan* meant someone of extreme stature. It took a century to learn the difference between *taipan* and *lopan.* By then, the foreigners had been so thoroughly humiliated that they continued to refer to themselves as *taipans.* In the West, *taipan* refers to an individual in control of an economic giant, like a Multi-National Enterprise or MNE.

Upon revealing the heroin trafficker, the control room watch, trying to enjoy Mid-rats, is inundated with inquiries on the actions we might take. Naturally, these queries are far beyond his level of expertise. But, nonetheless, the crew continues to probe. One proposed scenario has our submarine surfacing and boarding the cargo vessel like old, swashbuckling pirates. The senior personnel in crew's mess quickly discount that possibility. Most of us are too old, and we are fresh out of sabers.

After a few more inquiries, the control room watch reveals that we are tailing the cargo vessel until fast boats arrive on scene to intercept. The control room watch anticipates the interceptors will be here in less than two hours. Police crafts from Malaysia, Indonesia and Singapore will coordinate an arrest.

Our submarine will never be mentioned officially. The secrecy of our stealth needs to be kept silent. This is a repeat scenario for all submarine operations. The news never mentions our presence, yet there is seldom an area of action in which we are not the first on scene. If we could launch torpedoes, everyone would know of our presence. Unfortunately, we strictly are forbidden to fire upon any vessel unless fired upon. Since they never know of our presence, they would never fire upon us. We are relegated to the silent shadows of diplomacy. This is so unfortunate. We could end this cargo vessel's drug trading days right now. They are a sitting duck, and no one would ever realize what happened. They would just explode and sink unceremoniously to the bottom of the strait. It is unlikely that they have filed an accurate sailing plan, so no one would know of their demise. But, I suppose, the Malaysians, Indonesians and Singaporeans need some publicity to bolster their efforts against drug traffickers. I nod a few times to myself and select another piece of pizza.

At the berthing area conference table, I get a chance to discuss the cargo vessel with some of the other off-going, control room watch standers. From their description of the vessel, it is a twenty-year-old or so, Korean-made, ninety-foot, cargo vessel. The control room watch standers state that it has an identification label associated with Hong Kong as its port of origin. Although, they all doubt that the vessel homeports in Hong Kong. They believe it is a Thai-based, border-smuggler. However, those few crewmen that they observed milling about topside on the vessel did look Chinese.

After some probing questions concerning the seaworthiness of the vessel, the control room watch standers provide some rather negative appraisals. First, it has an unusual abundance of rust build up. The vessel has not been well maintained. Of course, many of the scows that ply the waters around Hong Kong have that appearance, so this vessel would blend right in as a South China Sea island hopper. In the Pearl Estuary, it might go about unnoticed; however, in the straits, it does stick out. Most vessels in the straits present an appearance that beams out a notion of seaworthiness. This vessel gives you the impression that it is traveling at high bells just to avoid sinking.

One of the forward senior enlisted personnel asks how we came upon this vessel. The senior, off-going, control room watch stander volunteers that we were provided intelligence to be on the look out for this vessel. Someone knew it would be in these waters. Communication with our squadron command confirmed the vessel's suspected identity. The control room watch stander asserts that we are following a drug trafficking vessel, and that the suspected cargo is heroin.

A vibration in the pop riveted stowage lockers alerts us that we have increased our propulsion orders. The vibration continues to increase in amplitude. We are answering at least a Full bell. Something is up! Before we can all interject our suspicions, the forward roving watch comes through the berthing area and informs us that the cargo vessel has sped up. The Malaysian intercept boat is on the horizon and caused the cargo vessel to try to make some distance away from them.

If the Malaysians intercept the cargo vessel, the crew in its entirety can be executed, if they are discovered carrying heroin. Malaysia has strict drug policies. All the punishments seem to terminate in some form of execution. We have been asked to trail the cargo vessel, until one of the police boats intercept her. We even feel for the crew of the cargo vessel. Most are contract laborers and have no knowledge of the cargo. Regrettably, the rules of evidence in Malaysia are not as strict as they are in our country. The crew could all be executed. We even pray the Indonesians or the Singaporeans appear on the horizon soon. It might behoove the cargo vessel to steer toward one of those police boats rather than be intercepted by the Malaysians. One thing is certain their heroin running days are over.

We remain at high propulsion bells for over an hour. Then, all of sudden we slow down. Word comes to us via the announcing system that we are breaking off pursuit and returning to our assignment. Some thirty minutes later, the forward roving watch informs us that the cargo vessel began a frenzy of dumping cargo overboard as it steamed away. A Singaporean police boat finally staffed it with 50-caliber machine gun fire. The cargo vessel surrendered and allowed the Singaporean police to board her. Whether there were any drugs left aboard or not we do not know; however, we have been asked to provide a copy of our surveillance video to squadron command for further transfer to the Singaporean authorities. Word from the forward roving watch is that our surveillance video caught the cargo vessel's crew dumping some 200 huge, 50-lb-cement-size bags overboard. That is a lot of heroin.

It is mid-watch now. I wonder what the crew is watching for the evening movie. We show films on the evening and the mid-watch in crew's mess. Generally, the same movie is shown for both watches. Only off-watch personnel are allowed to attend. Personnel behind in their ship's qualifications are prohibited from attending.

By the time I get to the crew's mess, the film is already started. It is one I have seen before, called *French Postcards*. It is a sweet story about college age kids doing a year of their education in Paris. I decide to watch a few frames, as I sip on some coffee. Popcorn is being hot air popped by the bushel basket, it seems. The cooks' assistants are going overboard trying to sate the audience. I grab a cereal bowl full of popcorn myself.

Projection of the movie consists of a 16 millimeter, reel-to-reel projector, mounted on a special, draw-out stand in the rear of crew's mess. The projector flashes images on a pulldown screen, attached in the overhead to the forward bulkhead. The alignment of the projector and pull-down screen follows the open area provided by the walk space between the tables in the center of the crew's mess. The audience occupies the tables and floor area to either side of the center walk space. It is a cozy arrangement.

Although the stalking of the heroin trafficker is on everyone's mind, they sit in silence, munching popcorn, and allow the Paris setting on the screen to enchant them. I have never been to Paris, but I must say, the director of this film presents the city pretty much as I would have envisioned it. A mixture of modern paved streets intersects the old cobbled streets described in the classic literature and the sagas on the French Revolution. Coffee houses spill out onto the sidewalks. Wine seems plentiful. The landmarks flash upon the screen as backdrops to the unfolding romantic story. If I had majored in French and gone to Paris, I, too, would have fallen in love with a Parisian gal much like one of the ones in this movie. It is hard not to think of love and romance when viewing the streets of Paris. I suppose every city has some allure, but Paris captures the market on love.

The special part in the movie that I cherish plays out, and I lose interest in the rest of the film. To me, movies that I have seen have special parts. The rest of the scenes are just buildup to these special crescendos. Life is like that I suppose. We cherish those special moments and discard the rest as refuse. I am glad I chose an interesting life in the submarine service, so I can experience many special moments. In life, we seem to be waiting for special moments to arrive. We waste so many hours waiting. Waiting for what? Waiting to die? We are alive, now. We need to enjoy that time because with every breath we take we are that much closer to death. In death, we will wait forever. I believe that I adore this movie for the special message it provides. Despite the pitfalls, the young college kids decide to experience life. Whether the outcome becomes good or less desirable, they seek out the experience. They will only travel this way once. It is best if they enjoy every minute of it and not allow the hours to pass by meaninglessly waiting and wondering where the excitement is. Life needs to be lived that way, every day.

Today, we tracked down a major heroin trafficker. This crew may never do that again. Together, we experienced the hunt. Together, we did something for the millions of kids back in the United States who might have been unfortunate enough to get hooked on this evil substance. Together, we succeeded. No one can take this from us. In our old age, we can say to our grandkids, we made a difference in the drug war. We did not just meaninglessly make holes in the water of the Malacca Strait. We apprehended one of the world's most notorious drug traffickers. As I get up and walk bent over out of crew's mess, so as not to disturb the projection, a smile forms on my face that I cherish all the way to my bunk. It is the smile of satisfaction for a job well done.

Life does not allow us that many days like this one. But, it did provide us this one, and I am thankful. I will nap early tonight. Mid-watches are best for sleeping. Besides, after today's excitement, I should sleep well. I will think of Paris, the love that could have been and allow soft music to ease me into sleep.

CHAPTER 7

Hostage Crisis, Strait of Hormuz and Persian Gulf

Is that pancakes, I smell? By God, it has to be. The roving watch has not woken me yet, so I guess I can ease out of this bunk and get a head start on breakfast. There is nothing as delicious as hot pancakes in the morning. I grew up on pancakes. Every morning before I went off to grade school, my mother would have a large pancake waiting for me when I sat down for breakfast.

Pancakes have a way of filling you up. In New England, especially in the winter months, the locals have a saying: "Pancakes stick to your ribs." It is a strange way to say it, but sure enough, pancakes provided whatever fuel you required to brave the winter winds in order to make it to school. Although it has been a long time since I have experienced a New England winter, I still miss the pancakes.

When I was younger, the pancakes always came with generous amounts of maple syrup. Nowadays, we have choices of boysenberry and coconut together with regular maple syrup. Somehow, I still usually choose maple syrup. I guess it is just a habit.

Intoxicated by the scent of pancakes, I make my way to the bathroom area. Once inside the door, I overhear a few other crewmen discussing our entrance into the Indian Ocean. Although I just go about my business, I do feel the stability of the ship in the deep ocean. In channels or straits, the ship feels edgy, as if it might need to maneuver quickly. In the deep ocean, the ship feels relaxed, as if she were at home in these waters. It is hard for me to explain, but an ocean allows the ship spherical freedom to move in whatever direction desired.

After cleaning and attiring for watch, I make my way down the passageway to crew's mess. Sure enough, the cooks are making pancakes. Since it is breakfast to order, I prepare my order slip for two large pancakes with bacon. I will skip the sunny side-up eggs that usually accompany my pancake order, just pour myself a cup of coffee and settle into a comfortable seat at one of the tables. As I wait my pancakes, the crewmen at the table are discussing the orders of the days for our watch. They are crewmen from the control room area, so they are familiar with the day's agenda. Interestingly, we will be steaming at full power to the Strait of Hormuz. From their conversation, there are targets of interests awaiting us in the strait. The Strait of Hormuz provides the access route for most of the oil cargo out of South Asia. It is always a potential hot spot for international conflict.

One of the mess cooks brings my plate of pancakes and bacon. Of course, the other crewmen at the table chide me that I should eat a full stack of three pancakes. I just shrug off their comments and apply generous amounts of maple syrup. It is as if I am in my own world. The conversation at the table distances from me, as if I were a sailboat departing a harbor. The more I eat, the more the conversation fades away until there are just buzzwords to remind me of the others at the table.

Full steaming means that we will be at upper propulsion bells all watch. We will be busy monitoring our equipment. Well, the morning watch, coupled with pancakes, will be just fine for arduous duty. Without noticing the time, I gobble down the two pancakes, refill my cup of coffee and head back aft to relieve the watch. As I walk aft, patting my belly as if to stow the pancakes properly, I ask myself how many people I know in the civilian world have visited the Strait of Hormuz. Few, I suspect. It is not exactly a tourist destination.

In a few days, we will be on station in the Strait of Hormuz, gathering data on the targets of interests. If this were wartime, the strait would become a shooting gallery. We would run out of torpedoes long before the strait would ever run out of oil tankers. Fortunately, for the oil tanker industry, we will be just taking pictures. Of course, the pictures that we take will have the crosshairs of our periscope upon them. In good taste, we never mail a copy of the oil tanker's picture to its captain less we traumatize his crew.

On watch, it is high bells extravaganza. We need to get somewhere fast. For the next six hours, we maintain Ahead Full, decreasing the bell only long enough in order to acquire a position fix. Touring one space after another in an endless effort to sustain plant parameters within specifications builds up my expectations for the noon meal.

Sooner than I had expected, my relief is on scene. The watch went by so fast that I even forgot how many cups of coffee I drank. If all my watches were this busy, my career in the Navy would be over in no time. But, I am glad to relinquish this watch. We are really hauling away toward the Strait of Hormuz. I guess our episode with the heroin trafficker took much more time than we were allocated.

My watch relief, however, provides another more realistic explanation for our sudden haste. According to his unofficial sources, there is a rumor that an American embassy has been overrun, and the ambassador has been kidnapped. I am in disbelief. Penetrating the confines of an embassy constitutes an act of war. This trip to the Strait of Hormuz could be a prelude to war. We might actually get to fire upon vessels in those waters.

My relief and I take a little longer turning over the status of the plant, as I probe him with questions over this new insight. Although he is reluctant to forecast any new information other than the scant words that he overheard, I continue to probe him for more details. After I am thoroughly convinced that I have exhausted his knowledge of the situation, I agree to allow him to relieve me.

With my empty coffee cup in hand, I make my way through the missile compartment to crew's mess. I know just the crewmen to sit next to in order to acquire additional information on this embassy crisis. Sure enough, when I arrive in crew's mess, the group I am looking for is busy discussing something in private at the far table. I quickly slip into the one remaining seat and listen in.

I am so interested in their conversation that one of the mess cooks has to nudge me in order to get my preference as to how I want my filet mignon prepared. I quickly respond "medium." Medium is fine. It means that the cooks have a greater leeway in its preparation. Besides, this conversation that I am overhearing is exciting. As the story goes, a band of Muslim religious fanatics stormed the U. S. Embassy in Tehran. The entire complement of the embassy has been taken into captivity. In other parts of Tehran, this same Muslim group has detained American and British businesspersons. So far, the number of Americans arrested is suspected to be in the fifties.

From the conversation, the United States has been caught with their pants down. We have no immediate military support anywhere in the area. The control room watch stander relating the story emphasizes at this point that we are the only American war vessel in the area. In a few days, when we arrive in the Strait of Hormuz, we will be confronting at least two Soviet cruisers. We will have no land or sea support for a few days.

The mess cook delivers my filet mignon with a baked potato and some corn. I just set the plate aside. We all agree at the table that, as a submarine, we will have the initial advantage over the two cruisers. From past experience, the two cruisers will not be working together. One cruiser will patrol the opening of the Strait of Hormuz from the Gulf of Oman while the other will remain just outside the international boundary to the country in question in the Persian Gulf. That means the inner most cruiser will be about three miles, at sea, outside the main oil terminal of South Asia.

Three miles is the accepted international sea boundary. This distance was selected in the days of old cannons, because it marked the furthest distance that a shore mounted cannon could extend its nation's power seaward. Of course, today, our cannons can fire much farther than that, but, out of convention, we maintain the three-mile boundary to international waters.

The fact that World War III could have commenced does not escape our conversation. Fortunately, if it does commence, we will have a ringside seat. We may actually fire the first volleys. What bothers us, somewhat, is that we will be all alone. But, we are a submarine crew. We are accustomed to operating alone. Given our penchant for lone operations, Squadron Command undoubtedly will want to micromanage our every move. Undoubtedly, our efforts in the Strait of Hormuz will constitute assurance to Squadron Command that we control the situation. Squadron Command will need to convey that certainty to Washington, DC. No doubt, this mission will become extremely tense.

The filet mignon is delicious. Listening to the conversation, as I cut thick slices from the bacon-wrapped, tender steak, I can image the chaos unfolding at Squadron and in Washington, DC. Here we are alone in the Indian Ocean, confronted with an act of war in South Asia. Our closest troops are in Japan. We have no bases set up to allow us to deploy troops into the hostile area. The Navy will oversee this entire predicament. Our closest Battle Group is on maneuvers in the South China Sea. Actually, the report from the conversation at the table is that the Battle Group currently is in port in Japan. We are alone. Of course, we do have a payload of nuclear missiles aboard.

After the noon meal, I decide to get ahead on reviewing the engineering logs. One of my collateral duties is to review the engineering spaces' log readings for accuracy. Given the upcoming assignment, my primary duties might demand my full attention while we are in the Strait of Hormuz and the Persian Gulf.

The previous day's engineering logs are collected after each morning watch and deposited in a special in basket in the administrative room. Once again, I find myself cuddling a cup of hot coffee and lodging into the administrative room. This time, I do not have a donut to keep my mouth occupied. Nonetheless, I settle in and commence reviewing the logs. It is early in the month, so there are just about ten days worth of logs here.

The shaking of the pop riveted shelves reminds me that we are answering Ahead Full. It will be a bit noisy this afternoon, but I am used to it. My coffee mug even shakes on the table. I remove a handkerchief from my rear pocket and place it under the coffee mug in effort to dampen the shaking. It works.

Since the logs already have been reviewed by the entire chain of command in the engineering spaces, I do not expect to discover any anomalies. The review mainly consists of checking that all blocks are filled in, all out of specification readings have annotations in the remarks section of the logs and all required review signatures have been affixed. As I peruse the log entries, I recall how those watches were conducted. I even remember where I was when a particular reading was registered. Although I stand one out of every three watches, I am able to decipher what occurred on the other two watches. Truly, it is amazing what one can interpret from the log readings.

After reviewing about four days of logs, I realize that one of the lower level aft pumps has not been rotated as required. There is no log entry to explain the absence of rotation. Although each system is designed redundant with pumps, we rotate the pumps to insure equal run time for machinery history. Yet, in this particular system, we have not been running the alternate pump. A quick check of the remaining six days of logs indicates that the pump in question has not been run at all. There must be something wrong with that pump. There is nothing annotated in the remarks section. It must be something that the watch standers are keeping to themselves.

Since the machinery division leader is on watch right now, I decide to call him up and confer with him on this anomaly. The phone rings in the engineering space where I believe he is cooling off from the excess humidity. Sure enough, I am correct, and he answers the phone. From the low-growl-like pitch in his voice, I can tell that he has been working. I relay to him what I have discovered. He tells me that he will look into it and hangs up the phone. Although he seemed genuinely surprised about what I told him, I suspect that he was aware of the problem to some extent. I will let him handle this and catch up with him after his watch to find out what to do about this abnormal run time of the one pump.

The rest of the log review does not produce any other anomalies other than I need three cups of coffee to make it through. Afternoon watches, doing administrative work and following a juicy steak meal, tests my ability to remain focused. It is about watch relief time now, so I will try to catch up with the machinery leader before I put my seal of approval on this batch of logs.

Unfortunately, the only sure place to meet up with the machinery leader is the crew's mess for chow. My belly is still wrestling with the filet mignon and baked potato, but I manage to slide into the seat right next to the machinery leader. The meal is Mexican. He is of Mexican ancestry and adores spicy food. Naturally, so as not to displease him, I place a couple of tacos in my plate. Seeing my interest in tacos, he offers me a dispenser of hot sauce. It is the real Texas, dirt-street-town-type hot stuff that warrants a pitcher of ice water to quench it. I decline, immediately. He teases me with something about hair on my chest.

Finally, after some ten minutes of watching enchilada sauce ooze out both sides of his mouth, I inquire about the pump. Our conversation is interrupted by a few of the crewmen at another table shouting "Olay!" as another crewman tries to horn, with his index fingers, a red tablecloth held up by some other crewmen. Mexican food does that to certain members of the crew. They believe that they have been transported to a bullfight arena in Old Spain. Apparently, two enchiladas, marinated in hot sauce, are the only qualification required to become a matador in crew's mess.

After the ruckus dies down, the machinery leader informs me that there is nothing wrong with the idle pump. Apparently, our alternate crew ran the idle pump for an extended period of time while they repaired the pump in question. It was a turnover item for our crew to operate the current running pump long enough to regain an equal run time for machinery history. However, he mentioned that it was not his intention to utilize that pump continuously. He specifically instructed the watch standers to run the pump three of the four watches per day. Apparently, someone forgot to start the idle pump each day on the morning watch, as he had instructed. He assured me that the idle pump was operating now and will be alternated as required. The fifteen days that it had been running caught up the machinery history time in arrears quite nicely. We both agree that the next annual Squadron Inspection will require us to explain this anomaly.

The rest of the meal, I force down the two tacos and lots of ice water. Apparently, the cooks applied generous amounts of sauce, unfortunately the extremely hot variety, to the tacos before they served them to the crew. I pray I am not so bloated with ice water that I cannot fit in my bunk. Our bunks have a depth limit, and my girth has expanded to accommodate the Mexican food. Seeing my discomfort, the machinery leader offers me up as a bull to the young matadors. How do I get myself into these situations?

Entering the Strait of Hormuz

During the next few days, the ship transits to its assigned entry point in the Gulf of Oman in order to enter the Strait of Hormuz. About two hours are spent preparing the ship for silent running. Naturally, to keep the crew busy, field day is held, as well. As we wait to enter the strait, we find ourselves with a greenie in each hand scrubbing the bilges and decks. I suppose there is a reason for the field day. It does keep us alert, and it does serve as a reminder that the operation to follow will not be a routine evolution.

Field day is secured just before the evening meal. The cooks serve surf and turf: lobster and tenderloins, with baked potato. Fortunately, I have the evening watch, so I get first dibs on the lobster. Only the lobster tails in their shells are served. The reason is that the Pacific Ocean lobster has no claws. Actually, it is called a *longusta.* However, the tails are as meaty and as delicious as any from the Atlantic Ocean. Melted butter with a slice of fresh lemon accompanies the lobster tails. There is no need for the manipulation devices required with Atlantic Ocean lobsters. One easy movement is all that is required to remove a tail from its shell. From there, it is just a matter of dipping the meaty tail into the melted butter and squeezing some lemon juice upon it. The lobster tails are delicious.

During the evening meal, the ship's commander announces the intentions of the mission. We are to evade the first Soviet cruiser, guarding the entrance to the Strait of Hormuz, and take up a position in the Persian Gulf to engage the cruiser patrolling the entrance to the oil fields. Our orders are to sink that cruiser if any hostile intentions are observed. Once that cruiser is sunk, we are to sink the remaining cruiser and engage all Soviet forces in the Persian Gulf.

The orders are clear. We will line ourselves up like a cocked revolver aimed at the cruiser patrolling the oil depot. We are good at doing this. It is unlikely that we will be provoked in any way. However, we have to be prepared to sink the cruiser in any event. Two torpedoes in his side should do it easily. I wonder if the Soviet cruiser skipper knows that death will reside merely a few minutes away.

After some deliberation upon arrival at our embarkation point in the Gulf of Oman, Ahead Standard is ordered. The strange, metal-stretching sounds emanate from the bulkheads. We are diving deeper. Apparently, we are commencing our entry into the Strait of Hormuz. We will be quiet now. Soon, chopping sounds of a large surface vessel's propeller are heard through our hull. We are passing under the first cruiser or some large oil tanker. To infiltrate a port area, sometimes it is best to follow underneath a large, surface vessel like a tanker. We have done this often. This could be how we are disguising ourselves in order to evade the first cruiser. It does make sense; an oil tanker would escort us right into the mouth of the channel leading to the oil reserves. We would veer off from underneath the tanker in order to take up a position of advantage on the second cruiser. Whatever that screw noise is it is very close above us.

For the first few hours, the status of the engineering spaces remains constant. The inlet seawater pressure gauges indicate that our depth remains constant, and there are no propulsion order changes. The seawater injection temperature is cooler than I would have expected for this area of the world. However, we are deeper than our normal operational depth. That might explain the colder inlet temperatures. It probably does!

Suddenly, the engine order telegraph rings up Ahead One-Third. After we respond and answer the lower propulsion bell, we feel the submarine rising. A check of the inlet seawater pressure gauges indicates lowering pressure. We are rising. According to the inlet seawater pressure gauges, we have leveled off at periscope depth. The propeller chomping sounds that serenaded us for the past few hours are diminishing in amplitude. Whatever we were following is distancing from us.

Within ten minutes, Ahead Two-Thirds is rung up. The inlet seawater gauges indicate increasing pressure. The pressure increase is meager compared to their previous transit readings. We are probably just a little below periscope depth. It would appear that we have sighted the second cruiser and are taking up an attack position along his patrol path.

Word is conveyed by a messenger watch from the control room that as many as one hundred Americans might be being held hostage by the rogue Islamic group in Tehran. This news evokes a chuckle from those of us in the engineering spaces. The Islamic group has maybe one hundred Americans in captivity. We, on the other hand, with our payload of multiple re-entry nuclear warheads, sitting in the middle of the Persian Gulf, hold all of Asia captive. Within a few hours, every major city on the continent of Asia would be destroyed, if we decided to launch. And, I mean every single one of them. We would execute billions of people. I guess diplomacy dictates that we should negotiate the release of our hostages. One has to wonder at the temptation though. If we released our nuclear weapons, right now, we would never need to negotiate anything in Asia again, particularly in South Asia.

The announcement of the propulsion order to reduce speed to Ahead One-Third communicates that we have taken up an attack position against the second cruiser. Like a cocked revolver with a hair trigger, we wait upon his every nuance for an opportunity to blow him out of the water. He is ours whenever we decide to take him. From this point on, we wait like a silent, steel shark admiring a lone, unsuspecting seal.

Watch after watch, our submarine tracks the cruiser above. Actually, the tracking is not that difficult. The cruiser has established a routine twenty-mile, sentry-like pattern. It travels in a straight line twenty miles to the West, then turns and returns the twenty miles eastward. The cruiser repeats the pattern back and forth along the same trek just like clockwork.

Sitting in our undersea lair, we have to wonder why these Soviet sailors risk their lives in this way. It is not like they will get to return to a life of leisure. According to the propaganda we have been told, their lives are quite restricted to their home base and its immediate environs. From the intelligence received on the two cruisers, they are out of some small port along the *Kamcatka* Peninsula. That place is cold all year round. Living there would be akin to residing in Alaska. Why do they do it?

Some of the officers from the Naval Academy have explained the dedication of the Soviet sailor as one of dependence. This type of labor is all they have ever known. The communist rule is altogether not all that different than the lives of their ancestors under the Czars. The big change in Russia produced a more equitable economy, but the sense of authority remained essentially the same. Also, there is this Mother Russia concept that enables each citizen to embrace a kind of motherly bond with his/her country.

The reasons for the Soviet sailors' willingness to endure such hardships are difficult for us to understand. They seem so much like us in many ways, yet they willingly subject themselves to sacrifices in this generation so that future generations, they hope, will reap the benefits. We, on the other hand, realize our benefits immediately in this generation. We are here to maintain our lifestyle. It is a strange comparison between the American and the Soviet sailors. They sacrifice everything for the future while we sacrifice to maintain the present. It would seem that we are much closer in our philosophies than one would imagine. But yet, here we are ready to blow each other out of the water and, unfortunately, billions of people right along with us.

By now, our sonar technicians have taped every sound emitted by the cruiser above. We could find this guy in the middle of the ocean in our sleep. The strange chug-a-chug sound of his propeller begins to imitate a heartbeat. During the turns at the end of his twenty-mile stretch, the strain of his internal machinery reverberates outward in the form of heavy chugs from his propeller.

During one of the turns, our periscope films the underbelly of the cruiser. We see, on the crew's mess monitor, the cruiser's two propellers and the strange design of its hull and keel. Years of marine growth cling to its hull, decreasing the cruiser's full steaming capability. Our engineers are in agreement that the cruiser is in need of a drydocking period in order to sandblast off the layers of barnacles affixed to its hull. Some fracture damage appears on one of the propellers as well. This vessel is in dire need of an overhaul.

Some of the fire control crewmen who constantly check range to the target inform us that the cruiser is like a sitting duck traveling along an amusement park, game channel. The consensus amongst the fire control men is that the Soviet cruiser has no inkling that we are here. If he did, he would be using evasive tactics and have the other cruiser come in to harass us. The Soviet cruiser is clueless as to our presence.

On some of the periscope passes that the control room allows to be viewed on the crew's mess monitor, the Soviet sailors milling about on the upper decks are so close that they positively could be identified, if we knew them. We have a still picture of one picking his nose and stealthily discarding the contents overboard so as not to be noticed by his shipmates. He is a young officer. I hope in his future career that picture is never declassified to the point where his navy would have access to the photo. It would be a tremendous embarrassment to him, if he were to attain the rank of admiral and be shown his folly as a youth. Of course, to realize how close the cruiser men were to their death would also be an awakening for the Soviet Fleet that they would respond to immediately.

If we are forced to attack this cruiser, it might be hard on our crew. We have gotten to know these Soviet sailors from our constant periscope surveillances. It would not be like sinking a tub on the horizon like in a video game. Even though we do not know these sailors personally, we have come to know them, as we do actors on a stage. We would miss them. They would haunt us forever. I pray we do not have to kill them. They are just doing what we are doing. From their mannerisms, we even might enjoy their company. I doubt we would chose to drink vodka with them, but certainly some other refreshments would suffice. We can envision ourselves with them enjoying a ship-to-ship, get-acquainted picnic. Although, I suppose, if we did meet them, we could never kill them. Somehow, we have to demonize them. We have to admire them though. Here they are thousands of miles from a friendly port aboard a vessel much inferior to ours in technology, as they hold the line gallantly and with dedication. There is nothing more their country could ask of them. It is difficult to slaughter brave men.

Suddenly, a conversation we are having in the engineering spaces is interrupted by the distinct sound of high-speed propellers passing above us. We know that sound is not coming from an incoming torpedo. Not even the Soviet Navy could miss at this distance. One of the engineering space watch standers decides to call forward and inquire as to the source of the noise.

After what seems to be an eternity awaiting a response, it turns out that the high-speed sound emanated from the propeller of a launch. From the best guess of the control room watch standers, the launch came from the other cruiser. The launch slowed and tied up alongside the cruiser that we are targeting. Four scrambled-egg hats disembarked to the sound of whistle salutes. Scrambled-egg hat is the enlisted men's affectionate reference to officers above the rank of lieutenant commander, or O-4. Commencing with the rank of commander (O-5), the visors of officers' formal headwear are embroidered with thick, gold threaded inlays.

From the description of the launch party, it would seem the cruiser that we are targeting is hosting a reception for the senior officers of the two cruisers. If there was any need for certification that our presence had not been detected, that was it. The Soviet Navy would never party with a potential threat alongside their bow. These poor souls are clueless.

Reports filter back to the engineering spaces that the sound of Russian music can be heard coming from the cruiser. There are even reports of watch standers appearing a little tipsy, as they make their rounds on the main deck. The Soviets are so naïve. They must suspect that the Americans would dispatch vessels to confront them. Apparently, our submarine passed under their surveillance before the Soviets were able to establish anything. This cruiser actually might have received confirmation from the other cruiser that no enemy vessel has approached their established outer perimeter. To support that position, we do hear sporadic sonar pinging emanating from the Strait of Hormuz. The Soviets truly might believe they are here alone. They must believe that to be holding a party and allowing their topside watch standers to become so lax.

Another report filters back to us that our sonar technicians have detected rapid pounding sounds emanating from the cruiser. They have interpreted the sound as Russian dancing where the performers squat and do quick duck-walk movements. All we need to hear now is the breaking of glass, as they toss their champagne or vodka glasses against their ship's hull.

Hearing all these reports dampens our passion for the hunt. The Soviets are coming across as hapless does and skippers that have wandered onto a shooting range. They are too stupid to torpedo. It is times like these that make us wonder why we need to train so much. Why we have to sacrifice so much? What are we doing here? These Soviets resemble recreational sailors like the ones that venture out a mile or so from shore just to drop anchor, heat up some Brie on French bread and sip wine. All we need now is for the Soviet cruiser to announce swim call. Actually, they might have a better chance detecting our presence from a surface dive from one of their apprentice seamen than with the use of all their antiquated sonar equipment.

As the evening turns into midnight, the Soviet crew under observation by our periscope just gets more and more relaxed. At one point, our control room watch standers express serious doubts that any of the cruiser's crew are functional. The boarding officers have not returned to their launch. It appears they are overnighting. Given this discouraging display of military preparedness by the Soviets, it is easy to understand why our navy has banned the consumption of alcoholic beverages aboard our vessels.

At Mid-rats, the general consensus of our crew is: what are we doing here? One of our crewmen offers a response: Who would be here to eat this delicious pepperoni pizza? Although the personnel in the crew's mess get a giggle out of the suggestion, it hits home, quickly. We are much better trained than the Soviets. We have superior equipment and weapons. Everyone aboard the submarine is thankful that it is this way and not the other way around.

When my uncles taught me to hunt in the deep woods of upper New England, it was a simple process. You scouted the area that you intended to hunt months ahead of deer season. This way you knew the deer trails, and where the game liked to settle in during the day. If the area was thick with brush, you employed driving tactics where one or two hunters took up ambush positions while the others in the group, usually three or four, drove the deer to you. If the area was open, you relied on tracking and your knowledge of the deer trails to intercept your prey. Either way, the task was clear and simple. You hunted the animal down until you got a clear shot at him and pulled the trigger at the first opportunity.

Hunting from a submarine in Cold War time is different. Much of the preparation is the same. The tactics of intercept are likewise similar. However, when you rendezvous with your prey, you keep him in your gun sights for days, weeks, if not months on end. And, you never shoot him. You just have to be prepared to shoot him.

The unfortunate side effect of waiting so long with your finger on the trigger, so to speak, is that you get to observe your prey. You begin to identify with him. Your mission, more and more, assumes the likeness of a laboratory experiment or field study. Given the backwardness observed in these Soviet sailors, we could translate our surveillance as some kind of anthropological field study. In this scenario, the Soviets resemble primates with their cruiser as their cage. Truly, under our gun sights, they are not that far from that description.

It is nearly noontime now. From the imagery coming in on the monitor in crew's mess from the periscope, it is a bright sunny day in the Persian Gulf. There are a few scattered clouds in the sky. Traffic through the gulf seems normal. Yet, the launch is still tied up alongside the cruiser. The officers must have had quite a party last night.

The noon meal today offers spaghetti with Italian sausages and meatballs. As we dine, practicing twirling spaghetti in our spoons with our forks, the periscope monitor in crew's mess presents a clear picture of the main deck of the cruiser. Suddenly, one of the diners gets the rest of the crew's mess' attention by announcing that there is a lot of quick movement on the main deck of the cruiser. Sure enough, the four officers are being escorted by what appears to be the senior officer staff of the cruiser to the launch. Slurping our spaghetti, we watch four officers climb down a makeshift ladder into the launch. As soon as the four officers have boarded, the launch crew tosses the mooring lines onto the cruiser and gets underway. Soon, the sound of the high-speed whining of their propeller passes right over us. The main deck of the cruiser clears up quickly after the officers have left. It is business as usual on the cruiser.

I suppose as long as I live I will remember the sound of high-speed propellers whenever I eat Italian sausages with spaghetti. Some little quirks like that seem to stay with you forever. I guess it is the spaghetti that makes the connection. Italian mobster movies always seem to plan assassinations over spaghetti dinners. There is some weird connection between gun sights and spaghetti.

How long do we have to watch these guys? It cannot be too much longer. Our rapid deployment forces (RDF) should be establishing a base of operations nearby. They are geared up to be full operation in less than two weeks. They must be setting up their command center now. Our support fleet should be arriving soon, as well.

The sentiment on the submarine is: why can't we just torpedo these two cruisers and go home? Unfortunately, diplomacy requires perseverance. We are here to shoot, if diplomacy fails. Our presence provides that prerequisite courage of conviction necessary for our foreign affairs effort to succeed. Simply, speak softly, but carry a big stick and be ready to poke them in the butt with it when necessary.

The monotony continues, as we follow the cruiser along its sentry-like pattern. By now, the cruiser's movements and ours have become routine. We could both reproduce them in our sleep. Whenever a task evolves this long, it begins to fade in importance.

During the last evening meal, no one at the table even mentioned the cruiser. The meal could have taken place somewhere in the middle of the Pacific Ocean. It is as if we are not in the Persian Gulf anymore. We have become complacent about the fact that we are sandwiched between two Soviet cruisers. The dangers that filled us with anxiety when we snuck into the Strait of Hormuz are no longer empowering our concerns.

The mealtime conversations revolve more about the upcoming sports season and evening's movie selection. Even on watch, though we are in silent running status, we seldom express any concern for the Soviet cruisers. To us aboard the submarine, the Soviet cruisers are no longer there. Most of the watch standers go about their duties, as if they were on routine patrol status. Often, I have to remind them of the danger above us. Often, I have to remind myself. It appears that we have become too complacent to be vigilant.

Fortunately, our latest radio reception informs us that an attack boat will be entering the gulf to relieve us. Radio reception on patrol status is restricted to passive. We only transmit in emergency situations, or when directed to do so by Squadron Command. Transmission would alert the cruisers of our presence. It looks like we will be leaving the gulf tomorrow.

Although we are aware of an attack boat entering our area, we cannot communicate with it. Our sonar technicians will have to be alert to detect a submersible craft. Fortunately, our most recent radio reception outlines the ingress and egress routes for the attack boat and us. Rest assured, it is a difficult task to traffic control submarines that are unable to provide feedback. Our egress route should be a few kilometers off the port bow of the relieving attack boat. Our submarine will represent the vessel leaving the harbor. The attack boat will keep the channel markers off its starboard side. Our submarine, on the other hand, will hug the opposing channel markers with our starboard side. Entering and leaving the Persian Gulf in this way should provide ample maneuvering space for both submarines.

Our departure from station has been timed to commence one hour after the attack boat enters the strait. This should provide the attack boat ample time to distance itself from the outer cruiser. We have one obstacle left on this mission: to evade the outer cruiser undetected.

At the prescribed time, we commence our withdrawal from station. The trip to the mouth of the strait is tense until our sonar technicians announce that they have detected the incoming attack boat some six kilometers off our port side. We breathe a sigh of relief. We have plenty of maneuvering space.

Within an hour, the echoes of sporadic sonar pinging can be heard through our hull. The randomness and duration of the sonar pings indicate the Soviet cruiser is probing in the dark. We lower our propulsion bell and wait for the pinging to cease. For a while, we even hover the boat to slow our progress into the cruiser's area. As predicted, the Soviet cruiser soon ceases his sonar search. Our bottom intelligence indicates we have another hundred-feet safe operating depth below us. We descend to that depth and slowly ease ourselves under the path of the cruiser. When we exit the strait, the cruiser is some five kilometers off our starboard bow. At that distance, the cruiser would have difficulty hearing us at the depth that we are operating. Our exit from the Strait of Hormuz goes undetected. About twenty kilometers from the exit area, we increase propulsion to Ahead Full and commence our transit back to the North Pacific Ocean in order to continue our original patrol assignment.

CHAPTER 8

Port Visit Western Australia

With the Strait of Hormuz becoming farther and farther from our wake, the commanding officer addresses the crew over the ship's announcing system. We have been granted a few days layover in Australia. It is welcomed news. A loud cheer erupts from crew's mess that can be heard one compartment away. Apparently, we are being rewarded for our performance in the Persian Gulf.

Recalling the world's geography, this new destination will mean that we will be transiting through the Indian Ocean and avoiding the narrow straits that intertwine themselves within the Indonesian archipelago. Sailing will be smooth. There are no landmasses of any size between our current position and the western coast of Australia. Furthermore, the transit area is not known for any Soviet naval activity whatsoever. Of course, that translates into drill time extravaganza.

We have been allocated nine days to veer from our present course. Transit time from our current location in the Indian Ocean to Perth, Australia should be about three days. If we spend three days in port, we should require another three days sailing to our new patrol area. Speaking with the control room watch standers, they seem to feel that we can make it to our patrol area in two days. For that matter, if we dispense with drilling, they feel we could make Australia in two days. Of course, few of us doubt that we will be allowed to skip any available drill time during our trek to Australia. It goes back to the old submarine saying: Sweat lots in peace in order to bleed less in war. If there is anything this commanding officer believes in, it is that saying. For certain, we will be drilling.

On my next watch, the engineering officer comes back to visit me. He is concerned about the electrical power situation in Australia. As he has been informed, we will be tying up to a pier. Australia's electrical power system is designed for 220 Volts Alternating Current (VAC) and 50 cycles per second (Hz), whereas, our shipboard system is designed for a higher voltage and frequency. After some discussion, we conclude that Squadron would not have OK-ed the port visit without taking this issue into consideration. And, seeing we will be in port for only three days, we can keep our steam plant operating at minimum power with minimum watch standers. Optionally, we could shutdown the steam plant, limit our shipboard electrical loads and run our diesel generator. Every morning before liberty call, we could start up to warm up the power plant and charge the battery, if depleted by the running of excessive electrical loads. We can do this. It will mean that more of the nuclear engineering complement will be required to remain aboard, but we can make this happen. Everyone aboard should get, at least, one day ashore in Australia.

The engineering officer is about to depart the engineering spaces when the first drill is announced. It is a simulated fire in the galley and, of course, it is in the boiling grease section. Our poor French fries are burnt again! The engineer and I commence the general emergency rig of the space that consists mainly of sealing off the compartment from the smoke generated from the fire and assembling the damage control equipment. If you are not in the effected compartment during a fire, the actions are routine. What is more, if the immediate actions in the effected compartment were completed quickly enough, you would not have to don a breathing apparatus. This turned out to be the case in this drill. Although, the grease boiling area of the galley is a sensitive spot for a fire, we have so many fire drills in that area that we respond with precision, like automatons.

The drill secures quickly, as a result of the rapid response from the galley crew. The engineer makes a comment, as he is leaving the engineering spaces, that it is unlikely that we will catch much sleep this evening. I chuckle in agreement. We have not drilled in a few weeks, so we need to catch up.

Sure enough, we barely recover from the fire drill when the collision alarm sounds. A collision alarm without any following announcement translates into flooding somewhere. Since the effected compartment was not announced, it means the flooding is severe and has overwhelmed the watch standers. Without question, this represents the worst type of flooding.

With extreme zeal, my watch standers isolate the engineering spaces and carry out general emergency procedures. In less than a minute, the engine room is sealed up tight as a drum. Just after I report the engineering spaces rigged for collision, the submarine takes on a downward incline toward the bow. Slowly, the angle of incline increases. It becomes difficult to remain standing without grabbing onto something. Some watch standers sit and pry themselves into a braced position between the piping systems and/or switchboards. The feeling of being subjected to such angles of incline is akin to trying to walk down a steep, slippery hill.

Once the submarine approaches a forty-five-degree down angle, the order is passed over the ship's announcing system to inject reserve high-pressure air into the ballast tanks. The actual action is not taken, as doing so would surface the ship.

The flooding was simulated in the bow compartment. The drill was secured upon the watch standers simulating the actions to blow the ship to the surface. The control room watch standers are ordered to achieve even trim. From that point on, the drill actions are restricted to the bow compartment in order to assess the casualty control actions. In the engineering spaces, we are allowed to continue with our routine watch standing evolutions.

Flooding is a very dangerous situation. In addition to adding more weight to the ship, the water enters the electrical system, causing short circuits. Short circuits soon evolve into disruptions of power. Electrical equipment is deenergized. Lighting is disabled. The crew ends up in darkened spaces being splashed with cold water under elevated pressures. It is a terrifying experience to be in the dark feeling the water level climb up your body, like death pulling you into the depths. Much training goes into creating a submariner's mind that can subjugate such horror and perform with precision under extreme stress. After all, underwater, one cannot just decide to jump over the side to escape the horror. There are no exits.

Surprisingly, the rest of the watch goes by without any interruptions. In the forward compartments, some evolutions are monitored and graded. Back aft in the engineering spaces, no one comes to disrupt our routine. We maintain elevated propulsion orders and make good time on our way to Australia. It would appear that the drill packages will be acute and of short duration. As for the log readings, the engineering plant equipment is operating within specifications.

I have never been to Australia. Although, I admit I have heard many stories. The story of most interest to the crew is the one about the female-to-male ration of 2:1. Despite our reservations about the story's validity, the thought of being immersed in such a social setting settles well with us. Time will tell. Another story that sparkles our imagination is the one about the western portion of Australia being separated from the eastern portion by thousands of miles of uninhabited desert. From a quick review of the geography of the Australian continent, this story appears to be true. What is more, of the projected fifteen million inhabitants living in Australia, 1.5 million people reside on a short strip of the western coast of Australia. That short strip is where our submarine will be mooring. To say that there is promise of romance here is an understatement. The crew, to a man, is eager to dock.

An in-port period in Australia will be a welcomed time for the Supply Department. We have been underway just long enough for our fresh consumables to run out. Our store of fresh greenery and milk has been depleted. We are approaching our bottom limit of fresh eggs, as well. Australia will enable us to restock these items. One thing about being asea for any length of time is that you come to savor your fresh consumables as long as they are available. Somehow powdered eggs and milk convey an alien and repulsive flavor that seems to reduce the quality of life to a refugee like status. Unfortunately, after a few weeks at sea, the lack of fresh consumables is the norm for sailors on extended deployment.

The ship's supply personnel painstakingly attempt to ensure that as much fresh stores as possible are on loaded and chilled prior to an extended underway. Storing of fresh consumables is an art in itself. The supply department strategically places these items within the chill lockers for timely allocation in order to extend their availability as long as possible while underway. Running out of a fresh consumable prior to two weeks underway is unacceptable. Every supply person is aware, from experience, of the fury of the crew whenever a fresh consumable runs out ahead of prediction. For the rest of the deployment, the supply department will have to endure the crew's mockery for such an oversight.

During this morning's meal, the senior enlisted personnel, on more than one occasion, have to remind the junior crewmen to mind their comments. Apparently, the new crewmen find cereal served with powdered milk unacceptable. Admittedly, it does present an unsavory flavor; however, it is one of the many sacrifices one learns to endure in the submarine force. Arduous duty in submarine life is not restricted to work and living conditions, it refers, as well, to the absence of life's usual accommodations. Fortunately, after a few weeks of complaining, the new crewmen adjust and adapt to the loss of life's privileges while underway. For some of the new crewmen, the loss of MacDonald's or BurgerKing, by just being underway, is an experience worse than death. If they can survive such a terrible adversity, they generally will be able to cope with life at sea.

Savoring the last of the fresh eggs at breakfast, I dream of how good a fresh salad would taste. Even a fast food, salad preparation would suffice. It does not have to be a salad made from the outer most greenery of a head of lettuce. The innermost parts, generally the aged portion, would sate me. In port, I seldom dine without a side salad. To me, the salad provides the roughage necessary for proper digestion. If I eat a chewy-textured meat, like steak, it does not settle well within me without a salad in accommodation in order to help within my digestive tract. Consuming steak at sea near the end of deployment produces the ill-desired, gut bomb sensation in my abdomen. During the after-steak-dinner watch, this unsettling sensation internally tortures me so much so that upon mooring, I am quick to seek out the nearest salad bar. Most submariners respond similarly.

Looking beyond the obvious distaste for cereal served with powdered milk, every food selection that requires the addition of milk is prepared with this powdery concoction. Pancakes, for example, are made with powdered milk. The extent of the replacement of milk with powdered milk is unlimited. All our meals are likewise affected. As a result, the crew's appetite wanes quickly. Coffee consumption increases dramatically. A general malaise seems to overcome the crew. The sooner fresh consumables are replenished the better. Recovery from this uneasiness miraculously appears after one meal containing fresh consumables. The submarine force truly operates on its stomach.

Within what seems like a few moments after closing my eyes for sleep, the ship's announcing system blasts a radiation emergency. Since I am the off-going watch, I am required to congregate the emergency response team. Flopping out of my bunk, as a cowboy would dismount a horse, slipping into my poopysuit and donning an emergency breathing mask, I am off to the engineering space bulkhead door.

What a sight to see! About a half-dozen, groggy-eyed sailors, hastily-dressed and sucking on low pressure air through their face-clamped breathing apparatus, are huddled about the bulkhead door, awaiting orders to enter the engineering spaces to assist the on watch personnel. I approach the disgruntled group, announce my leadership and make the call to engine room control center to request permission to open the bulkhead door and enter the engineering space. After speaking with the senior person on watch, my request to enter is denied. It is a drill, simulating excessive airborne activity. Opening the bulkhead door would contaminate the compartment in which we have assembled. We have been ordered to wait until an emergency ventilation of the engineering spaces has been completed.

To emergency ventilate a space submerged requires a change in the ventilation line up. The suction for the ventilation is provided by one of the major pieces of equipment that utilize the ventilation system for their intake, such as, the diesel. The submarine needs to rise to a depth that enables a ventilation mast to be raised above the surface of the ocean. The emergency ventilation procedure requires all hands cooperation and coordination. Often, one standing in a space under emergency ventilation can sense the change in airflow and sometimes feel the suction on the space. In the meantime, the emergency response team members settle onto a comfortable spot on the deck and suck on breathing masks. It is one hell of a way to pass a morning just after breakfast.

As the line up to emergency ventilate is proceeding, it becomes obvious to all of us in the emergency response team that as soon as the engineering spaces are emergency ventilated, the ship will secure from the drill. If we are not secured immediately after the emergency ventilate, then we will soon be secured after we enter the engineering spaces. These types of drills are designed to measure the ship's overall response. Once the engineering spaces are ventilated, the casualty becomes compartment specific. Since we will not be repairing any piping systems, if we are required to troubleshoot anything, it will be an administrative exercise to discover the cause of the airborne activity.

Airborne activity refers to radioisotope gases or particles dispersed in the atmosphere above a certain limit. The limit is based upon the notion that breathing this radioisotope for a specified period of time would expose the lungs to a level of radioactivity in excess of established body limits. These radioisotope airborne limits are quite small. Most of the limits are measured in amounts less than one billionth per milliliter. There are one thousand milliliters in a liter (about a quart). The quantities required to activate an airborne alarm are infinitely small.

To think that some medical personnel complain about having to wear a surgical mask. Here we sit with a hard rubber, octopus-like device clamped onto our faces, pulling on our hair and straining our lungs. Why? The ship needs to test the adequacy of our low-pressure air system in order to provide us emergency air during a casualty. There is a reason that these little experiences are not shown on submarine recruitment videos. They are downright nasty. All one can hope for is that the last user of the emergency breathing mask thoroughly cleaned it before he stowed it. If he had not done so, then this sucking exercise really does!

Fortunately, the ship is adept at emergency ventilating a space, and we are secured quickly. I remind the members of the emergency response team to clean their breathing mask prior to stowing them. The stowage locker provides the cleaning solution and the surgical patches to dry them. The cleaning solution resembles the fluids used to cleanse a body being prepared for surgical incision. Whatever it is called, it has a death sense about it. You know when you apply this fluid that it kills whatever germs you deposited on the inner surface of the mask. After the breathing masks are cleaned, I close the emergency storage locker and report to the control room that the emergency response team has secured from the drill. This exercise is a wonderful wake up, but I assure myself that I will not miss it after I retire form the submarine service.

Although I make a number of attempts to get some sleep, the condensed morning drill package prevents me. I suspect, at most, I managed fifteen minutes of uninterrupted shuteye during the morning watch. For some reason, I was tired on the morning watch. I do not recall overeating or working excessively during my on-watch time or the previous watch. Perhaps, I am just coming down with some kind of flu. One of my pre-flu symptoms is unusually long sleep sessions. At lunch, I find myself not impressed with the goulash entrée of macaroni and hamburger immersed in a pool of tomato sauce. I just settle for a cup of coffee.

The afternoon watch fares no better for me. We experience one drill after another. During this watch, however, the drills are designed such that they do not alter the propulsion orders. Despite the hectic responses by the crew to the drills, the submarine makes good time to Australia. Unfortunately, there was little time for sleep during the morning and afternoon watches. Since I stood the mid-watch, I will be the oncoming evening watch. Sometimes, the watch rotation draws you a lemon. This was one of those lemons for my watch section.

The evening meal entrée is salmon. I have never liked salmon, so I pass for a bowl of chicken broth. Broths are always available. They can be found in pre-made envelopes located inside the seating bins of the crew's mess tables. Just add some hot water from the coffee urn assembly, and presto, you have broth. With a few saltines crushed in the bowl, the broth seems to settle me.

The flu is difficult to cope with at sea. There is little the corpsman can prescribe to alleviate the effects. Once you catch the flu, it will latch on to you for a few days. The best remedy is to drink lots of hot fluids and take hot showers. Of course, like the plague, your immediate friends are thanking you, as the rest of the deployment unfolds, for inflicting them.

Upon relieving the watch, I receive the good news that only a battery charge is scheduled for the evening watch, and it seems we will be answering Ahead Full the entire night. This watch and the next will be unscathed by the drilling. That just suits me fine. We will have a fully charged battery when we arrive in Australia. What is more, the fact that we are charging tonight is an indication that the drill period is over; otherwise, we would be charging the battery tomorrow evening.

The news of the battery charge sits well with all my watch section. After a full day's session of drills, we are ready for some down time. We will cherish our rack time on the mid-watch. It is unfortunate, but more often than not, the at-sea requirements provide little time for sleep. A fleet ballistic missile submarine is not a sailboat that you can drop anchor in some isolate bay and allow the crew to sleep and lounge about for a few days. We have to be up and running all the time. There is no respite, especially submerged.

The watch goes by as routine as any watch that I have ever stood. Once the battery charge commences, the engineering spaces seem to go into automatic control. New personnel soon begin to appreciate the value of a battery charge. Since the ventilation line up throughout the ship cannot be altered during a battery charge, it follows that drills or interruptive type of evolutions are forbidden. During a battery charge, the crew settles in. For the next eight hours or so, the ship will be in interruption avoidance mode of operation. Submariners like it that way.

Little changes during the watch other than shifting the running engineering space machinery around to average out runtimes. Pepperoni pizza is a welcomed sight at Mid-rats. However, I just grab a few of the cooks' fresh dough selections and devour them quickly. My stay in the crew's mess is brief, and I am off to my bunk for some most desired sleep. Without even an adieu to my watch section, I am sound asleep.

Interestingly, some ten hours later, I awake fully rested. Although it seems like I just closed my eyes, ten hours have gone by without any sensation of the time. I truly must have been tired to lay still that long. I feel better as well. It seems the flu has departed me for another host body.

At the noon meal, before taking the watch, one of the crewmen sitting at the table mentions that we will be holding field day on our watch. He comments that it is a compensation for the two-watch drill package we had to endure yesterday. The news raises a round of cheer at the table. Our watch section has been awaiting the wheel of luck to bless us for some time now. Also, it is certain that we will dock alongside a pier in Western Australia tomorrow. The docking watch will be the morning watch. We cheer that news as well with even more enthusiasm.

The noon meal is not anything to brag about. The entrée is one of those UFO specials served with mashed potatoes. We just eat. No one even asks what kind of meat the UFO was made from. Probably, they are afraid to get a reply like: kangaroo. The meat is tough in texture, but if you cut it enough, some tender portions can be isolated. This is one of those sacrifice meals in which the crew takes ample portions of the entrée in order to discard enough to discourage any leftovers from reappearing at Mid-rats. UFOs are serious business for a submarine crew. If you shy away from them, they just keep resurfacing, denying you the more succulent entrees and side dishes. The affectionate phrase for the disposition of UFOs is: "Shitcan your fair share!"

Upon assuming the watch, I notice one of the lower level watch standers walk pass. There is something about his attire that catches my eye. He is wearing a makeshift, crossed-chest bandoleer with greenies stuffed into the slots where the bullets would normally be stored. Apparently, he is prepared for field day. The anticipation of an in-port period often evokes such carnival forms of expression. I just allow him to assume his watch standing duties without comment. He is a bit out of uniform, but it is an innovative, cleaning attire that will be utilized appropriately on this watch.

About one hour into the watch, field day is proclaimed over the ship's announcing system. Soon the engineering spaces are overpopulated with cleaners. A few more bandoleer-toting personnel make an appearance as well. One is even wearing a Mexican sombrero. I let it pass. This is our last day asea for a while, we can rejoice a little in fanciful expressions.

Songs begin to erupt throughout the engineering spaces. *Working on a chain gang* seems popular. One of the better chorus groups in the upper level engine room attempts a try at *Lara's Theme.* Interestingly, we sing with more feeling during a departure than we do for an upcoming in-port period. I guess sailors miss more leaving than returning. Returning seems to bring much promise, whereas, leaving carries more regrets. I pause a moment to contemplate what my regrets might be after leaving Australia. I pray that they will be good ones.

The rest of the watch is spaced out with portions of arduous cleaning, chorus and log taking. We answer Ahead Full all watch. We are told that the closet land is the continent of Australia. The thinly, elongated landmasses of the Indonesian archipelago are behind us. Open ocean is about us everywhere. Of course, the old salts remind us that one thing this part of the ocean is known for is that it is the playground of the great white sharks. We could wait a year or so after this voyage to hear that little tidbit of information. But, it is true. These are the royal waters of the great whites. I suspect we will not be running any man overboard drills in these waters. Well, paradise is often located next to hell.

The engineering officer nudges my shoulder, as I am cleaning. He informs me that Squadron has arranged for a diesel generator to be available to supply us our normal rated voltage and frequency. The hard spot of the news is that the diesel is not very large in capacity. It will be able to augment our diesel to supply our ship's electrical loads while we are in-port. We decide to split the ship's electrical distribution system so that the shore station diesel generator supplies only one side of our main electrical distribution while our on-board diesel supplies the other side. Of course, that means an extra watch stander for our on-board diesel. We can stand our diesel watch port and starboard, so they can get some time ashore on their days off. Since the diesel-powered, electrical lineup may consume some of the battery's available energy during equipment startups, the engineering officer recommends an engineering plant startup on my duty day to replenish the battery with our steam turbine generators. I expected that proposal, so I agreed. If we only have to start up once while we are in-port, we will have a good in-port period.

Field day is secured an hour before watch relief. All we have now is the evening and mid-watch before our arrival in Australia. The morning watch essentially will be the maneuvering watch to enter port. I wonder if we will see any dolphins playing in our wake.

Liberty in Australia

The three distinct blasts of the diving alarm awaken the crew this morning. Today is the day. In a few hours we will be amongst the kangaroos and koala bears. Every member of the crew expresses pleasantries, as he prepares for breakfast and the watch. Anticipation of an in-port period does that for the crew. Going ashore makes everyone happy. Entry into the crew's mess for breakfast resembles entering a high school auditorium on graduation day. Everyone is glad to see everyone else. Some crewmen practice the Australian greeting of "G'Day!"

To enhance the crew's anticipation, the periscope operator projects views of the Western Australian coastline on the crew's mess monitor. The terrain looks barren. We are informed that it is. The northern section of Western Australia is nothing but desert. The Australians have one lonely outpost in this northern section. It is a military based called Darwin. Its very name conjures up connotations of isolation and the far reaches of civilization.

From the continuous scan of our periscope, the seascape reveals no other vessels afloat about us. Usually, no matter what port we sail into the waters abutting the landmass are teeming with little flotillas of sail craft. This is not the case here. We are quite alone. One of the crewmen at the breakfast table comments that every great white residing off the western coast of Australia must be following us hoping for someone to fall overboard. The thought gets a chuckle. For certain, no one plans to test the crewman's suspicion.

Upon finishing with breakfast, a tugboat can be seen on the monitor approaching us from the southeast. It is an ocean going tug. We can tell from all the inner tubes fastened upon its bow. The inner tubes are used as cushioning devices to enable the tug to make contact with our hull.

The sea state is calm. This will be an easy rendezvous with the tug and a pleasant trip into the harbor. Some smoke seems to billow out of a stack near the tug's wheelhouse. The smoke is not coming from an exhaust stack. It is coming from a horn stack. We cannot hear the tug's horn, as we are in crew's mess observing a periscope image on a monitor. The smoke is pressurized air being forced through an orifice to alert our vessel of the tug's intention to come alongside.

The maneuvering watch is announced just before I finish breakfast. "G'Days" are voiced all around crew's mess. Accompanying chuckles enhance the ambience. We shall hear those words a good bit for the next few days, I predict.

The sea state is so calm that the boat barely rocks. Soon, the bumping sound of the tug attaching itself to our hull is felt with a slight jarring of the ship. The tug's engine is revving at high speed, as it tries to back down. We can hear the tug's engine whining through our hull. For the tug to attach to us so quickly, we must have surfaced right outside the harbor. Strange, we could not discern any port facilities on the crew's mess monitor. They must have been located further to the south beyond the current scan of the periscope.

The crew's mess is packed with sailors and "G'Days". It is standing room only. The crew is observing our entry into the Australian port. Sure enough, dolphins are jetting back and forth on our port and starboard wakes. The dolphins' daring captivates the crew. I never imagined they could swim so fast. Little attention is paid to the coastline and the scenery along the entry channel. The dolphins' antics are too distracting. The smaller dolphins are able to ride the waves backwards on their tails. How can they do that?

Soon, the ship slows to maneuver at a right angle. The dolphins submerge and leave us. The crowd in crew's mess begins to disperse. The periscope allows us to view the Australian sailors waiting on the dock with heevies and mooring lines. We are here. At the announcement that we are lowering our positioning motor, I grab a cup of fresh coffee and head back aft to coordinate the shore power hookup.

We have been at sea a while. It takes some time to clear the after hatch. As the roving watches open the after hatch, one of my electricians shines a flashlight through the opening and exclaims: "Yup, it's day out there!" The comment raises a round of laughter. God, I pray we never stay at sea that long.

I follow two of my electricians out the after hatch. Upon clearing the hatch, I notice television cameras are focused upon us. Apparently, having a submarine pull alongside these piers is an anomaly. The television cameras were focused on the procession occurring on the forward brow where the commanding officer and his senior staff are attired in dress uniform. I can sense from the commanding officer's grimace that we were early in popping the after hatch. It appears, in the middle of the welcoming ceremony, we distracted the television crew. Well, at least Australian TV got to see American sailors in their working uniforms. We are not all spit and polish.

My electricians are worried about our poor timing. I console them with the logic that the error has already been made. If we just go about our business, no one will think anything is wrong.

Sure enough, the Australian sailors hurry up getting the aft shore power brow over. The Australians sailors are professional looking. If I were to imagine a working sailor in a catalog, I would think of these fellows. They have the mustaches, the tattoos, the freshly pressed uniforms and the mannerisms of old salts. They could easily step into an Old Spice commercial. We, on the other hand, fall a little short of that image.

The exchange of information between the pier shore power squad and my electricians is slowed due to the strange accent of the Australians. They seem to talk through their noses and space their words oddly. Strange, we are allies separated by a common language. We look directly at their lips in order to decipher the meaning of their sounds. Unfortunately, they have difficulty reading our lips, as Americans seldom employ strong lip movement in speech. Fortunately, since we both are here to handle electricity, the randomness of our sounds is corralled eventually into meaningful expressions. To make matters easier, Squadron has provided joy connections adaptable to our electrical system.

Joy connectors resemble huge amphenols that enable one electrical system to be patched directly into another electrical system. Usually, we are required to splice the individual connections together. With a joy connector, all the connections are contained within a larger connector. One merely needs to slide the female connector from the shore power side over the male connector of our distribution system, tighten the connection and power is available. A phase rotation check of the two electrical systems passes, and shore power is connected to our electrical distribution system. Upon completion of bringing on shore power, the Australian electricians tour my electricians through their diesel facility in order to familiarize us with their operational and emergency procedures.

Interestingly, as our ship's officers cater to the Australian dignitaries, the Australian electricians invite my electricians into their club for pints. Pints are the Australian reference to spirits. The club is located right next door to the diesel facility. Tell me these Australians electricians have their priorities in order! Something about this arrangement tells me the duty crew will enjoy this in-port period a lot more than anyone aboard had predicted. Although tempted, I remind my electricians that we need to shutdown the engineering plant. Though some grumbling accompanies our walk back to the boat, I can sense my electricians plotting their clandestine rendezvous with these Australians and their pints. I can only pray that it will be only a few pints.

Climbing back down the after hatch, my electricians watch the forward crewmen cross the gangplank on liberty. It will be a few hours before my electricians can depart. Of course, I notice that all my electricians took a fond look at the Australian club before they entered the hatch. Liberty for them might just be across the gangplank in the club. Well, at least, they will not be hard to find.

The lineup of the electrical distribution system occurs without a hitch. The Australian diesel is supplying our starboard bus loads while our diesel supplies our port bus loads. A bus is an electrical term for a major section of a distribution system. With the electrical system addressed and the engineering plant shutdown, some of the senior enlisted personnel and I are ready to go on liberty. It is about noontime now. The shutdown and shore power arrangement took longer than we had anticipated. Some thought is given to staying for chow, but the suggestion to sample a pint at the Australians' club is too enticing.

It comes as no surprise to us, as we enter the club that the same Australian electricians who assisted us with shore power earlier are holding up the bar. From the lisps in the conversations, they must have mustered right over here as soon as they were secured. The interior of the club resembles that of a fancy pizza parlor in small town United States. The floor is sturdy. A somewhat cleaned, ten-foot long, red carpet adorns the welcome area. Two pool tables anchor each end of the open area. The bar stretches the length of the far wall of the entire establishment. It is a thick bar that gives the impression that four or five hand-bowling lanes were lacquered together. The bar has an incredibly fine finish. Beer mugs slide from one end of the bar to the other with ease. There are a few tables set up for private conversation against the far wall to our left as we enter. Today, they are empty.

We stride on in to cheers from the Australians sailors and some of our crew who moored themselves to the bar earlier. Without asking our preference, the bartender who is in working military uniform just begins pouring us draft beers. As we settle onto our stools, the bartender serves us with the comment: "No charge, mates." We nod our acceptance.

The music playing on the juxbox sounds familiar. They are popular songs in the United States. Although, at first, we believe the Australians are playing them to please us. It turns out that all of the songs have been composed and sung by Australian artists. Truly, none of my group had ever realized that before.

The draft beer is Swan Larger that is brewed not far from the military base. The other option on the tap is South Pacific Larger, or SP, another popular brew all over the South Pacific. Swan is a light beer that is soothing to drink. We enjoy it. To us, it closely resembles Olympia from the Pacific Northwest of the United States. From our conversation with the Australians, this time of day is popular for the consumption of a pint. Apparently, the Australian Navy has a program akin to alcohol rations in which members can consume so many pints per pay period. Accordingly, the beers that we are consuming are rations already pre-paid and accounted. These rations are extended to at sea personnel aboard vessels of the Australian Navy, as well.

After a few drafts, we have reconnoitered enough information on the opportunities ashore to call for a taxi to take us into town. Town is a little place called Rockingham, a typical wild west-like, dust bowl of a watering hole. It contains one bar. We decide to stop there.

Entering the watering hole, we are confronted with two doors. Neither door is labeled. As it turns out, one leads to the men's section, whereas the other door leads to the dancing area that permits women. The men's side resembles an American West-style, mining town saloon without the piano and the dance hall girls. Miners are standing about everywhere sipping beer. They still have their mining rigs attached to their waists. Some are even wearing their hardhats with a lantern affixed. Without exception, they have dust shadows on their faces where their goggles did not protect their skin. We endure one beer in this environment and decide to check out the other side of the bar.

The dance side of the bar is like walking into another world. The room is well kept. The bar surface reflects a pristine glare. Women immediately join us and buy us beers. After five hours of saying hello, we have not paid for one drink. We have all been invited for tea. In Australia, tea refers to a full course meal and entertainment for the evening. None of us refuse. We don't even pretend to check our calendars. One could get to like Australia!

The gal that got teamed up with me presents a face that has experienced many trying times. Her body looks great though. One glance is enough to realize that she jogs or spends a lot of time in the spa. Her personality is pleasant. Best of all, I have no trouble understanding what she is saying. She tells me her name is Mary, and she has two daughters: Elizabeth and Victoria. I find it interesting how these names are the same as the reigning and former reigning monarchs of England.

Upon leaving the watering hole, the gals split us up into couples. I find myself riding to points unknown with Mary and her two daughters. The daughters are in their late teens. Apparently, the three gals are members of the same softball team. They had stopped off in the watering hole after a game with a group of gals from Freemantle. Freemantle is the city next up the coast from Rockingham. The car we are in is a dark-blue, two-door Tercel. Of course, to frighten me, she drives on the wrong side of the road. But, so does everyone else on the roadway, so I lose interest in the anomaly.

It seems we have driven forever on a flat surface. There are no hills and no curves. Suddenly, the little Tercel pulls into what appears to be a desert area. The dirt seems to take flight as we pull in. We wait a few minutes for the dirt cloud to settle back down before we exit the vehicle. As soon as we are all out of the car, Mary unlocks the trunk to get some softball gear bags. When I lean over to grab one, the gals stop what they are doing and smile. I can interpret from their smiles that I have done something that pleases them. What that is, I have no idea. Their smiles continue the entire walk to the storage area inside their house.

They live in a three-bedroom, single-floor, ranch-style home. It has a huge living area that I can tell they designed for the parties. The kitchen area is small. The bedrooms are all the same size and equipped with queen-size beds. There are two bathrooms, yet only one is equipped with a shower. Of course, the fridge is packed with Swan larger. Either they were expecting company, or they are adept at beer consumption. Two minutes have not gone by before there is an open Swan larger bottle in front of me. They did not even ask if I wanted a drink. They just assumed that I did.

Sitting back in an extremely comfortable recliner in their living room, one of the daughters begins untying my shoes and removes them from my feet. Then, she begins massaging my feet. I take a swig of my Swan and realize that I can get used to this treatment. Mary informs me that the younger girl, Victoria, will entertain me while Elizabeth and her prepare dinner.

Taking great care to massage my feet, Victoria relates to me her junior college experience. She has commenced her freshman year in pre-nursing. Interestingly, Australia provides for all their education as far as they desire to go. If Victoria decides to become a doctor, as long as she passes all her examinations, the Australian government will pay for all her education and provide her a monthly stipend check to see her through. I am amazed. From time to time, Mary interjects that royalties from Australia's mining industry pay for all their education. Everyone in Australia essentially can be paid to pursue education as far as they decide to go.

The more my conversation with Victoria evolves, the more I am inspired by the Australian priority to educate their citizens. The government even has provisions for students who desire to change their career goals. They are allowed one career change in their education path. Now, that does not mean one career change during their education, but one career change after they have completed their education for a career. In a sense, if they find that they do not like the medical field, they can redo their education to become an engineer. In a lighter suggestion, Mary informs me that the Australian government also provides similar educational opportunities to Americans who desire to relocate to Australia and become Australian citizens. I let the idea pass.

Seeing my Swan larger bottle nearing the bottom, Victoria quickly fetches me another cold one from the fridge. One could get used to Australia. She opens the second bottle for me and then sits down on the foot cushion in front of my recliner. The conversation quickly changes to my residence in the United States, and where I grew up. Victoria wants to know all about me. As I relate my experiences growing up in the USA, Mary and Elizabeth take short breaks from their cooking to query me on different issues. Soon, it becomes apparent that the girls just want to hear me talk. The topic of the conversation is unimportant. They want to hear my voice. They even chuckle when my New England accent sneaks though. The conversation goes on for over an hour, before Mary tells Victoria to grab my beer and escort me to the dinner table.

The dinner entrée is lamb. I am surprised; however, the gals tell me that it is a favorite in Western Australia. On sampling the first morsel, I am further surprised that it does please my taste buds. I do not even desire to quench it with my beer. The lamb is even quite tender. Accompanying the lamb are side dishes of sweet potatoes and stewed tomatoes. There is even a little saucer of sweet jelly in which to dip the lamb. The jelly reminds me of the jellies that are served with Peking Duck in Hong Kong.

Despite my initial reservations with the lamb, the gals continue to press me to talk. They want to know my favorite sports teams, my pets' names, my high school, the kids' names from my neighborhood, etc. We even discuss bait fishing in detail. I surmised quickly that theses gals are tomboys.

The conversation slowly evolves into partnerships. Mary relates that her husband was a gold miner who died in a freak accident a few years back. Both her daughters have boyfriends who play Australia's version of football. American football is referred to as Grid Iron in Australia. When I inquire as to their whereabouts, the gals tell me that the boys are drinking beer some place. A few more queries into their relationships reveal that there exists a gender barrier in Australia. According to the gals, men do men things: whereas, women are for procreation and to serve the men. In example, they remind me of the separation between the two sides of the watering hole. Women are relegated to being at the convenience of men. Men, in Australia, enjoy the company of men.

Interestingly, when I relate the situation in America. The comment with which the girls respond is: "See, I told you, they are just like they are in the movies." Apparently, there is a belief in Australia that American men are exactly like the Australian men; however, they are portrayed differently on the screen. When I express my disbelief and amazement, the gals seem genuinely in awe. Here in Australia, the gals are reduced to servants. They even share with me that no man has ever helped them with their softball gear or luggage of any kind. Suddenly, I feel like someone has beamed me into a new world.

One of the issues that the gals seem to emphasize over an over is how spoiled American women are. The gals evoke a deep envy for the way the American women are treated. The word "pedestal" echoes through the conversation all evening. However, I must admit, although my words express sympathy for the plight of the gals, my mind admires the arrangements the Australian men have created.

For me, it is a four-beer dinner. The gals just keep feeding me. I cannot seem to consume enough sweet potatoes and stewed tomatoes. The stewed tomatoes are really good, and they mix well with the beer. After a pause to allow the lamb to settle, Mary presents me with a powder puff-looking thing that she tells me is dessert. She hands me a fork and invites me to sample. Amazingly, it is crème-filled and quite pleasing to the palate. Served chilled, it resembles a form of light ice cream in very thin crepe. It is delicious, and my smile conveys my approval. Interestingly, the dessert quenches my desire for beer.

Sensing my need to relax, Elizabeth and Victoria excuse themselves and begin washing the dishes. Mary escorts me into the living room where we settle in on her sofa and watch some TV. She goes through the channels explaining all the shows. We decide on a comedy that features some merchant seaman turned entertainer. He is hilarious.

One thing about Australian gals, they are forward. They do not wait for the gent to make a play for them. They convey their intentions quickly and directly. I am a bit nervous over the situation. Mary senses my apprehension and reminds her daughters that they have to get up early in the morning. Apparently, that is their cue to retire and leave Mary and I alone. They respond to Mary's suggestion far better than any of my electricians ever responded to any of my suggestions. The gals would make excellent sailors.

There is pleasantness to Mary. Had I met her in any other manner, I probably would have passed her by. My preference in women slants for those with a pretty face. I am a real sucker for a looker. Tonight, she has been so kind to me that I feel obligated to spend time with her. It is the sort of kindness that I have wanted from other women and never received. She has been good to me. From the manner in which her fingers touch and explore me, she intends to be a lot nicer, too.

My mind wanders off to Maria. Mary reminds me a little of Maria. They both have dark black hair. By coincidence, they cut their hair at about the same length. Mary's hair is a little curlier. They both have a hint of romantic Spanish in their eyes. As best as I can recall, Mary's lips are as moist as Maria's. Mary is more desirous of me. The way her body tenses as my hands sculpt her contours hints to me that Mary has not been with someone in a while. Maria's body never reacted that way.

Feeling my arousal, Mary quickly relocates us to her bedroom. There are stuffed animals everywhere on her bed. Soon, they find themselves with other less desirable accommodations on the floor. Poor fellows! There is a sense of haste in Mary's manner. I have never seen a woman undress so fast. More so, before I can open my mouth and gape, Mary attends to my clothing. I had never realized how easily small fingers could unbutton a shirt.

With my shirt in the company of the stuffed animals, my chest is greeted by Mary's. She has huge breasts. They weigh down my hands as I cup them. Somehow I never noticed she was this huge when we were dining and drinking. Some corset-like device that she wore under her softball uniform must have hidden them. She can tell from my smile that I appreciate them. I believe she was waiting for my reaction before she pounced on me.

Truly, I did nothing but lie there on her bed. Soon, I was immersed within her. She moved upon me to her desire, pumping up and down and swerving right and left in a random frenzy. Each time I tried to rise to exert my manly persuasion, Mary pressed me into the sheets with her breasts. A position, I admit, I got to admire. Thank God, I had consumed a lot of alcohol, because had I not I could never have lasted as long as I did with Mary siphoning me.

She had a habit of kissing my eyelids each time she leaned forward to press me down. I did not mind it, but it seemed strange. No one had ever spent so much time on my eyelids before. Actually, no one had spent much time on any part of me this much before. Mary really wanted me. I must have struck some sex crave nerve inside her. I could not believe her lower abdominal muscles could tighten, stretch and grasp me the way they did. At times, being inside her reminded me of a firm handclasp. Given the way she bounced about atop me, she could have hurt me if she desired. She moved like she handled the gearshift in her Tercel. If I had never known the gearshift pattern, I would have learned it being with Mary. I certainly appreciated the fine difference between first and second gear. Third gear took my breath away. Fourth gear stopped my heart.

Finally, she stiffened as if she were experiencing a seizure. I could feel her lower abdominal muscles clamping upon me. She was not breathing for a few moments. Then, she convulsed as if she had been stabbed in the chest. A second convulsion followed a few moments after the first. On the third convulsion she collapsed upon me. I held her firmly as she wiggled about randomly in my arms. As she calmed, I finally got to move a bit and finished off what she had enjoyed so much starting. Soon, her fluids began dampening my lower abdomen and legs. I sensed a lot of fluid flowing onto me. Mary's exhausted breath sounded wonderful against my ear. Her huge breasts comforted my chest. I felt victorious with her fluids draped over my lower abdomen. Mary fell asleep on top of me.

During the night, Mary bothered me twice. Amazingly, I felt up to the task each time. Although, I must admit I was more able the first time than the second. She explained to me that lamb gets her in the mood. I was thankful that she had only one helping; otherwise, I fear I would have failed to measure up to her demands.

In the morning, I was greeted with a full breakfast. From the little chuckles her daughters' made, I suspect my performance was appraised thoroughly. Waking up to a house full of women takes some adjustments. The best I could decipher from their mannerisms was through analogy with how men compare women that they have bedded. It felt odd being the object of comparison. The breakfast, however, was delicious. Once again, I took extra helpings of stewed tomatoes.

It was agreed at breakfast that I would spend the day with the gals. They offered to take me wherever I liked in Australia. I settled for seeing kangaroos and koala bears. They mentioned a park just north of Perth that kept a number of these animals.

Perth is the major city of Western Australia. With a population of over 1.5 million, it is the largest metropolis within a thousand-mile radius. We would have to travel through Perth in order to get to the kangaroos.

First stop along the trip was Freemantle. Freemantle was a popular American submarine base during World War II. Many of the namesakes of the attack submarines, currently stationed in Pearl Harbor, were homeported in Freemantle. They were members of the famous Submarine Squadron Twenty-eight that harassed Japanese shipping in the straits of Indonesia.

In Freemantle the gals took me to the piers where we sampled old fashion fish & chips. The fish & chips were served in a newspaper rolled up in a cone-shape. French fries (chips) were interspersed with slithers of deep fried white fish. Sprinkling some oil and vinegar on the mixture added an exquisite flavor. Quite frankly, the fish & chips were delicious. Unfortunately, fish & chips are never served this way in the United States. If I cared to repeat this dining adventure, I would need to reproduce it myself at home.

Following Freemantle, we passed though the outskirts of Perth. Perth looked as huge and as important as any American metropolis in the distance. Given the barren surroundings, it reminded me of Las Vegas more than any other American city. As we passed Perth, I could not help noticing the huge neon and regular road signs promoting American companies. The gals informed me that many of Western Australia's largest companies are American owned. The Americans have invested enormously into the heavy industry of Western Australia.

After we passed Perth, the Australian landscape really does change dramatically. There are few signs of civilization. It is worse than the trip from the Hoover Dam on the Arizona-Nevada border to Las Vegas. As we drove down this desolate, randomly-maintained highway, I expected to see aborigines pop up and toss spears at us at any moment. After some fifty miles or so of driving, a little oasis with a shelter appeared on the horizon. The closer we approached, the more the establishment discouraged me. Yet, this turned out to be the famous kangaroo place.

A cloud of dust erupted as the Tercel pulled into the parking area. Once again, we waited for the dust cloud to settle before exiting the vehicle. Upon exiting the vehicle, all I could see was barnyard fence stretching forever. There was one hut-like building that contained a turnstile and a small air-conditioned office area. As we approached the turnstile, a female exited the office area, attired in a park ranger uniform. She extended the usual Australian greeting and told Mary the price of entry was a few Australian dollars. An Australian dollar is worth about sixty cents American.

After passing through the turnstile, we were greeted with an expanse of shade grass separating a few date trees. The gals just walked on into the shade grass area. They seemed to know where they were going, so I followed. The tall grass bothered me, because I was aware that poisonous snakes were everywhere in Australia. The gals were wearing tall, leather boots, whereas I just had on my sneakers, offering my calves as potential targets for snakebites.

Some hundred or so yards into the shade grass, we came upon a family of kangaroos resting. As we approached, the entire family stood up to greet us. The little ones hopped while the adults walked toward us. Walking for adult kangaroos is odd. They use both hind legs and their tail. Pressing their thick tail against the ground enables a kangaroo to move its feet forward resembling a walking step. As a New England deer hunter, the similarities between the kangaroos and whitetail deer were striking. The best I could tell, kangaroos have huge hips, thighs and feet that allow hopping; whereas, whitetail deer have slender, pointed feet for running on their hooves. The facial features between kangaroos and whitetail deer are similar. It bewilders me why kangaroos evolved in the manner that they did in Australia. What is it in Australia that would encourage an evolutionary pattern of hopping around versus running? Obviously, many millions of years ago, there was a land condition that warranted such an evolution. What it could have been, I have no idea.

The kangaroos make no noises at all. They just hop or walk up to us. The gals feed them with treats they purchased from the park ranger. The larger kangaroos place their little upper arms on the gals' shoulders to remind them that they have not given them some of the treats. The entire feeding session is well organized. The kangaroos must have been conditioned by many visitors to remain calm. As I watch the gals feed the smaller kangaroos, a seven-footer grabs my shoulder. I turn to face him and am forced to look up into his eyes. Although he says nothing, the message is clear: feed me! The gals noticing my obvious apprehension in being confronted by such a huge animal come to my rescue and offer the beast some treats. After consuming three of the treats, the huge kangaroo releases his grip on my shoulder and slowly walks away. The breadth of the animal's backside exceeds twice mine. These kangaroos get huge.

Sensing my concern, Mary tells me that before they travel any further north than this site, they place a rooguard on their Tercel. A rooguard is a reinforced, metallic cage that covers the front end of the vehicle. In the event of a collision with a kangaroo, the rooguard protects the car and its passengers. Mary tells me that a collision with a seven-foot kangaroo, at highway speed, would demolish a car and kill most of the passengers. In the outback, herds of kangaroos hopping at high speeds often randomly skip across a highway. There is little time for a car to react to a kangaroo crossing its path at high speeds. Elizabeth provides some statistic that most car accidents in the outback are between huge kangaroos and vehicles. Victoria even mentions that sometimes a huge kangaroo will collide with a car and just keep on hopping. The car will be so damaged by the collision that it will be unable to run. The impression settles within me quickly that kangaroos present a potential danger.

Leaving the kangaroo family, we walk toward an oasis area surrounded by strange looking trees. Mary tells me that they are eucalyptus trees. Elizabeth points out a number of koalas in the trees. Koalas remain in their trees where they feed. My impression of the koalas is that they resemble drug addicts stoned on the streets of Waikiki. Mary laughs at my comparison and relates that the eucalyptus leaves contain a drug that keeps the koalas stoned. Koalas are not the friendly creatures portrayed in advertisements. They have huge, elongated claws in order to impale the tree branches and trunks. Mary advises me never to attempt to pick up one of these creatures. They are quite ferocious in defense. I agree.

We wander about the park catering to other kangaroo families for about an hour. Sensing my poor adjustment to the humidity, the gals recommend that we head back. I waste no time encouraging them. The same park ranger escorts us to our vehicle, and we are off on our return trip.

Most of the way back we have the ocean view to our right. A few sailboats tack about an endless expanse of ocean. This must be a paradise for sailors in sloops. Those asail today are miles apart, allowing for almost any kind of maneuvering imaginable. Out here, sailing does not mean venturing out a few miles just to drop anchor and sip wine. Here, they sail for hours. These are serious, blue-collar sailors who enjoy the sport. It is no wonder Australia produces such competitive sail teams for the famous America's Cup.

The gals are quieter on the way back than they were on the way up. I guess the heat got to them and wore them down. Elizabeth and Victoria take the opportunity to nap as we pass through the outskirts of Perth. I am sleepy as well, but I keep Mary company, as she navigates the only super-highway in Western Australia. Well, at least I can say that I have seen live kangaroos and koala bears. Few people where I grew up can say that.

Mary asks if I would like to stop off at the watering hole for a few beers. I decline. So, she drives directly to her place. I was not sure if she felt like a few beers or not. She does not seem to be the type that frequents the watering hole. When we arrive at her place, however, she is quick to open up a few cold beers for us. Her daughters excuse themselves and go to their rooms to finish some homework assignments for tomorrow's classes. Mary and I reminisce the day and sip beers. She is a quiet woman who appreciates the attention and company of men. The evening passes pretty much the same as the first evening: a few comedies shows, some foreplay and then some intense play. I could enjoy being around this woman. I doubt there would be a morning in which I would depart for work without a huge smile on my face and a belly full of chow.

The next morning, Mary gets her daughters off to the university, before she drops me off on the pier. We embrace goodbye and promise to keep in touch. I won't, but I go through the motions of expressing my thanks. We part, and I do not watch her vehicle drive off. I just hurry down the forward hatch to take over the watch. As I get into the control room, I stop to answer a phone that just keeps ringing.

There is a young Australian gal on the other end, desiring to date a sailor. Opening the "date" book laying on the control room table, I notice that her call will be the 44th entry. Our vessel has been here for three days now, and there are 44 requests for sailors from Australian women. As I enter her name in the date book, the 39th entry catches my eye. Some twenty-four-year-old had requested to have sex with the entire submarine crew. In the remarks column, someone entered that our renowned, well-endowed sonarman was sent to her address to comfort her in her time of need. Assuring the young lady who just called that a sailor would call her, I close the "date" book. Coming to Australia is like an open invitation to a meat market in which we are allowed to sample anything we choose.

Making my way back aft, I recalled all the boyhood rumors I had heard about Australia. Now, I discover that they are beyond the truth that I had believed as puffery. These Australian women really do come after Americans.

Back aft, I soon return to my senses and assume my duties as an engineer. We are starting up momentarily to warm up the plant and then shutting down. We accomplish the cycle in a few hours. During the entire procedure, we do not divorce for shore power or our diesel. In the breathers between evolutions, the watch section personnel are quick to volunteer their unusual experiences in Australia. Without exception, none of us have ever experienced anything like these Australian women. About half my watch sections vows to return to Australia upon arrival back at homeport in Hawaii. Some of the crewmen have even proposed to the Australian women. I have to admit, those gals are hard to beat. They know how to treat men. I will miss them forever.

The next day I remain aboard double-checking the pre-underway preparations. Sipping coffee in crew's mess, I am inundated all day with romantic episodes of the crewmen with Australian women. I doubt any member of this crew will ever forget the kindnesses of Australia. One of the crewmen returning from liberty is wearing a light blue t-shirt with a huge kangaroo sewn upon it with the words: "I'm an American, but I love Australia." Those words truly capture the essence of our experience during this in-port period in Australia.

The following day, we are underway. Some of the Australian gals are on the pier waving us farewell. It is not goodbye, because no one will ever say that they will not return. Something here will draw us back. Like sirens soothingly singing in our ears, we will remember Western Australia.

Once again, the playful dolphins return to our wake and escort us to the deep water. The periscope operator maintains the view on the Australian port long after we have cleared the breakwater. Unlike leaving a port to distance our worries, this sailing fills us with longing for the wonderful people we met and loved so passionately. Thank you Australia.

CHAPTER 9

End of Deployment Patrol

In no time at all, we arrive at our dive area. The periscope takes one last scan of the horizon, before the diving alarm sounds. In the distance, just barely visible, is the last glimpse of Australia. We watch our periscope dip under the waves. Soon, the familiar sounds of submergence creep through the metal of the hull, reminding us that we have rejoined the creatures of the deep.

Our exit from Australia will be around the northern tip of the continent, through the Torres Straits and into the Coral Sea. We will slip around the island of New Guinea and enter the Pacific Ocean via the familiar route of our naval fleets of World War II. For the most part, it will be open ocean sailing. Few cargo vessels transit these routes. Although there are scattered island chains along the way, we will ensure that they remain far off our bow. Within a few days, we should cross the equator into the North Pacific where we shall commence our patrol.

In the engineering spaces, we experience and note in our log taking the typical readings of the equatorial seas. Seawater intake temperature is high, making it difficult for us to cool our running machinery. Our steam plant efficiency has decreased, as well, as a result of our inability to maintain a high vacuum. Fortunately, we will be exposed to these environmental conditions for a short duration. It would be difficult for our submarine to operate efficiently in these waters indefinitely.

Since we did not take on any new riders in Australia, crossing the equator does not warrant any Shellback ceremony. The commanding officer acknowledges the crossing by scheduling surf & turf for the evening meal. What the shellbacks could not inflict on pollywogs, they will carve out of the entrée.

Shellback is a naval term for a carnival-like, equator crossing ceremony in which inductees, affectionately referred to as pollywogs, are subjected to forms of humiliation as a rite of passage. Trust me, you only want to experience this rite of passage once.

These waters around the equator seem so tranquil today. In the days of World War II, they were filled with excitement. Surface ships repelled sortie after sortie from Japanese Zeroes every day. Submarines filled these waters with torpedoes and left the remnants of their prey afloat everywhere. Marines bled all over the sandy beaches of the islands. Death feasted in these waters.

Two watches of ship's drills were scheduled just prior to entering our patrol area. I guess the commander wanted to remind us that we were a military organization again. Or, maybe he wanted to insure we remembered we were submerged on patrol. Either way, we got the message. From here on until our return to homeport, the order of the day is vigilance.

From the trek of our patrol area posted in the control room, slowly, we will steer our way toward the Sandwich Islands. Although we are officially on patrol, we navigate homeward. Gone are the special operations of the early part of our deployment. Until we moor, our only offensive action would be the deployment of our missiles. That is an action all of us hope we would never have to perform. Home would be meaningless, if we did.

The further north we sail, the cooler the seawater injection temperature becomes. Each degree decrease creates a cause for celebration. Forward watch standers are eager to ask the engineers when they come to crew's mess after their watch what the seawater injection temperature reads. Smiles and cheers erupt whenever a two-degree decrease is reported. They even cheer false readings, like when the ship dove deep and passed through a temperature layer. Some crewmen even raised cups of red Kool-Aid in a toasting gesture to acknowledge our good fortune to be going home. After five months of deployment, all sorts of little things, hinting at good fortune, are appreciated and amplified. One needs to experience a long deployment in order to understand. I wonder how many submariners in the future will retrace our sailing. I pray that it will not be many.

We are well passed the mid-point of our deployment. Apprehension begins to appear in our minds of what it will be like to return to our homeport. For many, they will simply resume their lives, as if the departure never occurred. For others, life will present unexpected circumstances. How many will return to divorce papers? Seldom is there a six-month deployment in which at least two crewmembers are faced with an unexpected divorce. Often, the sailor's wife encounters some sweet talking, socially-mobile individual who seduces them into comparisons. In comparisons of lifestyles, the military member always looses. We are paid much less than our civilian counterparts. Actually, we are paid less than entry grade menial laborers. It is a sad reality that the military is so underpaid and under-appreciated. For those sailors with attractive wives, it is just a matter of the number of patrols before she wanders off with a civilian of any stature.

The military is not well treated within the civilian community. In these times of post-Vietnam dislike for the military, sailors have to weather the discontent of their civilian peers. Being underpaid is just one of the disadvantages that they are forced to overcome. The lack of support from the officer corps and the civilian constabulary are two others. If there is an altercation of any kind in the civilian community, the sailor is presumed to be the guilty party. Why? It is more the bad taste everyone has in their mouths over Vietnam than anything the sailors have done.

For those sailors attempting to complete their college education while ashore, the troubles multiply. Often, in order to acquire acceptance in collegiate settings in which grade accomplishment is subjectively adjudicated, the sailors have to bend to the inclination, often anti-military, of their peers and instructors. Sometimes, it has been the case that an A+ paper will be graded as a C+ or less simply because of the sailor's affiliation with the military. Acceptance in some universities is often judged in the same manner. Regrettably, a sailor's attempt to get along with his collegiate peers will run him astray with the military's investigative branches and affect his security clearance.

The problems compound for a sailor leaving the submarine service. Though his training aboard a nuclear submarine far exceeds that of his civilian counterparts of any formal educational level short of a doctorate, he will be denied advancement without first obtaining a four-year-college, engineering degree. This may well be the worst injustice levied upon a military member. He receives no recognition whatsoever for his experience in the submarine force. There is hardly one engineer in the civilian sector that can match his intergraded power plant and interdisciplinary knowledge. Yet, he will squander in the lower pay grades until he completes an engineering degree. Usually, he will be assigned to an inexperienced college graduate being paid twice the sailor's salary or more. Truly, the sailor will earn both his own salary and that of the college graduate engineer. Of course, the college graduate engineer probably spent his time in the streets burning the American flag and dishonoring his country. Injustice is what America has embraced. The street protesters completed their education while they dodged their duty to their country. Now, they continue to protest by preying upon the unfortunate and forgotten few who stood by their country. America's cowards continue to keep America on her knees. For the most part, our nationally elected leaders represent these cowards and sustain the injustices perpetrated upon its military personnel.

When the submarine returns to homeport, these injustices await their crews. It goes without saying that the cowardly vultures of civilian enterprise will be perched right outside the main entrance gate to the military base eager to prey on the new arrivals. Like trash dump birds, they know when the good morsels come in. These are hard times for any military person. It takes great personal volition to look the civilian community in the face and discount them as the cowards that they really are and still hold fast to your beliefs in America. An American submariner is doing a job that his civilian counterpart could not even imagine beyond his marijuana-swapping, beer-guzzling, free-sex, slovenly existence. Yet, for the good America remembered by the submariners, the job gets done despite the plethora of injustices.

I doubt any of our universities, other than the military academies, produced any able leaders in the decades of the cold war. They produced cowards bent on one thing, self-aggrandizement. God only knows where these pseudo-leaders will take us in the future. One thing is certain, the American submariner had better win the deterrence race, because the upcoming generation of inept leaders will never take us anywhere except into a morass of malaise.

It is lunchtime again. Underway, it seems the meals become the meeting places. Like coffee houses of Europe or the fast-food burger shop abutting a school or work place in the USA, crew's mess serves as the gathering place. Here, we discuss the events that we experienced or old news that we received from our radio traffic.

The hostage crisis in Tehran is still fermenting. Now, we have a Battle Group on scene to provide a visible deterrence to the Muslim extremists. Somehow, the ability to see danger is far more effective than to have it unseen in your backyard. From the radio traffic, the harsh words of the early extremists' pronouncements seem to have abated. The presence of a Battle Group has that effect on the Islamic vocabulary.

Our part in the hostage crisis is done. We were there to provide diplomatic empowerment for our foreign affairs negotiators until a more visible inducement arrived. It is unfortunate that the publicity of the crisis favors what can be seen. It is the fate of stealth to remain silent. Apparently, to those in Washington, DC, the war baton of preference is a silent one.

Lunch today is a seafood combination, consisting of fish and crab in a New England clam chowder like sauce. This combination is always tasty. Seldom does anyone ever overeat this meal, but it does hit the spot. Served with mash potatoes and mixed vegetables, this meal is as balanced as you can get. I recall similar meals being touted as the day's special in New England restaurants. Interestingly, they were served with the same combination and manner. Some executive, right now, is ordering this meal, at elevated prices, in a New York City restaurant. He is even eager to receive it. It probably even is the highlight of his day. Yet, for us, it is merely another meal underway. We are accustomed to these types of meals. There are no choices for us. We dine as well as any clientele in New York City's fast serve restaurants.

Discussion during the meal is limited to basic greetings. Although, in our minds, we all know that we could have ended the hostage crisis and all the shenanigans of South Asia. Why we were not ordered to do so, we do not know? Somehow diplomacy prefers to draw out these conflicts. Many of us believe that it is economics at work. Nuclear war would be bad for the world economy. Besides, what could one hundred or so American hostages matter compared to the health and welfare of the world's economy? They are expendable, as we are. It is a sad situation, but it is true. The economic interdependence of the world has outgrown the rights of the individual. What is held as true in America is not so highly regarded overseas. I suppose that is another reason why this fleet ballistic nuclear submarine exists to remind the world to curb its aspirations and ideologies.

I decide on a bowl of chocolate ice cream from the dispenser for dessert. Splurging, I add nuts and some cherries. Savoring each spoonful, my tablemates and I wonder if life will be as kind to us after our naval service. Most believe our lives will be better. I disagree. I believe that the time we spend together underway will be the best times of our lives. These are times that we will cherish forever. We were there. When all is said and done, we can stand up and say we were there. We were not in a New York City restaurant dining during the hostage crisis. We were there. And, we could have made a difference beyond anything imaginable by any New York City restaurant patron. We were there.

The chocolate ice cream was so delicious that I take time to lick the bowl. I have not done that since I was a kid in elementary school. I can do that underway, because I am not out here to impress anyone with my table manners. My shipmates have the same liberties. No one chides them over etiquette. We are here for another reason, and we are damn good at it.

The afternoon watch is a normal patrol watch. The submarine is operating at missile launch depth. We are alert, awaiting the dreaded order to discharge our payload. This close to the end of our deployment, we pray that order never comes. It would be a shame to miss an in-port period on Waikiki Beach.

This time into the deployment what seems to captivate our imaginations is how many college beauties will grace the Hawaiian beaches. There are certain times of the year in which the coeds flock to the islands. They are everywhere. The University of Hawaii enrolls up to 6,000 short-semester coeds during these periods. Truly, the island of O'ahu becomes a bachelor's paradise, even for submariners.

I recall a tall blonde that visited the chess tables in Waikiki. She must have been 5'10", maybe 140 pounds with a gorgeous smile that was sweeter than the morning after. I remember she stared at me, as I played chess. Whether she knew the game or not, I do not know. But, she seemed interested that I could play. She waited for the game to finish. However, when I left the chess table, I could not manage to say a word to her. I wanted to so much. God, I wanted to say something. But, I didn't. After a while, she looked at me one last time, said something to her girlfriend and the two gals left the beach area. I never saw that gal again. But, every time I returned to the chess tables, it seemed that I could feel her watch me play. Why didn't I say something? My God, how many opportunities have I passed up like that? I guess I just did not want to get involved. Something inside me prevented me from speaking to her. It was like there was a mental ball & chain attached to my larynx, clasping my vocal cords shut. And, I let her walk away. Maybe I felt inferior, because I had not finished my degree before I joined the service. Maybe I felt inadequate, because the service paid us little, and our public admiration was weak. But, this gal did not seem to be bothered by all that. I believe she truly just wanted to meet me. And, I let her down. Had I said something, I would never have been able to let this gal go. Perhaps, given my self-appraisal, I suppose the outcome was for the best. It is so terrible how society hinders social interaction. Another time and another place, we might have been lovers. I would have liked that. Now, I have the regret that I just let her go.

Thoughts like these often fill my mind prior to a post-deployment, in-port period. I always vow to correct the mistakes of prior in-port periods, but somehow all my promises to change go unheeded. No matter how old I get, I never change. The constraints that withheld me from pleasure in the past continue to haunt me in the present. The future, I suspect, will not materialize my promises. I allow my opportunities vanish before my very eyes.

The contemplation on my sad state of affairs is interrupted by an order to line up the seawater systems for discharge. We need to do this so as not to permit the discharge of potentially radioactive isotopes to be entrained into the intake of our seawater systems. Although we insure that all our discharges are below the limits authorized for the release of radioactive materials overboard, we take added precaution so as not to contaminate our seawater systems. It is a simple, but necessary, procedure. We essentially line up all cooling systems to one side of the ship while we discharge from the other side. The ship undergoes a turning maneuver to insure the discharge fluids are expelled away from our hull. The procedure is the same when discharging human refuse from our sanitary tanks. These discharges occur far from any landmasses and far from any shipping lanes.

My roving watches and I commence the lineup of the seawater systems. Additional watch standers come into the engineering spaces to assist with the actual discharge. There are some sampling requirements as well to insure the chemical quality of the discharge. Radioactive discharges are well documented in order to certify our concerns for the ocean environment.

For the next hour or so, my watch standers and I will be in a repeat back mode, listing every valve we position for the discharge. Evolutions such as this require such demanding compliance. A repeat back refers to a supervisory watch stander ordering a valve positioned. The positioning watch stander repeats the order, positions the valve then reports the new position of the valve to the ordering watch stander. The ordering watch stander then acknowledges the new position of the valve in question and moves on to the next step in the procedure. This is a time consuming process, but it provides incredible accuracy and precision. The repeat back procedure is drilled into every nuclear trained submariner from the first day he commences training. By the time he reaches his ultimate duty station aboard a submarine, the procedure is ingrained into his mental framework. It is as common as the procedure he uses to relieve himself in the toilet. For some personnel, they know the repeat back procedure better.

During the discharge procedure, the routine transforms my watch standers into automatons. In the dead time between the orders and the report of their accomplishment, little distractions flood into our consciousness. For me, this close to returning to port, I think of the beaches on O'ahu. Huge waves carrying body surfers to the shore form a smile on my face. Re-experiencing the thrill of one of those wave rides makes me long for the islands. As a youth in New England, I never dreamed of even standing on a Pacific island beach. Now, in a few weeks, I will be there again with the feel of cold ocean water on my shoulders, beach sand stuck into my bathing trunks and the tropical sun permeating through my suntan lotion. Few young men get those opportunities. My shipmates and I experience at least five-months worth of endless summer a year.

Another valve positioning is reported, and another valve is ordered positioned. After ordering the new valve position, my thoughts return to the beaches. Will it be Hanauma Bay or Makapu that we visit first? These are East Shore beaches behind Diamond Head. Hanauma Bay provides breathtaking views of a coral inlet. The waves are small, almost akin to an interior, mainland, swimming hole filled with tropical fish. On the other hand, Makapu offers high surf and wave rides beyond anything imaginable for a body surfer. Unfortunately, the ebb and flow of the waves at Makapu are strong, resembling riptides. Weak swimmers should avoid this beach or end up as casualties. Many aspiring body surfers die here, including locals with much experience in the island waters. Hanauma Bay seems safer, after a six-month deployment. The coed population selection is far greater at Hanauma Bay, too. However, the presence of wild, more-than-willing coeds are a given on the shores of Makapu. It seems these gals desire the brave, half-crazed, waterborne-Adonises of Makapu. With a little audacity coupled with a daring performance on the huge waves, a body surfer can pick as he wishes from the litter of shapely, willing damsels sculpted in coconut oil on the sands. The promise of such easy success often drives desire to overwhelm reason. Sure things promote such daring.

One of my junior roving watch standers brings me a fresh cup of coffee. I thank him. Sipping the hot contents, its warm, thirst-quenching effect reminds me of the feel of the strong waves at Makapu, hurling me toward the shore. Like that first thrust into a gorgeous, willing, moist damsel, the warmth of the coffee makes its way into the sanctuary of my most cherished memories. I could use one of those women right now. I have to shake my head a few times in order to dislodge the thought from my consciousness, less I get aroused on watch. Sometimes, these desires are difficult to extricate from my mind. To experience one such pleasantry condemns one to an endless replay of fresh desire for repetition.

Another valve is reported positioned. We are ready to discharge. During the actual discharge, all the watch standers need to be attentive. The discharge is the serious part of the procedure. Potentially radioactive coolant will be discharged into the ocean environment. Everything must be done with precision. Pleasantries of the island beaches are replaced with a steadfast commitment of mind. We will discharge slowly until we achieve a particular operating parameter. Various monitoring devices will boundary our operation. Flow, temperature and pressure form the sides of our operating box. Juggling these three variables truly is a work of art. But, we do it with perfection. Trapeze artists have nothing on my watch standers. We perform flawlessly.

Upon reaching our ordered limit, we secure the discharge and commence a return to normal of the valve lineup. Similarly, we conduct a repeat back system. Slowly, the systems return to their original pre-discharge stati. As we are returning the systems, the thoughts of beaches, easy women and the thrills of strong, wave riding flood back into our minds. We are alive again, if only in our memories.

Memories of being underway are limited. Most are clumped into habitual performances. Although we make our way to the engineering spaces a few times a day, each day, our recollection of that walk is clumped into one experience. It is not one that we are particularly fond of either. It just happens to be one in which, as an automaton, we remembered for one inconspicuous reason or another. Truly, it is an inconspicuous one that we remember. Nothing of interest happened on that walk. We recall some of the valves, some of the missile tubes and other submarine implements along the way more vividly. That is it. It is just one uneventful walk that represents a few hundred, maybe even a thousand.

Other memories acquire the same pattern. Our watch standing, for example, clumps up in the same manner. Despite a few hundred tours conducted during our many watches, we remember one. I suppose it could be a composite tour, but more specifically, it is one inconspicuous tour that stands out in our memory. I suppose that it could be described as an ultimate tour distilled from many of our past tours. Even the drills and evolutions are likewise remembered.

For the many hours underway, we remember them like a civilian remembers the manner in which he travels to his/her workplace from his/her place of residence. There is so much left out. Like automatons, we just allow our autopilot to take us there. Most of the time, our minds are thousands of miles away. How much time in our lives do we compress into one experience?

The high points of the patrol are what we recall. I suppose life, in general, is much the same way. It is only the high points that stand out in our memory. To live a sedentary life means you will have few high points to recall and hours upon hours of boredom compressed into one or two experiences. Those individuals that share elaborate tales of exotic travels are those who have lived a life filled with challenges. I admire them, because they truly have lived. They did not tiptoe to their graves.

On this deployment, we experienced a few tense moments: a Soviet submarine encounter, a romance session in Hong Kong and one in Australia, a drug intercept in the Malacca Strait and the hostage crisis in the Persian Gulf. That is not bad for one deployment. Those five experiences will stand out forever in my memory. From fear to sweetness, each will mark the path of my life with advantages. What more could I ask for in a six month period? Few individuals repeat the romance sessions in one year of their lives. Some individuals will be unfortunate enough to acquire one such session in all their lives. Others will have many more, but they will be the kind of experiences that are compressed into one routine encounter. Like our walks to the engineering spaces, they will remember the inconspicuous parts of the experience. How pitiful such a life would be?

I suppose that is what they mean on the Navy promotional posters by the words: "see the world." We see the world as a buffet line. We get to choose sparingly what we desire. Our choices may be limited in quantity and quality, but they are choices. Like our meals, we get only a few selections of entrees per day, but over the entire patrol we overmatch the menu card at any New York City fast-serve restaurant. Our experiences are the same. Though we do not get the panorama of choices one would in New York City, over the entire patrol we will stumble onto comparable opportunities for these experiences. We see the world not as a gala banquet but as a buffet line. And, we have the good fortune of being able to run through the buffet line a few times in order to sample all the entrees and side dishes. It works out for us in the long run.

My watch is almost over. I suppose I will have to face another meal choice. From the odors seeping into the engineering spaces, the entrée smells like another UFO special. The evening meal, like the night skies in New England, seems to overpopulate with UFOs. That must be our curse. UFOs haunt us everywhere we try to hide. I hope these are served with French fries. I have a taste for French fries tonight with lots of catsup and mayonnaise. Here is my watch relief already.

He brings news of the potential for a shortened patrol route. It appears our submarine has been granted an early in-port for our actions in the Persian Gulf. Another fleet ballistic missile submarine will zigzag through our operational area, after we go off station. The news sounds even more delicious than the unpromising odor of the UFO on the grill.

Walking forward to crew's mess, my mind floods with ideas of what to do after we tie up. Squadron will be sure to advise our dependents of the change in patrol length. We can expect loved ones on the pier to greet us. And, of course, there will be the usual Hula dancers. It is a tradition in Hawaii to welcome a boat back off patrol with Hula girls. One time, we actually had Miss Hawaii on the pier to greet us.

Once in the crew's mess, my appetite seems to have abated. I smile when I recognize the sub-burgers on a serving dish being placed in the center of the senior enlisted personnel's table. Can I handle one more grease-burger? No, I can't! I will settle for coffee, take a seat and rest a while, while I listen to the forward crewmen discuss the early tie up. Somehow, I get a kick out of hearing them speak of a long patrol. There is something inside me that rides the waves of their joyous spirits. I cannot enjoy the news as well as they can. Something makes me hold back that kind of emotion.

From the very first sip of the coffee, it tastes good. Was it poured from a fresh pot? Or, is it just the news? Who really cares? The forward crewmen carry on while I settle in and sip my coffee. For the duration of the cup, I say nothing. I do smile, now and then. How can they be so happy? It is not like we won the war. We just went to sea and came back. So, we were out a little under six months. Surface sailors assigned to aircraft carriers stay deployed much longer. For the first timers, I can feel their anxiety for getting back to their loved ones. For me, I have been to sea too long to get all worked up over getting back. Back is always there. It is like jumping up, you always come down.

By the time I finish my coffee, a smile has permanently affixed itself to my face. It is a smile more of camaraderie than one of simple happiness. I am happy, because my shipmates are happy. And, quite possibly, I am happy, because I avoided the sub-burger gut bombs. Either choice, the coffee was delicious. It tasted like accomplishment or victory.

We will be back in-port in two days. We are to break off from our patrol area at midnight and haul back to port at Ahead Full. When I awake for the morning watch, we will be on our way back. We deserve to go back early. We did well out there.

CHAPTER 10

Mooring Pearl Harbor, Hawaii

"Ouga, ouga, ouga. Surface, surface, surface" blares over the ship's announcing system. This will be our last surface for this deployment. It will be a while before we join our undersea friends again. Two months, I think. We will experience a much-needed two-month, in-port period in order to overhaul the submarine. Six-month deployments take a toll on the ship and the daily-running equipment.

The Maneuvering Watch supervisor has just relieved me on the morning watch. On my way forward, the roving watch informs me that the Executive Officer (XO) wants to see me. That can only mean one thing: bad news for me or for some of my troopers. Since we are transiting homeward, we have received message traffic from Squadron. Unfortunately, not all the message traffic brings good tidings. Any problems that we will face upon tie up are forwarded to the ship to assist in their amelioration. That is what the XO wants to discuss with me at this meeting.

I make my way directly to the XO's stateroom. The stateroom resembles the administration room. There is barely enough room for two people to sit down comfortably. The XO's desk consists of fold-down panel that doubles as a pop-riveted, locker door. A shower stall and a one-sink-, one-commode-bathroom separate the XO's stateroom from the commanding officer's stateroom. I knock lightly on his door, even though I see him reading over some message traffic. The knock on the door allows him time to put away any sensitive information that I am not cleared to see. The XO invites me into his stateroom and offers me a seat on small cushioned, stainless steel cube. As I settle into the seat, the XO informs me that five Nukes will receive bad news when we tie up. Four are young men.

First, one of my senior enlisted Nukes had a family member die while we were returning from patrol. The XO informs me that it was determined by Squadron that the death notification was withheld because of the Nuke's unexpendable position. He will be notified right after the XO and I finish our talk. He will be issued emergency orders to travel back east and be off the boat as soon as we tie up. The Air Force has a plane waiting on the tarmac at Hickam Air Force Base to take him back east.

Second, a young second class petty officer who married his high school sweetheart will be receiving divorce papers shortly after we tie up. I know the person well. He will be devastated. He lived for that girl. Apparently, his young wife went astray while he was deployed. She fell in love with some college hippie and decided to file divorce papers.

Third, a young third class petty officer will be informed that his wife lost their baby while we were away. The XO confides in me that base medical personnel suspect that there might have been foul play in her miscarriage. It appears that she could not handle her husband being gone so long. She just could not take it. There might be a divorce in the making here as well.

Fourth, one of my senior second class petty officer's kids was arrested for dealing drugs out of their military housing apartment. The XO suspects that he may be ejected from military housing because of the incident. Since the boy in under age and a dependent of the sailor, the second class will be charged for the drug offense. The XO believes that the ship will be able to get the sailor cleared, but the dependent will face some form of charges.

Last, one of my single sailors is being sued over a paternity suit. Some college gal is claiming that he got her pregnant. She has no intention of marrying the sailor, but she demands that he provide for her and the baby after she delivers.

The XO and I comment on the sacrifices that submariners and their families have to endure in order to make these deployments. We both agree that getting news like this is unfair after a six-month deployment. Life is hard for a submariner and his family.

In passing, the XO comments that I got off easy. The bad news is a lot worse for many other departments. Divorce is the prime item of bad news. We have over a dozen divorces, even some from the wardroom. It is terrible how families are torn apart by long deployments. A submariner has to have a certain type of woman. If she cannot survive on her own, a submariner should never consider anything permanent with her. It gets worse for an attractive woman with kids. They have to fight off urges, fight off single men looking for partnership and handle the kids alone. It is a tough life for a submariner's wife.

The XO recommends that I inform the personnel affected as soon as possible before we tie up. He feels that they should be prepared. I realize that the news of the divorce for the young sailor will be hard on him. I recommend to the XO that he be afforded psychological counseling. The XO concurs with my suggestions and will prepare a request letter to Squadron Medical. There is even some discussion of providing the young sailor a leave of absence from the submarine environment until he can cope with the loss of his wife.

Divorces like this one are not uncommon in the submarine force. We hate to see them happen, but, unfortunately, they are a fact of life. Seldom does a deployment go by without at least one divorce waiting for some poor sailor upon his return to port. The wives are just too vulnerable when left alone for six months. Most young wives have never had to fend for themselves in their lives. The absence of their husband just overwhelms them, and they succumb to the lures of society. What they cherished most in high school or college was companionship with someone who took them around. Now, faced with no one to assist and entertain them they seek a replacement to fill in that gap. Often, that replacement comes with conditionalities of sexual favors. The gals offered those exchanges in high school and college, so they do not seem to object to doing so now. Soon, thoughts of their husband fade into the embraces of their new suitors. Pressures build as the young wives await their husband's return to port. The closer the tie up day approaches, the more the pressure accumulates to make a choice between remaining with their husband or following his temporary replacement. Often, the gal, rather than face her husband, just opts for divorce. Too often, the wife opts for divorce as the only solution to her infidelity dilemma.

The bad news takes away any appetite I might have had. It will be difficult for me to break such news to five of my personnel. It is almost as if my in-port period has been ruined. It is difficult to tell a young sailor that the love of his life has abandoned him; especially, after he has just sacrificed six months of his life in defense of his country. One would think the civilians would extend some form of reverence for deployed sailors. They don't! Instead, they circle around the deployed sailors' wives like starved sex-vultures, waiting for an opportunity to ravage their lives for their own self-ingratiation. Society does not even get involved. It is as if no one cared about the sacrifices that these young families endure for the sake of the safety and security of the American way of life. It kind of makes you wonder why anyone would be willing to sacrifice anything for such an indifferent society.

I will need a cup of coffee, as I mull over how to break the news to all these sailors. For some of the sailors, it will be harder for me to tell them than it will be for them to accept it. God, how I hate this responsibility! Why do I have to be the one to tell them?

Taking the first sip of coffee, I realize how bad the coffee tastes this morning. It tasted so good yesterday. I guess bad news has a way of distorting my flavor buds. I doubt even sugar and/or cream will help the taste of this bad brew.

The chief cook can see my disheartened condition. He has been on many deployments. He understands. In an effort to calm my concerns, he offers me a fresh cruller donut. I accept and dip it into my coffee. It is delicious. Fresh, warm dough always sates my taste buds. He pats me on the shoulder and says, "It's a tough life, isn't it?" I just nod and thank him for the donut.

There is never a good time to break bad news. Having just finished a six-month patrol is even worse. However, I have to do it. Working my way down the seniority ladder, I relay the bad news. Each man is affected deeply. It is particularly hard on the younger sailors. As I predicted, the young sailor losing his wife is distraught. He will need to make a trip to the psychologist before he returns to sea.

Tomorrow, we will tie up in Pearl Harbor. To some, it will be a return to paradise. Yet, to these five, hell would be a better representation. The young sailor even busted his butt to get his dolphins on this run. That is quite the accomplishment for the first deployment. But, he did it. He wears them proud, too.

"Getting your dolphins" is the submarine slang for qualification in submarines. All qualified submarine personnel are distinguished from other sailors by a set of dolphins affixed above their left shirt pocket. A set of dolphins consists of a single insignia promoting two sea carps riding on the wake from a submarine's bow.

Somehow when this young sailor goes ashore, his accomplishments will fade when the memory of his wife overcomes him. For him, it is not the comfort of Navy housing that awaits him, but the rough cots and cold floors of the World War II era barracks. It is so unfair, but life seems to turn out that way. I feel for him. I hope he survives.

How do you lose someone you really love and recover? I remember losing my dad, and I never recovered. I suppose it is the same way with other loses for other people. Death is certain, but something like the young sailor losing his wife, how will he recover? As long as she is around, he will have hopes of her return. They will be vain hopes, but they will be hopes that keep him going. I pray he forgets her soon; otherwise, we will have a basket case on our hands.

Maybe I should invite him over to my place a few times for dinner? I should invite a number of the younger guys over for the holidays. They have no place to go, unless they take leave and go back home. Few actually do who are stationed in Hawaii. The plane changes, irregularities and overbooking by the airlines really discourage holiday travel off the islands. If they do brave the trip to the Mainland, they select travel days in advance and arrears of the holiday to avoid the congestion days. It sure wastes a lot of leave time.

Speaking of holiday leave, it has been almost a decade since I returned to New England during a Christmas holiday. Christmas is the best time to see New England. Since we have no snow in the tropics, Christmas in New England sates two desires: one for the holidays to be with family and old friends and to see snow. I miss the snow. Yet, not this year, I have not been away from snow long enough to drag myself back to New England.

How will the young sailor go back home? He married his high school sweetheart. He could never go back without being overcome with emotion. Every place he goes will remind him of her. His hometown will bring so much sadness to him. I pity him. I hope he recovers.

From the periscope monitor in crew's mess, we can see the channel markers identifying the entrance to Pearl Harbor in the distance. They seem huge, even from our distance away. Like beacons inviting us to comfort, we steam toward them. Two tugboats are exiting the channel. They will be our escorts. As the channel markers get larger, the closure of our deployment approaches.

In the distance, we see what appears to be air quickly exiting the high-pressure air stacks of the tugboats. They are signaling us to come about to allow them to latch onto us. We feel the boat budge a bit as the first tugboat latches to our starboard side. Another nudge from the port side indicates that the second tugboat has tied up alongside.

Soon, the channel markers pass our bow. We have returned. Now, it is just a matter of navigating the channel into the quarry area of the harbor. The periscope sights Alpha Landing to our starboards side. Ford Island appears on our port side shortly thereafter. Two ferry launches cross our bow ahead of us. We are in the main loch now. The Sierra piers of the Naval Submarine Base lie ahead of us. We can see dependents and Hula girls on the pier. A large crowd has gathered to welcome us home. Well, for some of us, the welcome will be bitter sweet. For others still, the welcome will down right bitter.

I offer to allow the young sailor awaiting divorce to be exempt from the shore power party, but he refuses. He prefers to stay with his shipmates and do his job. I suppose he is right. If he can immerse himself in his work, it will help take the loss of his wife off his mind.

We tie up quickly. The brow is over even faster. Forward crewmen are disembarking at a record rate to meet with their loved ones. Few Nukes go over onto the pier. I allow the married personnel to greet their loved ones while the single personnel shutdown the plant and take on shore power. It will be another hour or so before the Nukes can join the liberty party. Then, there are the duty section personnel who must stay aboard until tomorrow morning.

Reflecting on the deployment, it was a good run. First, we all came back alive. Second, we experienced some fairly important missions. Third, and most importantly, when we were called, we were there. We were ready.

By noon, I don my civilian clothing and prepare to depart the ship. The engineering spaces are in shutdown status. The shutdown watches are stationed. We are in a steady state condition. I say my last adieus to the ship before I cross the brow. As I step onto the pier from the brow, I take one last look at the submarine. Nodding my head in approval, I thank the ship for keeping us safe during the deployment one more time.

The walk to the bus stop is peaceful. The weather in Hawaii is typical, tropical paradise. I walk slowly so as not to build up any perspiration, a trick in the tropics. The bus stop is just outside the main gate. The bus will take me within a few hundred yards of my residence.

At the bus stop, two college kids are discussing their experiences in a basic math class. I cannot help but overhear their conversation. One is chiding a fellow student for starting his college education so late in his life. Apparently, he is an ex-serviceman in his late 30s. Both these teenagers seem to find humor in such a plight. They seem to think that one should attend college right after high school. After ten minutes of overhearing them downgrade the old serviceman, I cannot help myself from contemplating what the fathers of the two young men did to enable them to attend college right after high school. I doubt their dads wore a uniform during the Vietnam Conflict. The ex-serviceman defended his country. Their dads did something else, and the young students will not be proud of what their dads did. My bus arrives, and I board without comment to the two young students. I take the first seat near the entrance and gaze out the window. Although I am glad to see the rich vegetation and familiar places along the route homeward, the young students' conversation haunts me. I shake my head in disgust over the legacy their dads' generation left to the American youth: You can desert your country, burn the American flag and grow up to be elected President. The ex-serviceman in their math class didn't do that.

At about the halfway point of the bus ride to my residence, I realized that some fifteen minutes had passed. That was the time it took to launch most, if not all, of a fleet ballistic missile submarine's payload. Given Hawaii's location in the center of the Pacific Ocean, the first touchdowns would greet me as I disembarked the bus. By the time I walked to my residence, cities around the world would be crumbling. I would turn on the TV to receive the estimated time of the Soviet's response touchdown on Hawaii. Any hour could be the last one. I will endure the rest of my life on earth knowing that fatalistic truism and understanding that I can never share it with anyone. In truth, fleet ballistic missile submarine crewmen never surface.

Epilogue

Deployment duration for a fast attack submarine requires some six months away from homeport. For a fleet ballistic missile submarine, the deployment duration is three months twice a year.

Divorce rate amongst the submarine community was rated as the highest in the armed services.

Prior to 1981, some military personnel on deployment were paid less than entry workers at MacDonald's.

A nuclear submarine can stay submerged up to seven years. Food and personnel sanity are the only limitations.

The electric power generated from a nuclear submarine's reactor plant is enough to power a small city. If all the steam generated from the reactor plant were directed to shore turbine generators, a city with a population of some 250,000 people could be satisfied.

Detection of a submerged nuclear submarine is near impossible.

One fleet ballistic missile nuclear submarine could destroy over one hundred cities.

One nuclear fast attack submarine could destroy an entire battle group.

One nuclear fast attack submarine, armed with a sufficient number of the right torpedoes, could destroy ever port facility (harbor) along the west coast of North America. The same is true for a nuclear fast attack submarine operating along the east coast of North America.

Missile accuracy is unimaginable. From anywhere in the middle of the Pacific Ocean, a fleet ballistic missile submarine could touchdown a missile in one of the end zones of the Oakland Raiders' football stadium. The lowest scale for missile target entry calibration is measured in feet. And, a fleet ballistic missile submarine does not qualify for a sharp shooting badge.

Fleet ballistic missile submarine crewmen are distinguished form other submariners by an additional insignia worn below their left shirt pocket, called a patrol pin. The patrol pin consists of a side view of a submarine with an intercontinental ballistic missile protruding upward. Silver and gold stars are affixed to the patrol pin to indicate the number of deterrent patrols a crewman has experienced. Each gold star represents one deterrent patrol, and each silver star represents five deterrent patrols. Seven patrols would be represented by one silver and two gold stars. The author wore this combination.

Due to the secrecy of nuclear submarine operations, nuclear submariners are not considered qualified to join the Veterans of Foreign Wars (VFW). This is likewise true for many campaign medals that are awarded to other military personnel. Consequently, nuclear submarine crews earn Navy Unit Citations, Meritorious Unit Citations and Navy Expeditionary Medals for services in theaters of operations.

In 1989, the Cold War ended with the dismantling of the Berlin Wall without one intercontinental ballistic missile being fired in anger by a fleet ballistic missile submarine.

The current arsenal and accuracy of the United States' fleet ballistic missile submarine force is sufficient to blast, in less than an hour, the entire world civilization back into the Stone Age forever.

Abbreviations/Definitions

Aft	Rear of a vessel
Amidships	Naval term for middle of the vessel
Attack boat	Submarine term for fast attack submarine: also called Hunter Killer
Bell	Naval term for a propulsion order
Boat	Affectionate submariner term for submarine
Bow	Forward end of a ship
Brow	Walkway like bridge from the pier to a vessel. Also, gangplank
Bulkhead	Wall in shipboard terminology
Camel	Large rubberized cushion used to space vessels tied up next to one another
CNMI	Commonwealth of the Northern Mariana Islands
Cold Iron	Term used to describe the shutdown condition of a steam plant
Coner	Affectionate term for a submarine non-nuclear-trained crewman who stands watches in the forward part of the submarine
Cruiser	War vessel larger than a frigate but smaller than a battleship
Deck	Floor in shipboard terminology
Deployment	Submarine patrol assignment of three months or more in duration
Dolphins	Affectionate term for submarine qualification insignia
Dragon Ass	The burning sensation as formaldehyde passes through a rectum

Escort	Slightly smaller Destroyer-size war vessel: also called Destroyer Escort
Fairwater	Tower extending upward from the top deck of a submarine: also referred to as the Conning Tower.
Fast Attack	Same as Attack Boat or Hunter Killer submarine
Fast boat	Patrol craft resembling a speedboat mounting a 50-caliber machine gun
Field Day	Naval term for an organized clean up of the ship
Frigate	Fast Destroyer-size war vessel
Gangplank	see Brow
Greenie	Hand-held cleaning device consisting of a sponge and green-colored abrasive pad
Gunwale	Upper edge of a surface ship's side
Heevies	clothesline-like ropes with a baseball size knot at the heaving end used to enable mooring lines to be exchanged between ship and pier
Hatch	Door in shipboard terminology
Keel	Main support frame running along the bottom centerline of a ship
Ladder	Stairs in shipboard terminology
MOS	Military Operations Specialty
Mung	Bilge debris resembling intermeshed mud
NROTC	Naval Reserve Officer Training Cadet
Nuke	Affectionate term for nuclear-trained submarine crewman
Old Salts	Senior fleet sailors
Overhead	Ceiling in shipboard terminology
Poopysuit	Submarine underway attire
Port	Left side of a ship when facing forward
Quarterdeck	Formal entrance and exit area to a naval war vessel
RDF	Rapid Deployment Force

SSBN	Silent Service Ballistic Nuclear: fleet ballistic missile submarine designation
SSN	1. Silent Service Nuclear: fast attack submarine designation 2. Affectionately, the acronym refers to: Saturday, Sunday and Nights, suggesting the extra time fast attack crewmen work
Starboard	Right side of a ship when facing forward
Stern	Term for the rear end of a ship
UFO	Submarine slang for Unidentified Frying Object
Wheelhouse	Naval merchant term for a bridge or control room: Place on board a ship where the steering wheel is located.
White Death	Affectionate submariner term for sugar
XO	Executive Officer: second in command: functions as administrative officer for a submarine

0-595-32902-0

Printed in the United States
21422LVS00005B/295-297

9 780595 329021